rain

rain

karen duve

translated from the german by anthea bell

BLOOMSBURY

This edition first published in Great Britain 2002

Copyright © 1999 by Karen Duve

First published by Eichborn AG,
Frankfurt am Main, 1999 under the title *Regenroman*

English translation © 2002 by Anthea Bell

The moral right of the author and translator has been asserted

Bloomsbury Publishing Plc,
38 Soho Square, London W1D 3HB

A CIP catalogue record for this book
is available from the British Library

ISBN 0 7475 5745 4

10 9 8 7 6 5 4 3 2 1

Typeset by Hewer Text Ltd, Edinburgh
Printed in Great Britain by Clays Limited, St Ives plc

And behold I, even I, do bring a flood of waters upon the earth to destroy all flesh, wherein is the breath of life, from under heaven; and every thing that is in the earth shall die.

(Genesis 6.17)

There is no such thing as bad weather, only the wrong clothing.

(Proverb)

Evil flourishes in the damp.

(Sister Mary Olivia)

1

Skies overcast, occasional showers, sometimes heavy, highest temperatures between 11 and 14 degrees. North-westerly wind decreasing, force 2 to 3.

'What? What did you say?'

The thin young woman strained her eyes and ears as she looked down the slope. She was in an empty lay-by on the main road, alone with a black Mercedes 300, an overflowing rubbish bin and a caravan with no wheels, its windows boarded up and a wooden notice on its roof saying SNACKS. The thin young woman's name was Martina Ulbricht. She had married a few weeks ago, and her husband Leon Ulbricht, with whom she was going to look at a house with a view to buying it, had vanished into the bushes a quarter of an hour earlier and had not yet emerged. She had waited in the car because it was raining so hard. But then she began to worry, and when the rain slackened slightly she got out. It was cold. In fact it was definitely too cold for the end of May. Martina wore nothing but a short yellow suede skirt, the kind that does up with a row of press studs, thin nylon tights and a limp green sweatshirt which was much too large for her. The back of the sweatshirt bore the legend

FIT
FOR
LIFE.

After only a minute out in the rain, Martina's chin-length red hair was plastered to her face. A strand of it described a calligraphic flourish on her forehead, from which water licked its way down to her mouth. She had a large mouth, with teeth like sugar cubes and lips sore at the corners, their skin flaking slightly. It gave her face a disconcertingly predatory look. However, she had a perfectly straight nose of average size above that mouth, and her eyes lay in their sockets looking as exposed and alarmed as if this were not their accustomed place, only a temporary refuge, and the rightful owner could come along at any time, stake a claim and pocket them like a couple of marbles. Taken as a whole, the details of Martina's physiognomy added up to such an attractive impression that wherever she went men perked up like pointers finding a scent, while the sight of her made women slump like sad cakes.

The rain was now falling gently and evenly, running over the smooth tarmac without forming puddles. The lay-by had only recently been asphalted. When Martina went over to the place where Leon had disappeared from view, clutching a packet of tissues, loose chippings crunched beneath the soles of her shoes. A trodden mud pathway led down the slope on the other side of a knee-high fence of plain wooden laths. This path was so narrow and overgrown that it was impossible to say if it was only a few metres long or went all the way down the steep bank to the river, which had been running parallel to the road for the last few kilometres. Martina called to Leon. An answer came from unexpectedly far away. It sounded something like, 'Come down here.'

'What? What did you . . . ?'

He called something else, but at that moment a train rattled by on the other side of the river, and once again Martina failed to catch his words. Undecided, she rubbed one nylon-clad calf over the other, creating a little warmth with the friction. Would it be a bad idea to leave the Mercedes behind unguarded? It wasn't locked, and Leon had the key with him. Martina crunched a few steps over the chippings towards the bend where the road gave access to the lay-by, craning her neck to see if there was any other car about to pull in with a potential thief inside it. A white minibus was approaching – windscreen wipers working frantically, curtains over the side windows – and shot past, splashing up jets of water. Then all was quiet again, apart from the rain and the regular clatter of the train in the distance. Martina went back to the slope and started to climb down. The path was so overgrown that she was under a canopy of dripping foliage, passing between walls of stinging nettles, elder and the huge leaves of something like rhubarb. A tunnel, a green tube. Drops pattered down on the leaves. Fleshy, cold plant stems brushed against her hands. There was a smell of mud, rotting wood and fungi. Leon's boots had left their imprint on the soggy ground; the pattern looked like the ribbed fossil of some Palaeozoic arthropod. Martina clutched the bushes to the right and left of her, clinging to the branches of the little birch trees to keep her yellow suede pumps from sinking too far in as she put her feet down. But they had smooth soles, and she had not taken ten steps down the steep bank before she slipped and lost her balance. She fell on soft, dead leaves and slippery mud and landed on her back, legs ludicrously splayed, skirt hitched up over her hips, among Fanta cans, crumpled grey paper, empty Haribo bags and half-decomposed heaps of animal droppings. She lay there for a moment, stunned, bit her lower lip, and looked at the branch she was clutching in her right hand. When she let go it sprang back, and a barrage of heavy water drops pattered down on her. Martina struggled up, straightened her skirt and assessed the damage. Her sweatshirt was sticking to her back like clingfilm, she was muddy all down her left side – her arm, her skirt, her tights, everything! Her left shoe was probably ruined. It had been driven right into the ground, and now looked as if she had been using it as a mould for making mud pies.

'Shit. Oh, shit,' muttered Martina, wiping her left hand on the white bark of a tree trunk which had fungi the shape and colour of children's ears growing on its trunk near the root.

She went on, less cautiously now and not clinging to any of the plants. When the path stopped sloping so steeply and levelled out, so too did the thick undergrowth. She had only a few metres more to go across sand and gravel before reaching the river. It flowed slowly on under the rainy sky, broad and dull-hued, while countless circles of ripples on the surface ran out from their centres, quivering. Leon was standing on the bank, almost in the water. He wore heavy black boots with metal rings in the sides, black jeans and a black anorak, its hood firmly tied under his chin. Against this landscape he looked like an inkblot on a photograph. Leon was holding a broken branch and looking at something lying in the river in front of him. He turned to Martina, startled. Drops of water were running down his round face and the round glasses perched on it. He was thirty-eight years old. Martina was twenty-four.

'I shouted up that you weren't to come down. What are you doing here?' he said.

'I'd been waiting for ages. I thought something might have happened to you. What have you been doing all this time?'

Martina pushed a strand of hair away from her face with the back of her hand, leaving a brown streak on her forehead. She looked past Leon and at the water beyond him, where something large, white and soft lay in the reeds, looking monstrous and disgusting.

'What on earth's *that*?'

Leon turned his head as if to find out what she meant, and did not answer. There was no need. Martina could easily see for herself what had been washed up in the reeds: a naked woman.

'Is she dead? She is dead, isn't she? Oh, my God, a dead body! What are we going to do now? What on earth are we going to do?'

'Don't look,' said Leon. 'You'd better go back. I'll be with you in a moment.' Then he asked suddenly, 'Did you fall over? You're all muddy. Have you hurt yourself?'

Martina took a step back, looked at him, looked at the drowned woman, looked back at him.

'What are you doing with that stick in your hand?' she asked, with a touch of hysteria. 'What do you need a stick for? She's dead, isn't she?'

Leon dropped the long branch which he had been tapping nervously against his boot, undid the strings of his hood and pushed it back from his head. He had short brown hair, less of it in front than behind, and some grey was already showing at the sides. He put an arm round Martina's shoulders and kissed her on the temples. He had to reach up slightly to do so.

'Come on. You're wet through. I don't want you looking at this. I'll take you back to the car and we'll be on our way.'

He meant his voice to convey concern on her account, but it merely sounded hoarse. His lips felt as wet and cold as if he had been in the river himself for quite some time. Martina went on staring at the corpse. Its dead skin was pale and bloated, especially in what had once been the hardest parts: the soles of the woman's feet, her hands, knees and elbows. The flesh looked crumbly, as if you could pick it off with your bare hands. Martina wondered if the woman had been young when she died. Yes, very likely. She had probably been good-looking before she turned into this slimy mass. She had very long hair. Black hair. Pitch-black hair which must once have fallen to her hips, and was now drifting in the slow current. The corpse lay on its back. It was looking up at Martina – if a corpse can be said to look at anything at all. It had no eyes. At first Martina thought it was just that the eyelids were closed, because the woman's eye sockets were not red and bloody but as white as the rest of her body. It looked so soft, that body, so vulnerable. Fine strands of green waterweed were entwined in its pubic hair.

The woman was lying in the reeds from her hips down, her feet among them. All her toes had been nibbled. Bone stuck out here and there from the rags of skin. Martina felt sick. At the same time she was suddenly reminded of her old handicrafts teacher and the lace doilies they cut out of white paper with nail scissors in year three at primary school. First you folded the paper a couple of times, then you cut zigzags and semicircles into the edges, and when you unfolded the paper you had a lace doily with a perforated rim. At least, all the other girls did. When Martina unfolded her lace doilies they either had a single huge hole in the middle or fell apart in two halves.

'Well, Martina, so what are we going to do wrong next?' Frau Weber used to ask.

'You didn't just leave the car up there unlocked, did you?'

Leon's voice brought her back to the present. 'I don't believe it! Are you out of your mind?'

He whirled round, raced along the strip of bank, sending sand flying, and barged his way up the slope. Martina followed. When she got back to the lay-by Leon was already walking round the Mercedes, which was exactly as she had left it. The rain was beating down on its black roof faster now. Martina opened the passenger door, but Leon got between her and the car and slammed the door shut again.

'Do you want to get mud all over my upholstery?'

He opened the back door and started rummaging around among the things on the back seat. Apples, his camera, a bag containing three pounds of asparagus which they had bought by the roadside, from which soil trickled when he picked it up; a net of undersized oranges, the road atlas, a silk cravat with a butterfly print, the rubbish bag, which had a Christmassy smell of orange peel, his notebook, and a book entitled *You Just Don't Understand Me*. The book was Martina's. Ever since she and Leon had been together he kept finding her with books like this, which she read to help her solve the riddle of the male sex. He had made several attempts to wean her on to *real* books, had read aloud to her in bed at night, given her books to read; careful not to overtax her to start with, he had promised to massage her back if she would at least read *Perfume* all the way through. No use. Whenever he saw her with a book in her hand it was a women's self-help manual.

Underneath *You Just Don't Understand Me* was a weekly paper which Leon had not yet read. He decided to sacrifice the Travel section, and spread it out on the passenger seat.

'Anyone would think I was a dog,' said Martina, sitting down on the Travel section, and she added, 'We must call the police.'

Leon was reluctant; they had driven a long way to look at this house and now they were nearly there. He didn't want to be held up by the police.

'She's already dead, isn't she? She's in no hurry now. Someone else will find her tomorrow, someone keen to feel important and happy to spend hours filling in forms. Why spoil his fun?'

He started the car. The windscreen wipers swept water aside.

'But we *must* call the police,' repeated Martina, crackling as she sat on the newspaper. 'We simply have to. Anonymously anyway.'

Ten minutes later the black Mercedes stopped in a small town called Freyenow, which was as quiet and empty as if it were suffering the aftermath of a nuclear disaster. Leon went into a phone-box and tapped his forefinger three times on the One of the metal keypad.

'Yes, a dead body,' he said into the crackling receiver, moving his lips distinctly and looking at Martina through the lenses of his glasses, the glazed side of the phone-box and the passenger window of the Mercedes, which were all steaming up fast with condensation. Martina put the sun visor down and wiped her face clean with a handkerchief in front of the make-up mirror, but she was still watching him out of the corner of her eye. When Leon got back into the car he gave her cheek a friendly pinch.

'Well, happy now?'

She nodded. 'I think I'd have dreamt of that woman every night if we hadn't called.'

Leon took a chamois leather out of the glove compartment and wiped the condensation first off his glasses and then off the windscreen on the driver's side. He handed the leather to Martina, turned the ignition key, and switched the blower on full blast. The engine started as usual, the fan whirred, but the windscreen wipers would not budge. Leon tried all the different speeds, and switched the wipers off and then on again.

'Aren't they working?' asked Martina.

'You can see they aren't working!'

Raindrops streaked the windows, quivering as they flowed into each other and parting company again as they grew heavier. Leon was not knowledgeable about cars. Although he considered himself a very good driver, he knew nothing at all about repairs. He had never carried out an oil change in his life, or even changed a tyre. He took his car to the garage for every little thing. He remembered seeing a grey and purple filling station just beyond the sign for Freyenow, so he turned and drove back.

The cash desk of the filling station was staffed by a skinny youth of seventeen with an earring and crew-cut short blond hair, left long only at the nape of his neck. He was leafing through a motorbike magazine, and did not look up as Leon came in. Leon cleared his throat and took off his glasses, which were steaming up again.

'Hey, can you take a look at my car? The windscreen wipers aren't working.'

The young attendant raised his head. His black Heavy Metal T-shirt was printed with a death's head and barbarian women swinging axes. He inspected the man waiting at the counter with steam rising from him, cleaning his glasses with his thumb, and it took him only a second to realise that this was someone he despised. It was the way he stood there.

'Checked the fuses, have you?'

'Fuses?'

The boy put a blister pack containing some longish blue, red and yellow bits of plastic on the counter.

'Change the fuse first. Mostly that's the trouble.'

He went back to his magazine.

Leon took a deep breath and assumed a forced grin. 'Look, couldn't you do it for me? I don't know how to do that sort of thing.'

The boy leaned back.

'Nope. Can't leave here,' he said calmly, with a certain relish. 'On my own in the shop, see. You can change a fuse, can't you?'

At this moment Martina came in and placed herself behind Leon, looking embarrassed.

'Is there somewhere here I can wash my hands?' she murmured.

The boy jumped up, closed his magazine and took a key down from the hook. The key was tied to a large, hollow marrowbone with a piece of string.

'Here you are,' he said. 'Toilet's on the left beside the car-wash. No, wait a moment – I'll show you the way.'

He held the door open for her.

'Hey, you're in a bad way,' he said. 'Had a fall, did you? I'll give you my T-shirt if you like.'

The boy was smiling and perspiring as he desperately racked his brains for something amusing to say. He did not spare Leon so much as a glance.

For one faint-hearted, wretched moment Leon wished he was a woman, a long-legged blonde with red-lacquered vampire claws who would never be expected to know how to change a fuse or find the way to the toilet on her own. Then he took his wallet out of his jacket, and when the adolescent attendant came back and was about to sit down and return to his magazine, Leon placed a fifty-mark note on the counter.

'OK, take your car into the workshop! I'll just lock up here.'

It took the boy all of four minutes to change the fuse. He worked in a pointedly casual way, not bothering about Leon's presence while he stared at Martina's long legs, clean again now, as she sat in the passenger seat. Then he wiped his hands on a cloth which was much dirtier than they were. He imbued this process with all the bitterness he felt at encountering someone who couldn't even change a fuse but drove a Mercedes 300, while he, who knew everything there was to know about cars, wasn't yet old enough for a driving licence.

'There you go, then,' he said, planting himself in front of Leon with the cloth over his shoulder. 'Saw how it's done, I hope? You'll be able to deal with it yourself next time.'

Leon bent down and into the car, switched on the windscreen wipers, which went back and forth twice – swish, swish – and switched them off again. Then he slowly straightened up and calmly grabbed the lanky youth by the collar. The lad was not much taller than he was.

'You just listen to me,' he said, so quietly that it was almost a whisper, pulling the boy close to him. 'I don't need to know how to do these things. Not me. I'm not cramming my head with proletarian skills just to please you. I believe in a society based on the division of labour, understand? There are people like you to repair cars, thousands of people like you, every last one with an earring and a crew-cut and a rat's tail down the back of his neck. And there are people like me who pay people like you to repair their cars and keep their mouths shut. Clear about that, are we?'

'Yeah, OK man, OK!'

Leon let go of the attendant, got into his Mercedes, and reversed out of the workshop without giving him another glance. Martina giggled appreciatively and kissed Leon on the cheek. He put his arm round her shoulders. Having money made up for a good deal.

Leon Ulbricht could still remember very well what it was like *not* having money, because he had only just left that state of affairs behind. He was a writer. He wrote short stories about disappointed men very much like himself, and poems which neither rhymed nor sold.

'I hate rhyming verse,' said Leon. 'I always wonder what the point of it is.'

He lived in Hamburg, and until recently had rented a fusty flat on the third floor of a neglected old building without any fancy stucco work or ornamentation. He shared this flat with a trainee slaughterman, with whom he had nothing in common but the fact that they were the only Western Europeans among the tenants in the building. The slaughterman had been there first and occupied the larger and better of the two rooms, with a view of the yard behind the building. Leon's room was on the side overlooking the street, with the abattoir opposite. He could see part of it from his window. When he had been working all night he would see the trucks arrive with animals' noses pressed to the ventilation gaps in the sides, sometimes double-decker trucks several metres long and full of pigs. They came early in the morning, when the city was at its quietest: soap-pink pigs with absurdly long bodies, obscene hindquarters, and their tails bitten off. He had once seen a pig break loose and stumble aimlessly round the site until blood-spattered men caught it and dragged it back by its ears. When he opened the window to air his room and the wind was blowing the wrong way there was a smell of blood and death – particularly in summer.

Harry had suddenly turned up at his place on one such summer evening the previous year. Harry Klammt was Leon's best and only friend. The fact that they almost never saw each other made no difference. Leon knew he could phone Harry any time – even at three in the morning – say: 'Come and give me a tow; my car's broken down on the motorway,' and Harry would set off at once and be glad to, even if he was 500 kilometres away.

When the doorbell rang Leon was lying on his bed, the only comfortable piece of furniture in his room, watching a film about Komodo dragons on TV. The flat had got very hot during the day, and he had left the window open, although the air coming in was so saturated with blood that he had a constant taste in his mouth as if he had just eaten two raw steaks. Leon left the slaughterman to answer the door, because visitors were nearly always for him. Leon did know a great many women, but when he went to bed with them he preferred to do it in their flats rather than his own. He found just getting up and leaving easier than throwing a woman out.

When the door of his room opened and Harry came in, the Komodo dragons were in the process of cornering a stag against a cliff. Harry wore a charcoal-grey suit with wide trousers; it looked both expensive and casual. He had shaved off the beard which used to soften the ruthless set of his mouth, and he now wore his hair in a ponytail tied with green pipe cleaners. Harry had grown thinner. His angular cheekbones stood out, and the whites of his eyes had taken on a yellow tinge.

'Hey there, old mate!' he said, and Leon jumped up, crying, 'Hey, man!'

They punched each other's upper arms and grasped one another by the shoulders. Harry was a head taller than Leon, and there was no resemblance between them in other respects either. Leon was stocky, with soft features, and sometimes looked almost tearful because he suffered from allergies which made his eyes red and swollen. The only distinct lines in his face were the contours of his glasses. He was wearing a pair of black jeans and a black T-shirt, as he almost always did. Leon was about to turn off the television, but when he reached for the remote control Harry stopped him and took hold of it.

'No, leave it! Leave it on! Hey, just look at those crazy creatures. They're those lizards that can push a whole goat off a cliff and then tear it to bits. They go on and on at it. I saw something about them before. Break your legs with a flick of their tails.'

They both sat down on the bed and leaned back against the wall, and Leon, who had seen the beginning of the film, was able to add that Komodo dragons also dug up corpses from cemeteries.

'Charming,' said Harry. 'Tell you what, it stinks in here a bit. I hope it's from outside.'

'No, it's me,' said Leon. 'I've given up washing.'

Something else Leon valued in his friendship with Harry was that even if they hadn't seen each other for years, they did not go in for lengthy explanations when they met again, but acted as if they had parted only the evening before.

The Komodo dragons had brought the stag to bay, and were attacking it, all six of them. They did not break its neck at once, but swarmed all over it, biting little mouthfuls of flesh out of it as it uttered shrill screams. One of the great lizards lay sucking at a leg, another was tearing pieces from the stag's chest, and one ripped its belly open, plunged a snake-like head inside, and came out with its scales glistening with blood. And the stag kept screaming all the time, screaming and screaming, until the lizards had buried it entirely beneath them and its cries died away.

'Filthy brutes,' said Harry. 'Filthy brutes – amazing, though.'

A blonde wildlife expert appeared on screen. She inspected the holes in the ground where the lizards lived and showed how deep they were by getting in herself, legs first. She was in luck: all the Komodo dragons were out and about killing stags. A few camera shots later, the wildlife expert, carrying a plastic bag, was making her way over to a somnolent group of lizards. She threw eggs and meat on the ground and stayed close to the creatures as they ate. One lizard swallowed a whole chicken, feathers, feet, beak and all, and when the woman took another egg out of the bag, thinking it was still busy with the chicken, it made for her. She only just managed to jump aside, but the lizard snatched the plastic bag from her hand and swallowed it and its contents as rapidly as it had eaten the chicken.

'Wow! went Leon.

The woman wasn't giving up. She kept feeding the weird lizards, getting closer and closer to them all the time. She poured water from a plastic bottle over their heads to cool them off, and finally she sat on top of one, stroking its wrinkled throat.

'Shit, what's she doing?' asked Harry. 'What's her idea? Why's the silly cow doing that?'

The lizard shot a long, forked tongue out of its mouth, and the woman caressed the tongue as well, letting it wind itself round her hand, praising the dragon lizard for its beautiful organ.

'This is just perverted!' said Harry.

'Komodo lizards don't like that kind of thing,' said Leon. 'Reptiles don't fancy people canoodling with them anyway. It just gets them down.'

The woman produced a pair of tweezers and removed dead scales and dirt from the lizard's skin. Then she kissed the Komodo dragon on its mouth.

'Oh, switch it off,' said Harry. 'I've had enough of that pushy cunt. Anyway, I want to show you something.'

Leon stood up and switched the TV off. He took a crumpled hundred-mark note out of a desk drawer and put it in his trouser pocket. Harry was already waiting at the door.

'We're going to the Mai Tai,' he said.

This rather unsettled Leon. The Mai Tai was a bar in one of the side streets off the Reeperbahn. This was Harry's world, not Leon's. The company in the Mai Tai – apart from the staff – consisted exclusively of men: men who always paid even large bills in cash, and whose professions were all bound up in some way or other with prostitution, drugs, or massage parlours. It was a place where the legal system of Germany was unable to make much headway against the pitiless and far older law of the physically stronger, swifter and more brutal, and a place where it was good to know you had Harry with you. He worked as a kind of business manager for the bar. Leon suspected that once again Harry had turned up with some definite end in view. The last time Harry took him to the Mai Tai, Leon was asked to make a false statement in court on his behalf. He didn't like the idea of doing anything like that again, but if Harry asked him, then he would unhesitatingly say yes.

This time, however, it seemed to be about something

different, because they went down to the boxing ring in the basement of the bar.

'That's Pfitzner,' whispered Harry, jerking his chin in the direction of the two men dancing round one another in baggy shorts, their torsos solarium-tanned. Leon nodded, although the name meant nothing to him. Pfitzner had silver-grey, shoulder-length hair, as impressive and terrifying as the magnificent coat of an adult male baboon. He must have been over sixty, and was at least ten kilos overweight. A large spare tyre hung over his golden trunks, and he obviously moved more slowly than his opponent, a young Turk. But even Leon could tell that Pfitzner must have been a really good boxer once. He was giving the Turk a good many problems. Leon inhaled the smell of fresh male sweat, and listened reverently to the quiet pounding of soft sports shoes and the slap of leather on flesh, now and then accompanied by panting. Every time Pfitzner's massive, hairy skull jerked sideways, Leon ducked too. He had tried boxing only once in his life – against Harry – and he had been floored immediately. (Curiously, being knocked out had been rather a pleasant experience, and hadn't hurt at all.)

'Right, that'll do,' said Pfitzner at last, and the young Turk immediately stopped fighting. They both held their gloves up at head height and knocked them gently together. The Turk climbed through the ropes, picked up his purple and black striped bag, and disappeared through a door which Leon had not noticed before because, like the walls, it was covered by boxing posters. Pfitzner, nostrils widened, came over to the corner where Harry and Leon were standing and got Harry to undo and remove his gloves. His knuckles were scarred. Harry handed him a towel, and Pfitzner rubbed his neck and wiped his belly down.

'This is him, is it?' he asked, having given Leon a perfunctory glance. Pfitzner's eyelids drooped so low that they covered part of his irises, giving his face the look of a melancholy viper.

Harry nodded, with a nervous laugh.

'And you reckon he'll do?'

'He's my best friend,' said Harry.

Leon swallowed. Whatever Harry's idea was, he would never let him down.

'Your friend likes to wear black, right?' said Pfitzner. He blew his nose into the towel, examined the mucus, and then told Leon, 'OK, Blacky, bring me my bag!'

Something in Leon rebelled. Pride required him to stay put and let the old sod fetch his own bag. At the same time, however, he sensed that Harry would not have hesitated to carry out the order, and now Harry was not expecting him, Leon, to let him down. Leon went back to the stairs, where he saw a sky-blue Adidas bag, and brought it over to the fat old boxer in the golden shorts. He was doing it for Harry. Pfitzner took the bag. He opened the zip, took out a bundle of banknotes, and handed them to Leon.

'Here's 50,000,' he said. 'That's the advance. You get the other 50,000 when the book's finished.'

Leon looked at Harry. Harry was grinning as if some vital part of his brain had been surgically removed. Then Leon stared at the money. He was amazed to see what a thin bundle 50,000 marks in cash amounted to, and he was amazed to see that thin bundle lying in his own hand.

From then on everything had been different.

Leon took his hand off Martina's shoulders and put it back on the steering wheel, since the bridge mentioned in the estate agent's directions lay just ahead of them. It was a straight wooden bridge made of stout, dark-brown planks roughly fitted together. It crossed a canal off the road a few kilometres beyond Freyenow. On the far side of the bridge there was a minor road which no one had thought merited a signpost. It was flanked by two ditches, one on each side, from which murky rust-coloured water flowed into the canal. The road was paved with round cobblestones, but two tracks of flat stones had been laid down the middle, making driving over it a little more comfortable. In low spirits, Leon and Martina observed the scene bumping past them on the other side of the wet car windows. Beet fields alternated with lush meadows, to be followed by more beet fields. Then the beet fields came to an end, and long ditches ran through the meadows into which the ground bled its reddish-brown water. Leon switched the radio on. He had to change stations twice before finding any music he could tolerate. He expected Martina to complain about the old reggae piece that was playing, but instead she started on about the drowned body again.

'What were you holding that stick for? You still haven't told me what you were doing with that stick.'

'You think I ought to have touched it with my hand?'

'Why did you have to touch it at all?'

He shrugged his shoulders. He would rather not explain that he had used the stick to push the dead woman's arm under the water and watch it drift up again, and to find out whether the skin would tear if he prodded it. (It didn't.)

'For God's sake, I had to make sure she was dead. And she is. Stone dead, get it? She didn't feel anything.'

'You could have told that by looking at her. *Anyone* could see she was dead. And you stayed there so long.'

Leon did not answer. Martina turned away from him and

looked out of the window again. The rain was falling from ever darker clouds. Dusk took over the whole sky at the same time. The animal kingdom was not a cheering sight either. Once she saw black and white bull calves pressing their mud-encrusted bodies against a metal fence. A solitary brown horse stood in another meadow, its right hind leg held at an angle to take the weight off it. The horse looked limp. Its ears pointed sideways, and although its teeth met, its grey lower lip hung down heavily, forming a small, soft bowl into which no doubt the rain was falling. Martina sighed deeply.

'It'll look quite different here when the sun's out,' said Leon, trying to cheer both her and himself. But Martina looked at him as sullenly as if the whole thing were his fault and his alone – the rain, their bleak surroundings, just about everything.

Martina was prettier than any of the other women Leon had ever slept with. None the less, he had never wondered how this long-legged lovely with her racehorse elegance had come to fall in love with him of all people, a short, myopic writer. Once, when he was asked in an interview: 'What do you consider your greatest talent?' he had replied, 'I can get any woman I want.' Whereupon the magazine received quantities of indignant letters from its readers – mainly from women who described Leon Ulbricht as an arrogant bastard, a four-eyed dwarf and a nasty male chauvinist pig. He relished such attacks and the helpless resentment behind them. However, he was not as proud of his greatest talent as it might seem. Of course Leon liked it when other men envied him, when they racked their brains trying to work out how this ugly little fellow, who wasn't even rich, managed to snap up their own women. Perhaps that was the best part of it, but it did not give him a feeling of superiority, quite the opposite. To Leon himself, his erotic talents – his charm, his capacity to empathise, even the technical skill with which he satisfied women (in fact that skill most of all) – seemed slightly undignified. About as worthwhile as the ability to juggle plates, or balance a tray of twenty full glasses on your head while riding a unicycle without holding on to the handlebars. A real man – and here he wasn't even thinking of Harry or Pfitzner – a real man should have other qualities. A real man was someone who earned big money, had a house, fathered children, knew how to repair cars and never failed to open a jar of pickled cucumbers. A real man could always get a hard-on when it mattered, and that was that.

He had met Martina at a local TV talk show on to which Leon had been invited to present his latest volume of poetry, *Create Or Cry Aloud*. The presenter's questions, however, were concerned not so much with the poems as with the rumour that a pimp was paying Leon Ulbricht to write his biography. Martina was sitting in the audience. She was really an editorial assistant on the show, but during transmissions the production manager always put her among the spectators, right at the front where she would frequently be in the shot. As a result, Leon had at first taken her for one of the photographic models who got free tickets through their agencies so that they could display their long legs in front of the cameras, now and then pushing back the hair from their exceptionally lovely faces. Besides the usual physical attractions of those in the modelling profession, it was Martina's eyes that had struck him most.

'You have eyes like a hunted deer,' Leon had told her when he was standing next to her at the buffet after the end of the show. He told all women, on principle, that he thought they were unhappy. If a doctor gives you the right diagnosis you trust him to treat you, and in Leon's experience beautiful women were no happier than any others. In fact their unhappiness differed from that of ugly women only in that the ugly women thought they knew why they were unhappy.

Four weeks later Leon had packed his books, his computer, his desk, his zebra skin and a suitcase into a rented VW van, and moved into Martina's large, light flat. He left the surprised trainee slaughterman the rest of his furniture and his old sound system, along with his black vinyl records (he took the CDs with him), explaining that all really great writers had lived in well-ordered surroundings. It was the same with competitive sportsmen.

Four months later he married Martina. Leon pictured himself leading a quiet, serious life in a little house far from the superficiality of the big city. He wouldn't give any more poetry readings. And he wouldn't write any more magazine articles, only books. The thick, weighty books of a mature, judicious man. First the book about Benno Pfitzner, then others. And meanwhile he would watch his children growing up. He and Martina began going through the property ads in the newspapers in search of a cheap house in the country. They had already looked at two. One was a miserable hovel, and the other was less than 200 metres from a motorway. But the last ad Martina had read out to him sounded good, even though it had been put in the paper by an estate agent. It said the house was on the outskirts of a small East German village, with nothing beyond it but marshes unsuitable for development, a nature reserve. And it cost only 40,000 marks. So they had set out again on a journey which this time took them quite a long way into the former German Democratic Republic. It had been raining when they started out.

*   *   *

And it was still raining when they reached Priesnitz. Priesnitz was so small that it had neither a school nor a church. Twenty-six houses and cottages and a grocery shop stood along the single village street. Currant bushes and crooked fruit trees grew behind wire fences. Just before the signpost which had once borne the name of the village, the land rose slightly without actually becoming a hill. The roadside ditches ended here. Instead, on the right-hand side of the road, a lively stream splashed its way towards Leon and Martina, disappearing into an underground concrete pipe every time it came to the entrance of a house. The stream changed from flowing above ground to flowing underground like a needle swiftly stitching. Apart from the freshly plastered grocery shop, where a youth sat on his moped under the dripping roof of its porch, staring after the Mercedes for a long time, and apart from a shed which some farmer with time on his hands had decorated with old car tyres cut in half and sprayed white, all the buildings were made of dark materials. Some of the roofs had been repaired with black tarpaulin. A broad strip of red plastic running diagonally across the window of one house, advertising videos for hire in white lettering, looked startlingly garish in these surroundings. Where the road was no longer lined by houses, tall birches grew beside it, and beyond them stood a manor house, a castle-like building which must have been a hundred years old, its right-hand side falling down and overgrown with ivy and creepers, its left-hand side sporting seven satellite dishes. On reaching the birch trees the stream struck off into the fields – or rather, as it was flowing towards them, this was where it emerged from the fields. The paved road became a gravel track and made for the manor house as if planning to run right through it. At the last moment, just in front of the flight of steps up to the house, it swerved sharply right, went straight ahead again for another few hundred metres, and petered out in a field of knee-high maize. The brook ran on, gurgling, by the side of the maize field. A path running through the meadows to the left in front of the field led to a grey house a little way off. The path was unpaved and was not even a proper path; after a few metres it consisted solely of two deep ruts gouged out of the wet red mud by the tyres of a tractor. Tall grass grew between them, slurping and scraping along under the Mercedes. Leon was afraid of getting bogged down and damaging the underside of the car on a stone, wrecking something important and expensive. The tank. The gearbox!

Pfitzner had given him the Mercedes. After that first meeting in the boxing ring, he had visited Pfitzner at least twice a week. They usually went into the back room of an amusement arcade where not even Harry was allowed to join them. The room had red wallpaper, and aluminium-framed black and white photos of naked and half-naked women adorned the walls. They were either lying on their stomachs or turning their backs to the viewer, all of them with their buttocks raised so high in the air that you feared for their backbones. Here Pfitzner indulged in the clichés which went with a life like his and seemed to please him. He always sank into a worn, yellow velour armchair, took off his woven shoes, undid the top button of his trousers and chose a Toscani cigar from one of the cedarwood boxes standing around the poorly lit, poorly aired room. His lips wrinkled as they clamped around the cigar, he took several puffs, then stuck the Toscani between his fingers, which were laden with rings, and began talking. Leon, hunched in the velour armchair opposite, opened his ring-bound notebook and wrote down the stories of the great Benno Pfitzner, prince of the red-light district, brothel owner, former boxer, who once almost had a World Championship fight. A magnificent life which would make a magnificent book – vivid, hard-hitting, with a touch of sentimentality too.

Leon felt flattered that it was to him Pfitzner was entrusting his story. It pleased him to think that his work – the work of a writer – was of value in the eyes of an ex-boxer. Sometimes he imagined that Pfitzner, who was superior to him in everything which mattered to a man, might actually think he was superior – if only in this single field – and perhaps even admired him. It was true that Benno Pfitzner's reminiscences gave not the slightest grounds for thinking that he had ever admired anyone but himself, but at their penultimate meeting for the time being, after Pfitzner had told the rest of his story and Leon had said he was probably going to move to the country, to the East, Pfitzner suddenly handed him the key of the black Mercedes.

'So that you can get back to Hamburg quickly now and then. I was going to buy a new one anyway. This one's older than I like them now.'

'How do you mean?' Leon had asked, his mouth dry.

'Go on, take it. It's OK,' Pfitzner had said, handing him the papers for the car too.

Although Leon was driving no faster than walking pace, dirty water from the potholes sprayed right up to the windscreen. Soil grated beneath the windscreen wipers. The tractor ruts which had been guiding the car along like railway tracks turned in the direction of the maize field just outside the garden fence, and when the Mercedes climbed up out of them, exactly what Leon had been fearing the whole time happened: the sump scraped on a stone. Leon gave a start, and Martina looked anxiously at his face. But when he drew up outside the rusty garden gate, switched the engine off and raised his eyes for the first time – they had been intent on the treacherous path until now – he forgot the sump and the stone at once. There were the marshes. Leon got out. He went round the house, following the fence. Directly behind the house began a matted carpet of bright green tussocks of vegetation interspersed by circular, dark-brown pools. A meadow of tall swamp grass adjoined it, stretching a long way, up to a row of pines. The overcast sky had taken on a pastel-blue tint. Above the trees two long, diagonal rifts broke through the cloud cover, with yellow sunbeams descending from them to earth, neatly bunched together like water flowing from the perforated rose of a watering can. There was a purple haze over the marshes, making most of the outlines blur in psychedelic lighting effects. The skeletal trees of a drowned wood stood out against this background as clear and black as if a patient with a choleric condition had drawn them in his art therapy group, breaking his pencil several times in the process. The grass growing out of a tree stump and the fat cigars of the reed mace just beyond the garden fence were all as sharp as scissor cuts. A creature of some kind uttered a strident, jarring cry.

'When did it stop raining?'

Martina had joined him.

'Coming? I want to see the house. Or at least take a look through the window before the estate agent turns up.'

'You go first. I'll be right behind you.'

When Martina opened the garden gate she discovered that the iron fence had sharp spikes in it at regular intervals.

Rather dangerous. Children playing here could impale themselves on those spikes, and then you'd have their parents suing for compensation. She decided that Leon had better paint the main part of the fence blue, and the rings and spikes gold. She would grow sunflowers by the gate. She went towards the house, the wet grass brushing her calves. There was no path any more. The garden beds were overgrown too, and rhubarb leaves and a few faded daffodils suddenly appeared in the middle of the lawn, which had run wild. The single-storey building had a steep pitched roof and a veranda, which was protected from the wind by corrugated green plastic. That would have to go, of course, and be replaced by wooden walls which Leon could then paint white. Martina hoped he would be capable of doing that much at least. She walked round the house rattling the window frames, beneath which thriving clumps of stinging nettles flourished. The kitchen window had been smashed recently, and gaped open like a large, ugly wound in the plaster. The swollen and flaking frame pushed in easily. Martina hauled herself up on the window sill and clambered inside, crawled over a dirty table beneath the window, and landed in a pile of broken flowerpots. Passing a stove on stilt legs, she reached a dark narrow passage. Martina felt about for a light switch, but there were no bulbs in the five-branched ceiling lamp. To the right was a room with a worn yellow fitted carpet. She could see Leon through the window. He was still staring at the marshes with a happy grin on his face. He looked silly. The next door led to a small bathroom with loudly patterned orange wallpaper which had come away from the walls at the edges and was rolled up like the tip of a fern. An unframed rectangular mirror with at least one dead insect per square centimetre hung above the washbasin. The washbasin itself was encrusted with stains of some white substance which might be either dried toothpaste or dried bird droppings. There was a slimy piece of red rubber tubing on the end of the tap. Disgusted, Martina pulled it off and dropped it in the bathtub, which had a greasy brown rim showing the last tidemark on its scratched enamel. There was a fine display of mould, like a Chinese firework display, in one corner of the room. Leon could tile the bathroom green and white. It would be better to use small tiles because it was such a small room. Perhaps they could find an old-fashioned tub standing on lion's claws somewhere.

The room opposite must be the living room. It was the largest. Someone had pulled up one corner of the faded and formerly red linoleum, exposing damp wood shavings and rotting floorboards which gave off a strong smell of mushrooms. There was no window looking out on the veranda, but the room had a large fireplace. On the other side a door led to a smaller room with wallpaper depicting elephants in pink and blue dungarees dancing round each other, out hunting with butterfly nets. There were no more rooms, which meant that this one would be Leon's study, unless he preferred to put all his stuff in the first room, next to the kitchen. This was where he would write the book which had brought him the money he was so touchingly proud of.

Leon was the first man Martina had ever really fallen in love with, and the first man in her life to have no money. For to Martina, 50,000 or even 100,000 marks were not real money. Leon was extraordinarily sensitive on the subject. He would never let Martina settle the bill in a restaurant, and he had insisted on paying for the wedding himself, which meant no bridesmaids, no church and no wedding cake. In the end it was just eight of them in a Chinese restaurant: Leon, Leon's mother, Martina, her parents, her sister Eva and the witnesses, a make-up girl from the talk show and Harry. Martina found Harry rather repulsive, and couldn't see why he was Leon's friend. Luckily he had come to visit them only once so far. When they moved out of the city perhaps she wouldn't have to see him at all any more. She herself had no close friends. Her beauty made a rival out of any woman who might have been a friend, and one of her many boring admirers out of every man.

The wedding was a disaster. Martina's father couldn't stand Leon. It was he who had made sure a prenuptial contract was drawn up dividing their property. He got drunk on rice wine in the Chinese restaurant and told Leon, 'Treat her right or I'll tear your balls off.'

'Yes, OK,' said Leon.

'Bastard,' said Martina's father. 'Never done a proper day's work in your life. Can't even wear a decent suit to your own wedding. What is this anyway? Call it a wedding? More like a fishing trip.' He stood up and threw his fork into the huge goldfish aquarium, which was bubbling much too loud. Leon's mother, who wore a black wool dress and looked small and shrivelled as a dry nut, began to cry. Martina's mother swept over to her in billows of orange tulle and took her in her fat arms. She looked anxiously and reproachfully at her husband.

'Oh, really, Dieter! This isn't the time or the place.'

'Piss off,' said Leon. 'Piss off to your scrapyard and sit in one of your old wrecks and jerk yourself off.'

Harry laughed so hard he got hiccups, and Martina's sister took the opportunity to move away from him and avoid the arm which Harry had placed round the back of her chair. Martina's father looked as if he might have a stroke any moment, but he did not throw himself on Leon; instead, purple in the face, he simply marched out, waving an imperious hand to indicate that his family should follow him. Martina's mother and Eva silently obeyed. He had looked at Martina as if expecting her to rise to her feet too. But now her name was Martina Ulbricht.

When she met Leon at the buffet after the talk show, her name was still Roswitha Voss. Leon had told her Roswitha was a terrible name, she might as well have the words SOCIAL MISFIT tattooed on her forehead, and supposing she ever decided to work in a bar with bedrooms for hire by the hour, she'd have no need to think up something different. That was how he had put it, and he hurt her feelings. It was a new experience. Normally men showered her with compliments because they were too indifferent towards her – apart from a certain pride of possession, and the greed they felt in their trousers – to go to the trouble of hurting her feelings. And since Leon was a writer into the bargain Roswitha had fallen in love with him at once, and from then on called herself Martina. She lost her old surname when she married him too.

A floorboard creaked. Martina looked round in alarm. Suddenly all the corners were full of eerie shadows, thick black shadows like something alive and damp. She hurried through the mouldering living room and along the dark passage, and thus back to the kitchen. Some plaster fell from the ceiling. An insect rattled its wings. Martina climbed on the kitchen table and scrambled out of the window into the garden. When she landed she saw something moving beside her foot. She bent down to look at it.

Leon was still standing in the same place. He was wondering how he had ever stood life in the city. How could he have written there? He'd be able to write better here than anywhere else. The sight of the marshes filled Leon with helpless longing. You could possess a woman's beauty by sleeping with her. You could shoot a fine animal, or buy it or eat it. What could you do about a landscape, though? He felt like throwing himself on the ground and burying his face in the moss. But that would have looked very foolish, so he refrained.

The garden gate creaked. Martina came through it. She was carrying a charred stick, longer and thicker than her lower arm.

'Just look what I found,' she cried, holding the stick in front of his face. Now Leon saw that it was not a stick at all, but a lizard, a fat, velvety-black salamander of tropical size. Two rows of flat warts ran down its back. A revolting creature.

'Isn't it sweet?' said Martina. The sweet amphibian glared malevolently at Leon and opened its mouth. A drop of milky slime ran out of its jaws and dripped on Leon's right hand. It burned like acid from a car battery. Leon screeched.

'Throw the disgusting thing away,' he roared. 'Chuck it away! It's poisonous!'

He wiped the back of his hand on the grass. There was a dark-red burning mark on the skin. Martina put the salamander carefully down on the grass. It waddled a little way forward on its crooked legs. Leon kicked it, and the salamander flew through the air to the edge of one of the pools of water, where it pushed off with its hind legs, plopped in, and disappeared.

'Why do you have to pick up everything you find and cart it around with you? Like a small child,' said Leon crossly. He went over to another pool, not the one into which the salamander had slipped. But when he looked at the clouded, brown, almost black surface of the water and imagined what kind of creatures might perhaps be lurking down below, he didn't feel like putting his hand into it. Martina fetched a tissue from the glove compartment of the car and spat on it. Leon stretched out his burnt hand.

'We ought to have kept the salamander,' said Martina, rubbing at the red mark. 'Look, all the hairs are coming off there. Perhaps we could have invented a new depilatory cream from its spit. We'd have made our fortunes.'

'Or perhaps it's *your* spit stinging me. Why do you women always have to use spit? I remember my mother always spitting on a handkerchief to wipe my face. Yuk! Disgusting!'

Martina stopped rubbing.

'I was only trying to be helpful.'

He took her by the chin.

'Come on,' he said, 'let's have a little more of your spit, then!'

He kissed her, a deep kiss. She resisted at first, then gave in and put her arms round his neck.

Just before it was completely dark the estate agent drove up in a Landrover and Leon bought the house.

2

Skies overcast, with rain. Highest temperatures around 15 degrees. Wind moderate. Cold for the time of year.

The house soon turned out to have drawbacks. It groaned. Usually it groaned once between three and four in the morning, and sometimes again at around four-thirty. The sound woke Leon and Martina up on their first few nights. Then they integrated it into their dreams, which from now on were full of creaking bridges and falling trees. There was also the new wallpaper. It did not stay stuck everywhere. Water oozed from the wall in various places, dissolving the paste or leaving tidemarks which resembled unsightly patches of sweat. Water dripped down the insides of the window frames.

'It will get better when it stops raining,' said Leon.

After all, the house couldn't be held responsible for the fact that it had rained almost every day since they moved in. And the bad weather did have one advantage: Leon's immune system did not have to cope with airborne pollen. Far worse, from his point of view, was the fact that there was another house barely 700 metres away, beyond the drowned wood. On the day they had come to look at their house the outline of the neighbouring building was blurred by the dim light, and Leon had taken it for a particularly dark patch of mist. Now he felt cheated of his marshland solitude.

'No, no, it's all in order,' said the estate agent, when Leon finally got him on the phone after three weeks. This time he had called quite early in the morning, when the estate agent appeared to be alone in the office and was incautious enough to pick up the phone. 'If the nearest house is over 400 metres away it's perfectly legitimate to describe a property as isolated. Anyway, what's so bad about one house? Two ladies living quietly together. What are you so worked up about?' he asked, yawning down the phone.

'What's so bad?' shouted Leon. 'One house is a thousand times worse than twenty neighbours. Very likely the old ladies have been longing for company for years.'

He let the receiver drop and hit the side of the phone-box, and marched out into the rain. The mark on his hand was beginning to itch again. Leon stopped, gave the weeping red area a good scratch, and cast dark glances at the dangling telephone receiver. Then he set off back to Priesnitz.

Every time he wanted to make a phone call he had to go to Freyenow, because there was no phone line in his house, and the only public phone in Priesnitz was in the grocer's shop. The grocer's name was Guido Kerbel, and he laughed on the slightest provocation. His laughter consisted of a hoarse screech and the display of a vast amount of pink gum. Exactly the sort of person Leon preferred to keep at arm's length. Martina, of course, had let Kerbel rabbit on to her at length on their second day and find out all about them. In the process she had acquired not only vegetables for soup and a packet of Miracoli but had also found out that their neighbours were sisters. Their name was Schlei and they were said to be rather peculiar, although Kerbel did not expand further on their peculiarity.

As Leon parked outside his garden gate he glanced suspiciously at the Schlei house. A thin plume of smoke rose from its chimney. The sisters themselves had not yet shown any signs of life, which was a good thing, although also odd, since they would have to pass Leon's house to get to Priesnitz or indeed anywhere else in the world. He climbed up to the veranda, which had not yet been painted. The rain never stopped for long enough to let the wood dry out. A brown slug was leaving a slimy trail as it crawled along the rounded balustrade. Leon bent down to look at it. A small, perfect organism, emitting bubbles. Infinitely vulnerable, nothing but a bit of muscle in a slimy skin, yet able to crawl over broken glass without suffering a single scratch. The slug waved the longer pair of its four feelers with deliberation and then contracted itself. Leon straightened up again and opened the front door.

'Well, what did he say? Will you get any money back?' called Martina from the living room. Leon took off his shoes, hung his jacket on the coat rack, and wiped his damp face with the sleeve of his sweatshirt. Then he sniffed, and went in.

'Still no one answering the phone,' he muttered.

Four unpacked boxes stood on the living room rug. A *Ficus benjamini* had fallen over, and the damp black compost from its pot had spread over the rug in crumbs and clumps. Martina, in her houndstooth check trousers, was kneeling on the floor, busy arranging Leon's books on the bookshelves in alphabetical order. She picked up his volumes of Schopenhauer and put them on the second shelf from the bottom, after Rilke.

'Hey, that's nice, you're in just the right position,' said Leon. He kneeled behind her, took her hair and wove and kneaded it into a miniature ponytail, which came undone again at once. Martina uttered a foolish giggle and leaned back against him. Leon rested his chin on her right shoulder and pressed his cheek against hers. They stayed there perfectly still for a minute.

'I'll clear out the toolshed today, if it stays dry,' said Leon at last. 'Nail up a couple of boards and so on. And then I'll fix the waste pipe in the bathroom.'

Martina suddenly stretched, picked a book out of the nearest box at random – it was Wondratschek – and put it on the shelves in completely the wrong place, next to Montherlant. When she straightened up again she had shaken free of Leon's embrace.

'Then do you mind if I take the car and drive to Hamburg?' she asked. 'I've still got to collect the boxes with my childhood things. My mother threatened to throw them all out.'

Leon fished the car keys out of his trouser pocket and dangled them in front of her face.

'Bring me back some more rawlplugs. The little red ones.'

'Thanks,' she said, relieved, and took the keys. It was really generous of Leon. She knew how much the Mercedes meant to him, and as a result she was always afraid of denting the bodywork, and borrowed the car only in emergencies. This was an emergency. She must get out of here before she had to watch Leon knocking nails in crooked again, or missing his target with the screwdriver. She just couldn't bear the stupid things he did. She would have liked to sink his toolbox in the marshes.

Although it was still drizzling she did not put on a coat, only her pale green suit jacket. Leon stood the *Ficus* up again and with his fingers scraped black compost out of the fringes of the rug. Martina leaned down and gave him a goodbye kiss on the forehead. The kiss struck Leon as faintly condescending. He stood up and kissed her on the mouth, carefully keeping his dirty hands away from her and touching her neck only with his wrists. Then he accompanied her to the front door. When he opened it they both got a shock. There was a large dog sitting outside, a dog with floppy ears and a short coat as brown and velvety as reed mace. He stared at them with shining round eyes. He was thin. On seeing Leon and Martina he put his tail between his legs and trotted off.

'Well, at least we've met the *dog* next door now,' said Martina. She tried to tempt him back, but the dog made his way through the fence where two iron uprights were missing and ran off into the marshes without once turning round. Leon whistled, but either the dog was hard of hearing or he considered Leon's whistle of no significance.

'We really ought to have called on those women ages ago,' said Martina. 'Even if you don't want to know them. It's only polite.'

'Are you mad? Don't you dare do any such thing, or we'll never be rid of them. Anyway, I don't think the dog belongs there. It was very thin. Perhaps it's a stray. Perhaps it doesn't belong to anyone.'

'Shall I put a bit of meat out for him? If he gets used to us then we'd have a guard dog.'

'No,' said Leon, 'you'd only be asking for rats.'

Crouching low with the collar of her jacket turned up, Martina ran to the car. As she turned into the maize field she opened the glove compartment and took out the road map. Leon's sunglasses fell out. There were red fruit drops stuck to the road map. The car heater also heated the glove compartment and had melted the sweets into the model of a molecular structure. Martina threw them out of the window and smoothed out the road map on the seat beside her.

Ten minutes later she reached the village street. Kerbel was unrolling the awning in front of his shop to protect his lettuces from the rain. He bared his gums and raised a hand. She waved back. The empty village signpost at the end of the street. The beet fields, the somnolent horse, the calves, the drainage ditches, the cobblestones. Martina switched the windscreen wipers on and then immediately switched them off again. It was raining so slightly that she couldn't find a setting with long enough pauses. She remembered that she had to turn right when she reached the main road. Over the wooden bridge, then right. And the river would be on her left, and would accompany her like a reliable nanny for the next few kilometres. Nice, good river.

Here was the wooden bridge where she should turn right. But to make quite sure she glanced at the map. Yes, right it was. Satisfied, she switched the indicator on. Right. Exactly. Just as she'd thought.

If all went well she'd be at her parents' house at around two. They always had lunch at twelve noon, so there was no danger of having to eat with them. She would put her boxes in the boot, stay for an hour or so, and then drive into the city. A car came towards her. The sight of it raised her spirits. The first car she'd met. Technology. Civilisation. People without gumboots on. She drove through Freyenow. The filling station. Then the lay-by. She could never pass it without thinking of the dead woman. Those feet among the reeds. Martina drove along beside the wide river for an hour before trees cut it off from view, and half an hour later she reached a junction.

'Right, I have to turn right again,' Martina murmured, but she stopped by the side of the road and looked at the map none the less. The world was full of things you could do wrong. Yes, she must turn right. She'd been perfectly correct.

After another half an hour she saw the first sign for Hamburg. By now there was a good deal of traffic. She didn't have to go into the inner city: her father's house and scrapyard were on the edge of town. Martina drove without having to consult the map now, turned off the main road and into the suburb where she had grown up. The streets and squares of her childhood. The meadow where she used to collect food for her rabbits, which was not a meadow any more but the Aldi car-park. The stationery and sweet shop, which was now a mobile phone store. The church with the parish hall where Pastor Spangenberg used to have his youth club disco on the first Friday in the month, to prove that the Church was a modern institution in touch with the young. Not far from the church was the Meyerdorfs' flower shop. Their daughter Susanne had been in Martina's class at school, until she shot herself in her bedroom with her father's sporting gun. She had stuck a note on the door first: 'Dear Mum and Dad. I'm sorry. I hope you don't get too much of a fright. Love, Susi.' The ceiling was spattered with her brains, and her parents had indeed got a terrible fright.

Martina stopped to buy her mother a bunch of flowers. The place now had a buzzer instead of the old-fashioned doorbell, but it still retained the musty, churchyard smell of all small florists' shops. A wreath was leaning against the counter, with a ribbon on it saying: 'A Loving Tribute From . . .'. The names meant nothing to Martina. Frau Meyerdorf came out of the back room where ornamental grasses and twigs, a pair of garden scissors and some raffia lay on a large kitchen table. She smiled her careworn smile and gave Martina her hand, which was so soft after years of working with wet flower stems that it felt as if it were decaying.

'Roswitha, how nice to see you,' said Frau Meyerdorf.

Martina didn't believe it. She was sure the florist really meant: 'Why are you still alive? Why didn't *you* shoot yourself?'

It was a mistake to come in here, thought Martina. Let's hope I don't make any more mistakes. How awful it would be if she began talking about the body in the water near the lay-by! However, she managed to tell the florist about the house in the marshes and her husband without mentioning a body at all, although she used the word *water* with striking frequency. She bought a bunch of blue irises. They were the only really attractive and elegant flowers there, among all the African violets and begonias, carnations, marguerites and vulgar florist's roses. Martina's mother liked such things: cakes of soap costing twenty marks each, patisseries where salesgirls in starched white aprons used little silver tongs to put the cakes in cellophane bags.

With the bunch of flowers on the passenger seat beside her, Martina turned into Rebhuhnstrasse – a long street, although it contained only two addresses: Dieter Voss's scrapyard and Dieter Voss's private house – and the same thing happened as usual when she visited her parents: something settled on her chest like a wet rug, making breathing difficult, something that felt increasingly oppressive the closer she came to her parents' house. Involuntarily, Martina changed down a gear.

The scrapyard was fenced in with wire netting and smelled of oil, petrol and burnt rubber. It was run like a supermarket except that the customers did not wheel trolleys round between shelves stacked with packets of cornflakes and low-sugar jams, but drove their own cars along the rows of derelict vehicles arranged by make.

Most of these customers were young men in blue overalls and old cars. Now and then they stopped and looked more closely at a rusty Honda or a crumpled Golf. When they found what they were looking for they got out and lay down under the car, or bent over the gaping jaws of the engine. Sometimes they would have girls hanging around beside them, freezing cold or with arms folded and obviously bored. The young men would drive back to the hut near the exit with a gearbox or a rear light they had removed from a wrecked car, and showed it to old Heinz. Heinz wrote out the bills and lent them tools, and had sat in this place as long as Martina could remember with his fox terrier – the present dog was his third – which looked like a much-petted stuffed toy. Sometimes Heinz checked the customers' car boots. Small spare parts were stolen all the same.

Behind the scrapyard lay what Dieter Voss called his garden. The site was as big as a football pitch. No fence, no lawn, no flower beds. No gooseberry bushes, rhododendrons or conifers, no birch trees, no broom or juniper bushes, no pansies, not a tulip, not so much as a tiny little lily of the valley. Instead, uneven sandy soil bleaker than a steppe after the dry season. Sparse tufts of grass appeared among puddles of water gleaming with oil. Low-growing, hairy foliage plants like tundra vegetation crept over the yellow sand here and there. The house was twenty metres further on. To the right there was a garage for several cars and a workshop. Dieter Voss was not a man to draw a strict dividing line between his profession and his private life. Eleven cars with their prices in the windscreens stood at the side of the road, cars which were still worth repairing. Only one stood out from the others. It was a pale yellow Audi which had occupied the same spot for over ten years, right at the front where the entrance to the garden would have been if it had been fenced. Its price was faded to illegibility, and by now the patches of rust took up as much space as the places where the paint was still intact. The few harsh grasses grew more densely around it, pushing their way through the bumpers and the radiator grille. The tyres had been flat and punctured for ages, the windows were broken, the upholstery was mouldy and stank. No one would ever buy that car. No one was intended ever to buy that car.

Roswitha had been thirteen when the business with Thomas Marx happened. Thomas Marx was fifteen; he had stayed down a year at school, so he had only just joined Roswitha's class. He had a mild case of acne, straggly fair hair which came down over the collar of his greasy Erdmann leather jacket, and he was thin as a tree frog. Outside school hours there was always a cigarette clinging to his dry upper lip; it didn't fall out of his mouth even when he talked. All the girls who had stopped liking horses and ponies better than boys agreed that he was really cute. Roswitha sometimes met him when she went to the disco in the parish hall.

One day, when she was just showing her forged school ID card at the cash desk, she saw Thomas Marx standing beside the glass case containing the pottery group's exhibits. He was holding a magazine. Four boys surrounded him, giggling. Roswitha put her jeans jacket down on the heap of other coats and went over to the rest of the girls from her class.

'What's up with them?' she asked, pointing her chin in the direction of the group of boys.

'Looking at smut, of course, what d'you think?' said Susi Meyerdorf who was to borrow her father's gun three years later, pushing a strand of hair back behind her ear. Roswitha went over to the boys and craned her neck. But Thomas Marx rolled up the magazine at once and put it in the inside pocket of his leather jacket.

'It's nothing,' he said, and the cigarette in his mouth, which was not filter-tipped, still clung to his upper lip as if held in place by a magnet. The other boys looked embarrassed, but at the same time there was a touch of malice in their expressions. Roswitha knew all those boys. They were in the class next to hers. One of them had kissed her once; the malicious expression was particularly marked on his face. Roswitha shrugged her shoulders, pretended to take a sudden burning interest in the ashtrays, piggy banks and vases in the glass case, and then walked back to Susi Meyerdorf.

'Idiots,' she said, and danced with Susi for a bit. Then there was music for slow-dancing, a song by Paul Young. Susi Meyerdorf, who was slightly shorter, drew Roswitha towards her and laid her head on her shoulder. But at the same moment Thomas Marx tapped Roswitha on the other shoulder, and she immediately let go of her friend and danced with him instead. Thomas Marx did not dance well and was always a little too quick when dancing close like this. Nor did he dance close enough, although he was sufficiently close to whisper in her ear, 'I'll show you the magazine outside if you really want.'

Roswitha did really want. She found her jeans jacket in the pile of coats and followed him. Pastor Spangenberg was standing beside the glass case, trying to recruit a boy for a study group; the boy hadn't slipped past him quickly enough. Spangenberg's language was larded with youthfully trendy expressions which the members of his confirmation class had either abandoned long ago, or used in a completely different context.

'It's vital to have an aim in life,' the pastor was telling the embarrassed fourteen year old. 'You know, I sometimes get the feeling that young folk today have no aim in life any more, if an old crumbly like me may say so.'

He could say whatever he liked. Meanwhile the lads who still featured as teddy boys in his vocabulary were dealing in marijuana and stimulant slimming pills behind his back.

When Thomas and Roswitha left the parish hall it was still light. Only nine o'clock. There was a white half-moon in the sky.

'Not here,' said Thomas, taking out his packet of tobacco to roll himself a cigarette. 'Got to be somewhere we won't be disturbed.'

'The scrapyard,' suggested Roswitha. 'I know where there's a hole in the fence. We can sit in one of the cars.'

As they turned into Rebhuhnstrasse Thomas Marx put his arm round Roswitha and caressed her shoulder. They reached the scrapyard around nine-thirty. It lay in blue twilight. Grasshoppers chirped. Metal creaked. The light from the little hut painted a yellow rectangle on the ground. It looked as if Heinz had stayed later than usual. The fox terrier would start yapping immediately if they tried slipping past.

'I really ought to go home anyway,' said Roswitha.

They went to the end of the fence in silence.

'Why don't we just sit in one of those old crocks?'

Thomas Marx made for the row of cars in Dieter Voss's garden and tried their doors.

'It's no use. Don't!'

But the right-hand back door of the yellow Audi opened. Thomas slipped inside and pulled Roswitha in after him. They closed the door and slid down far enough on the back seat for their heads not to show. There was a smell of plastic and some kind of lemony cleaning fluid. Thomas took the magazine out of the inside pocket of his leather jacket and opened it. In fact it was only part of a magazine: most of the pages were missing, and the others were crumpled and had watermarks. At least, Thomas Marx hoped they were watermarks; he had found the magazine in a bush. The photograph was still just visible in the dim light. It had a caption printed in ornate red script underneath, saying *Sucking a Bagful of Sweeties*. Roswitha looked at the picture, surprised and rather shocked: it showed a penis with its veins standing out spread over two pages of the magazine. A pair of wrinkled testicles dangled like saddlebags one on each side of the penis, and below its gleaming tip you could see part of a woman's face licking them. The woman wore orange lipstick, and her teeth were yellowish. She was sticking her tongue out so far that the frenulum looked as if it would tear any moment.

She doesn't want to touch that thing with her lips, thought Roswitha.

'That's fellatio,' said Thomas. 'Know what fellatio is?'

'I think so.'

'No, you don't. You don't know what it's like if you haven't done it.'

She looked at him, and then back at the photograph. Thomas rolled it up and put it back in the pocket of his leather jacket.

Roswitha liked Thomas Marx because he looked so cute, but it wasn't easy to make out what went on inside his head. What did he expect her to do now?

'Have . . . have you ever . . . ?'

'Of course.'

'Shall I do it to you?'

Bull's-eye first off, thought Thomas Marx, struggling to control himself. He nodded. Roswitha slipped further down towards the floor of the car. Her jeans jacket got in the way;

she raised herself again and took it off. Thomas unzipped his jeans. Roswitha got down on the floor once more and put her hand into his flies. Although what she brought out was limp and wrinkled and had a musty smell, she immediately put it in her mouth and wrapped her tongue round it. Thomas Marx was in a state of near-hysteria. Of course it was with intent that he had told Roswitha you had to do it before you knew what it was like, but this was just too easy. Usually he had to work on a girl for hours on end before she even let him touch her breasts. He might as well have dipped his penis in a glass of iced water. He felt his genitals trying to retreat into his abdominal cavity. Roswitha made desperate efforts, but all Thomas Marx could think was: Stop it! Oh, please, please stop it!

He tried to conjure up some sure-fire image in his mind's eye, something which might yet give him an erection and salvage his reputation as a stud. He failed.

Then, all of a sudden, someone flung open the back door of the car. It was Roswitha's father. Dieter Voss was a giant of a man. He didn't need to be a giant of a man; he could just as well have been small and puny, he could have had an amiable, round, full moon of a face, and he would still have scared Thomas Marx to death. But Dieter Voss was over one metre ninety tall and his shoulders filled the door frame. He was wearing blue workmen's overalls and carrying a crowbar, and he stared down at Thomas Marx out of small, angry eyes. It was almost twenty seconds before Thomas Marx was in any position to move and put his soft, maggot-like penis back in his flies. Roswitha wiped the spit off her lips. She tried to free her feet, which were wedged under the front seats, and she dared not raise her eyes above her father's knees. Finally Dieter Voss broke the silence, took a step back from the door, and said, 'You get out of here or I'll break your neck!'

His voice was hoarse, and he had to clear his throat directly afterwards. Thomas Marx's face turned from white to red. He stumbled out of the Audi, fell flat on the ground, jumped up again and ran off like a shoplifter being chased. As he fled along the road he began to lose his breath, which got him into a calmer state of mind again, and a question which was to occupy him for months to come formed in his head: would it have been better to have been found with an erect penis, or would that have made matters even worse?

Roswitha stood in front of her father, head bent, clutching her jacket to her chest like a naked woman trying to cover herself up. Dieter Voss let go of the car door and staggered back as if he had been hit on the head with a shovel.

'Go on, then, do as you like,' he said, turning and going back to the house. 'And have fun!' he shouted.

He never mentioned the incident again, but from now on his conversation with Roswitha was confined to such remarks as 'Yes', 'No', and 'Pass the butter.' He spoke to her as you might address an old aunt who is part of the family but to whom you feel completely indifferent. And whenever she asked his permission to go to a party or sleep over at a girlfriend's house he repeated the same words with the same intonation as he had used the first time: 'Go on, then, do as you like.'

He even said the same when she told him she wanted to get married. The pale yellow Audi had never been sold. It was an awful warning, a memorial to Roswitha's depravity, something which could not be forgiven until the scene of her transgression had been entirely resolved into its component parts by the weather and razed to the ground.

Martina turned into the garden and drove over a courageous dandelion which had had its leaves amputated several times, and was already used to being regularly flattened and rising again. The advantages of the garden's sandy soil became evident in this weather: it didn't turn muddy, and the ground was washed as clean as a bathing beach. You could also drive right up to the front door. Martina turned off the engine, took the bunch of flowers out of its paper, and pressed the bell. Two chimes sounded inside the house, and soon afterwards there was a rapid shuffling of slippers. Her mother opened the door. Renate Voss was small and plump, with flabby cheeks and short hair tinted black. Reading glasses dangled from a gold chain round her neck. She was wearing pale trousers and a red pullover with an appliquéd motif of the skyline of New York in paste gems. Her small feet were stuffed into red plush slippers.

'Roswitha. How nice! And guess what, Eva's going to look in later as well. I'll have both my girls here together.'

Martina's sister Eva was studying veterinary medicine in Hanover. She was the clever one of the family, and the sole comfort of Roswitha's mother, who came from a family of teachers and could share her taste for books and the theatre with her younger daughter. Apart from the self-help books, Martina never read anything but women's magazines, and Dieter Voss possessed only a single book, *Do It Yourself*, a manual for DIY enthusiasts.

Martina handed her mother the bunch of flowers.

'Oh, how pretty,' said her mother. 'That's so kind of you. What a shame we're going to the Harz mountains the day after tomorrow. I'll give Eva the flowers to take home this evening, if you don't mind. She can get some pleasure out of them then.'

'Fine, do that,' said Martina. She went into the living room, where her father was sitting leafing through the *Hamburger Abendblatt*. He folded the evening paper in the middle, looked round the side of it and grunted, 'Hello.'

'Hello, Dad,' said Martina, and stayed where she was on the edge of the rug, not sure whether to sit down with her father or rejoin her mother. But then Dieter Voss unfolded his newspaper again and forgot her. Martina turned and went into the kitchen. The heat of the oven met her. There was a smell of warm yeast dough. Her mother was cutting up a baking sheet of buttered almond cake.

'Time for cake already?'

'Yes, Dad and I skipped lunch today. We're trying to lose weight.'

'Can I do anything? If not I'll go and get my boxes up from the cellar.'

'No, that's all right, off you go.'

The three boxes, about the size of parrot cages, were stacked ready for her at the foot of the cellar stairs. Martina had packed the first one and stuck it up with tape when she was ten and had decided that she wasn't a baby any more. But she had opened it again several times since then. *Sandman* was written on it, in her neat childish script, *Jelly Baby Bear, Sleepyhead, Pixie Books, Froggy, Mr Toad, Hoppity, Fairy-tale Records*. She had packed up the other two boxes when she was fifteen and had decided that she wasn't a little girl any more. *Barbie dolls*, said one of them, *Steiff stuffed animals, piggy bank, Sandman, Hanni and Nanni books* . . . The third was labelled *school exercise books, Billy Goat Gruff, printing set, Dragon* . . .

Martina was briefly tempted to tear the sticky tape off the box and see what kind of a dragon she had put away in it.

Then she remembered that it must be another moneybox. She took the lightest box, hauled it up the stairs and out into the rain, and heaved it on the back seat of Leon's Mercedes. While she was still busy loading her boxes in, a Mini Cooper drove into the garden. Her sister Eva got out and gave her an exuberant hug. She was three years younger than Martina, just as tall, but more of an athletic type and not so fragile. She wore jeans, trainers and a blue anorak with the hood of a grey sweatshirt hanging out of it. Her hair was as long and red as Martina's, but there was nothing exceptional about her face.

'Well, so what's it like being married?'

'Exhausting. We're still papering the walls and moving furniture. Will you help me get these boxes up?'

'What boxes? Oh, your old things? Why not leave them here? You won't need them until you and Leon have children anyway. Or is something on the way already?'

'No. No, definitely not. Mum said she'd throw it all away if I didn't come for it.'

'Nonsense. I mean, my things are still here. It can't make any difference if your boxes stand on top of them. Let me have a word with Mum.'

'No, don't. Please! I came specially for them. Don't say anything to Mum, just help me upstairs with this stuff.'

They went into the house together. Frau Voss came out of the kitchen with a tea towel tucked into the waistband of her trousers.

'I'll soon have coffee made. You two go and sit with Dad in the living room.'

'In a minute,' said Eva. 'We're just going to get Martina's boxes out of the cellar and put them in the car.'

Eva was the only one in the family who accepted Martina's new first name.

'Do you have to do it now? Oh, Roswitha, you always cause such a commotion when you come to visit. Really, those things can wait!'

'Back in a tick!' called Eva, running down the stairs.

A quarter of an hour later they were all sitting round the living room table with steaming coffee cups. Eva was telling them about her new flat in Hanover, her studies, and that she'd joined a student group protesting against the killing of frogs for dissection. Dieter Voss had folded up his newspaper and put it down beside him, and was spilling crumbs over his working overalls.

'Bloody hell,' he said, 'you think I'm paying for your room and your studies and all the rest of it, just so you can get chucked out on account of a couple of frogs?'

'Dad's right,' said her mother, 'you've got to get your priorities straight.'

While Eva volubly defended the rights of frogs, Martina ate four pieces of buttered almond cake and emptied half the dish of biscuits standing on the table. Then she suddenly said, 'Did you know Leon and I saw a drowned body?'

She had promised Leon not to mention it, but now it was out.

'What?' said her father.

'Oh really, Roswitha,' said her mother, 'do you have to tell us about that just now? We're still eating.'

'Sorry,' said Martina, standing up. 'Shall I put more coffee on?'

'Oh yes, would you? I see Eva so seldom. I don't want to get up again now.'

'What was that about a body?' asked Eva.

'Yes,' said her father, 'you and Leon found a body?'

'Of a boar,' said Martina. 'A huge, drowned wild boar. Right near our house.'

'A wild boar!' Dieter Voss snorted scornfully.

Martina went into the kitchen, her head bent. She poured water into the coffee machine and switched it on. Then she opened the fridge. It smelled of an open can of sauerkraut. There was a whole regiment of full-cream yoghurts standing to attention on the top shelf. Martina took a yoghurt, removed the lid and tipped the contents into her mouth, scraped the remains out with her forefinger and licked it. She saw a bottle of diet Coca-Cola, poured herself a large glass and swigged it down. There was a biscuit tin on top of the fridge. She reached for it, put her hand in and stuffed a handful of biscuits into her mouth, chewing, swallowing, forcing them down. Then she set to work on the contents of the fridge again: two more yoghurts, the remains of a blancmange, a chocolate bar, five slices of salami, a chunk of cheese and a large piece of smoked sausage disappeared into her stomach like stars, comets and rays of light disappearing down a black hole. Martina's hunger grew no less, just as a black hole is never any smaller however much matter falls into it. Now and then she drank more large, greedy gulps of Coke. She looked round. There was a Snickers bar on the window sill. Why had her mother left a Snickers bar on the window sill? She tore the wrapper off and bit into it. At that moment she heard a noise outside the kitchen door. She stuffed the chocolate bar into her mouth whole and swallowed it with a single convulsive movement, like a snake swallowing an egg. She had been mistaken. No one came in. By now the coffee water had run through the machine. Martina opened the oven door and broke a piece of the almond cake off the baking tray, stuffed that into her mouth too, swallowed it down the wrong way, coughed, sending crumbs sputtering out all over the kitchen, and fought for air. Enough? Had she finally had enough? It was never enough.

Before Martina went back into the living room she drank one last glass of Coca-Cola. Her stomach was taut as a drum; it was impossible to pull it in. She took her T-shirt out of her trousers and let it hang over the waistband. When she put the coffee pot down on the living room table she murmured that she had to pop out for a moment, she'd be right back. But her parents and sister were too deep in conversation to notice her absence at all. Martina went back to the kitchen once more and stole a banana from the fruit basket. Then she went to the guest loo. Not the bathroom; it was too close to the living room. The guest loo was right at the far end of the corridor. It had brown tiles with white dandelion clocks on them. Martina locked the door behind her and listened, in case there was anyone following after all. No. She peeled her pullover off over her head and took a towelling hairband out of the bathroom cupboard, one of Eva's. Her hair was just long enough for a tiny ponytail, a stump of a ponytail. Martina tied it tightly back to keep it from hanging into the lavatory bowl when she bent over it. All her moves were practised; she had made them a thousand times before. Then she stuffed the banana into her mouth. She always ate a banana last.

Baby shit, she thought, bananas taste of baby shit. There was no heating in the guest loo. She was cold. Wearing only her bra and her houndstooth trousers, she kneeled down on the tiled floor, put up the lavatory lid and seat and bent her head. *Father, I have sinned*. She sighed, stuck her forefinger in her mouth and sucked it. Her body reacted to the ritual in the guest loo as promptly as a Pavlovian dog to the sound of the food bell. Her stomach convulsed, her mouth produced

53

thick mucus instead of saliva. She took her pretty, slender finger out of her mouth again and examined the strings of mucus hanging from it. Then she crooked her finger slightly, so as not to scratch her tonsils with her nail, and put it back in, further this time, right down her throat. It didn't work at once. Her head felt very heavy because she was bending it so low. Impatiently, she moved her finger faster, more roughly, further and further down her throat. Her diaphragm convulsed painfully. She opened her jaws – *Go on, then! Have fun!* – her oesophagus twisted like a caterpillar, but instead of the contents of her stomach all that came out of her mouth was a loud, obscene belch.

Oh God, thought Martina, oh God! And then: I hope they didn't hear that. She mustn't stop. If she didn't succeed in throwing up, then everything she had stuffed into herself would stay there in her stomach. It would make its way into her bloodstream, be diffused through her cell walls, fill her fat cells to the brim, and then new fat cells would grow and never go away. It would take root in her body and make her fat and ugly, soft and shapeless. She would get a huge, drooping, blue-veined bosom and a fat, wobbly bum; her thighs would feel like bags of slushy fruit. She would look like the fertility goddess of a pygmy religion, or – even worse! – she would look like her mother! Martina bent her head even lower, although the blood was already rushing in her ears. She put her finger down her throat again, working away at the little flap that keeps the oesophagus and windpipe closed in turn. Saliva as thick as wallpaper paste was running down her lower arm and dripping off her elbow. Her eyes were streaming. The glands behind her ears were swollen. They would stay swollen now for at least a week, and they would hurt. Serves me right, thought Martina. With the next belch she brought up the banana. Half a nut got stuck in her nostril in the process. It hurt, but if she stopped now to extract the nut she would have to begin all over again, building up her nausea from scratch. She put her finger down her throat once more. A torrent of brown liquid shot out of her mouth. And another. It was vital to drink plenty of Coke if you wanted to throw up. The carbonic acid helped to bring up the stomach contents. Chocolate, being heavy, usually sank to the pit of the stomach all the same and came up last of all. Martina wished she had eaten another yoghurt or some quark instead of the Snickers bar. At least she hadn't eaten any pasta or meat. Spaghetti always got up her nose when she vomited. Meat was the most painful thing to bring up. Chocolate was the most disgusting. Her body convulsed spasmodically, and a slimy brown clump the size of a ping-pong ball splashed into the lavatory bowl. Water spurted into Martina's face. The taste in her mouth made her vomit again at once. She clutched the lavatory bowl. Finger down her throat again. More vomit splashed into the bowl this time. The more of it left her stomach, the better Martina felt. She would have liked to vomit herself out too and flush herself away. When it was all gone she felt almost happy. The pain in her throat didn't matter. She was empty. Her stomach was still swollen, but that would right itself in the next two hours. When she stood up again her legs were shaky. She flushed the loo, wiped the rim of the bowl clean with paper, flushed the loo again until the dirty paper had gone down as well. She opened the little opaque glass window, let fresh air in, and inspected her swollen face in the mirror. How ugly she could look! She put her face under the tap, washed out her mouth, held first one and then the other nostril closed and snorted the nut out. Finally she sprayed the guest loo with some perfume she had found in the bathroom cupboard, a penetrating old ladies' fragrance called after an opera, examined herself critically in the mirror for the last time, and decided that she could face her family again. She went back to the living room.

'I'm not feeling well,' she said. 'I think I'll go home now.'

The further Martina went from her parents' house, the more easily she breathed. The rain was beating against the windscreen; her childhood treasures lay on the back seat. It wasn't even four yet, but she felt no desire to go on into the city and do any shopping. Leon would just have to get his own rawlplugs. Her throat hurt, she was limp and tired and felt slightly unreal, as if she were under the influence of a harmless drug. As she was passing the former stationery and sweet shop which now sold phones she stopped, got out, and bought a mobile. She would tell Leon her parents had given it to her. If she admitted to buying it herself Leon would probably read a hidden reproach into her action. He would insist on paying for it, although he had already spent all his money. Before Martina joined the main road she stopped briefly and consulted the map. She had to turn left. Yes, just as she remembered it. Left, and then straight on for a long way, and somewhere or other the river was waiting to escort her home. When she reached it the rainclouds had turned so dark that cars were already driving with their lights on. The river was broad, very broad. She hadn't noticed that so much on the way to Hamburg. Beyond a bend Martina saw the blue sign for the lay-by. She turned into it. No one was stopping there in this weather. The nailed-up snacks van stood abandoned in the rain. She drove slowly past it, and on to the wooden fence beyond which the trodden path lay.

Switching the engine off, she stared at the streaks on the windscreen. What was she doing here anyway? Still, as she *was* here she might as well get out. She stopped by the fence and stared down. Only now did she see how high the river had risen. The path reached the water only six metres down the bank. If the police hadn't already collected the corpse, the river would have washed it away. Martina put her head back and looked up at the dark sky until she was drenched through. How much longer was it going to rain? This was like the great Deluge which came to wash all sins off the face of the earth.

Dripping wet, she sat in the Mercedes, started the engine, turned the fan up higher, glanced at the road map again, wiped the condensation off the inside of the windscreen, and drove off.

When Leon had hauled Martina's boxes up to the attic he turned his attention back to the waste pipe in the bathroom. He lay on the floor with his head under the washbasin, so that he was looking at the underside of the yellow porcelain bowl, and the waste pipe and the spots of white paint which had fetched up there, unnoticed, when he painted the walls. The smooth chill of the floor tiles penetrated his blue overalls and cooled his sweaty body. Since moving to Priesnitz, Leon had not written a single page. There was always something to be renewed or repaired. His fingernails were cracked and dirty, but he felt good. The slight muscular stiffness with which he always woke up in the morning made him aware of his body as an efficiently functioning machine.

There was a spanner between Leon's teeth. He was clutching the waste pipe with his hands, trying to stop up a crack from which evil-smelling water seeped. He had a pink plastic bowl balanced on his stomach, and the oxblood-red suction cup of a sink plunger was clamped in position above his head. Leon had been working away at the washbasin waste pipe with it, and was initially successful, but when he washed his hands afterwards the water refused yet again to run away.

Leon called for Martina, who had wrapped herself in a woollen blanket as soon as she got back, lain down on the sofa, a pot of camomile tea within easy reach, and was now leafing through a number of women's magazines. Of course she had forgotten the red rawlplugs.

'Mhhina!'

No reply. He spat out the spanner and called again. 'Martina!'

'Yes?'

'The combination pliers!'

It was some time before two long sinewy legs came in, emerging from polka-dot knickers and ending in slender naked feet. The feet stopped beside Leon's face, and Martina, who had draped the blanket over her back like an old shaman, bent down to him and handed him a selection of five different pliers. He took one hand off the silvery waste pipe and picked the combination pliers with the red handle. Opening the pliers, he put them carefully round one of Martina's big toes and pinched it gently. She squealed and dropped to the floor beside him on hands and knees. He pushed her chemise up with the pliers, softly stroking the skin above the waistband of her knickers with the cold metal. Her flat stomach contracted. The pink plastic bowl balanced on Leon's flies tipped over and fell to the floor. Leon took his other hand off the waste pipe too, but black slimy fluid immediately seeped out again, and when the stink reached him he said, 'No good. I must get on with this,' gave Martina one of those kisses meaning *go away for now* with which she was only too familiar, and pushed her gently aside. Martina stood up and wrapped the blanket more tightly around herself.

'It'd look much nicer in here if you'd tiled it green and white,' she said, and shuffled back to the sofa. Leon once again turned his attention to the blocked pipe. The combination pliers gripped the diamond pattern of the silvery clamp round the pipe. The damp, mouldy smell was stronger now. Leon sat up and pushed the plastic bowl under the pipe before undoing its two ends. The clamp and a half-disintegrated rubber seal fell into the bowl with a clatter, followed by a flood of dirty water which spattered Leon's glasses. The stink immediately infested the whole bathroom. A clump of dripping, matted hair hung from the upper end of the pipe; the lower end was stuck up with green gobbets of something gelatinous which looked like giant frogspawn. Retching, Leon staggered to the window, pushed the awkward catch down and opened it wide. Cool, freshly washed air blew into his face, and at the same time the gurgling sound of raindrops falling into the water butt outside the house grew louder. Leon breathed deeply. Then he pulled himself together and approached the two gaping ends of the pipe again, armed with a roll of lavatory paper. After wrapping lavish quantities of the white tissue round his right hand, he took a firm grip of the matted, wet bunch of hair and dropped it in the plastic basin. There were probably millions of bacteria, protozoa and every imaginable virus swarming around in there, whirling around one another with their various protuberances, like debutantes at the Viennese opera ball.

Suddenly Leon had the uncomfortable feeling that someone was staring at him. He turned and saw the brown dog's head resting on the window sill, with one paw on each side of it. The dog's muzzle was pointing not at Leon but in an entirely different direction, and in order to look at him the dog had to twist his brown eyes so far round that you could see their whites, shaped like slender crescents. The animal kept staring at him, but showed neither fear nor curiosity.

'Well, fatso,' said Leon, 'want to pay us a visit, do you?'

The dog went on staring at him as emotionlessly as a hired killer. Nose quivering, he breathed in the stink of the slime from the waste pipe, and then his head disappeared and his claws scraped on the masonry as he dropped to the ground. Leon went into the kitchen, took the sausage tin out of the fridge and went to the front door. When he opened it the dog was already sitting outside, giving off the smell emitted by all wet dogs and staring straight ahead autistically.

'Well, what have we here, then?' asked Leon, opening a packet of sliced *Jagdwurst*. He held a slice up in the air, dangling it above the dog's head. The dog stared at the sausage.

'Now then,' said Leon, 'now then . . .'

Martina came out of the living room.

'Oh, don't be mean! When he's so thin and hungry!'

She took the sausage from Leon's hand and held it right in front of the dog's muzzle. The dog took the slice very carefully in his teeth and withdrew it from Martina's fingers.

'Make him fight for it a bit,' said Leon. 'That's the natural way. You don't get anything for free in nature.'

'It's not natural, it's horrid.'

The dog licked its lips and looked at Martina with its expressionless eyes, although Leon was holding the packet of sliced sausage. Leon took the next slice and waved it in front of the dog's face.

'Come on then, fatso, come and get it!'

This time the dog snapped at the sausage and snatched it from his hand. Leon took the next slice, held it up and let it drop. The dog picked it up. Leon took another and then another, letting them fall one by one into the dog's snapping mouth until the packet was empty. Then he hesitated briefly and looked at Martina.

'The pork loin too?'

'Yes, everything,' said Martina. She went into the kitchen and came back with two sandwiches, which the dog, who had just been sniffing sadly at the empty sausage pack, gulped down as well.

'That's all there is,' said Martina. 'You'll have to come back tomorrow. I'll get you something in the supermarket.'

The dog looked through her and then turned round, but he stayed on the veranda, as if he were afraid of getting wet.

'Why don't we bring him in?'

'If you like. But then we'll have to find out whose dog he is.'

'Perhaps he belonged to the people who lived here before we bought the place. It can't be coincidence that he keeps coming back.'

They tried to entice the dog into the house, but he stayed in the doorway, and when Leon attempted to drag him in by the scruff of the neck he growled. Finally Leon picked up the spare mattress from the floor and took it out on the veranda, and Martina put an old sky-blue duvet cover on a quilt which ought to have been thrown out long ago anyway. The brown dog lay down on it with his front paws crossed. Martina decided to call him Noah.

3

Skies very overcast. Sporadic showers, sometimes heavy, in the latter part of the day. Temperatures up to around 17 degrees.

Leon passed a restless night. He snorted, sweated, and tossed and turned in bed. Then he flailed his arms around like someone sending semaphore signals, whimpered and shouted, 'No, no!' At about four in the morning he woke with a start, sat up, and stared around him, eyes wide open, heart thudding, until the sight of the flowered curtains through which the light of the new day was now seeping made him realise that he was safe in his own bedroom. Leon had always dreamed like a man awaiting execution, and always in the same way, although he was never prepared for it. His dreams themselves were different every time, and afterwards all he could remember was that he had almost suffocated. A soft, grey mass had rolled over him, although how this came about he could not recollect. Leon's teeth were chattering. He felt terrible, and wished there was someone to put an arm round him and hold him tight. He looked at Martina. She was lying naked beside him, the crumpled duvet clutched firmly to her breast, her thin back with its angular shoulders turned to him. She was in a deep and soundless sleep. Her backbone was not, like most people's, embedded in a groove between strands of muscle; the spinal vertebrae stood proud, giving her a little crest on her back like a primaeval animal's. Leon ran his finger down it. A shudder ran over the taut skin. Martina sighed once in her sleep, and then her regular breathing continued. There was no comfort in that back. Leon dangled his legs over the edge of the bed and fished for his own duvet, which had slipped to the floor. He wrapped himself in it and waited for the thudding of his heart to die down. As he sat there like that, swinging his legs, he realised how damp and sticky his skin was, and felt an overwhelming need to take a shower.

Barefoot, he made his way over the zebra skin, which was now being used as a bedside rug, and at the same time tried to tread its edge flat. The humidity kept making it roll up. The light in the corridor wasn't working again. Probably a loose contact. Leon groped his way to the bathroom, where he switched the light on. Dazzled, he narrowed his eyes. When he did that he could almost see clearly. He was short-sighted, with a prescription of −3.4 in the left eye and − 4.1 in the right eye, and he was not wearing his glasses. Except for the scratched tub with its persistent rim of dirt, the bathroom now appeared clean and inviting. But he did not like the look of the pale man with the round, unshaven cheeks and swollen eyes staring back at him from the bathroom mirror.

'Don't know you, won't wash you,' he told his reflection with a nasty grin, and moved his nose forward until it met the cold glass. He was still sweating so much that the mirror immediately clouded over with condensation. Leon opened the small window. He took off his pyjamas and stood naked, legs apart, in front of the lavatory bowl. As his urine splashed into it he looked out of the window. It was lighter now, but you could hardly say the sun had risen. At least it wasn't raining. Sparrows twittered noisily in the pear tree. Leon pressed the knob of the new cistern and was pleased to see how promptly it flushed. With one fingernail, he smoothed out an air bubble which had formed beneath the new textured wallpaper. Then he got into the tub and pulled the shower curtain round him. His next job would be to replace the rusty, immovable shower head. He turned the tap on. There was a gurgling and glugging in the pipe, which ran straight out of the wall, a little water emerged from the shower head, stopped, and spurted out again hysterically. Then a regular flow of water sprayed down on Leon, but so feebly that he had to hold each part of his body under it in turn. Once again there was a gurgling in the pipe, the shower stopped running, and the water that came out next was brown and had a musty smell. The water had been slightly brown yesterday too. The house had its own well, and obviously, given the marshy surround- ings, it couldn't always run perfectly clear. But yesterday it had merely been tinged with brown, not as brown as this. This was liquid manure. Still, Leon went on showering. He hoped the water would eventually run clearer, and applied plenty of shampoo to make up for it. The water got no cleaner, and left dirty foam in his navel. Worse still, it didn't run away, so now the bathtub was blocked up too. Soon he was standing ankle- deep in foaming brown soup. Leon turned the tap off again and reached for the snow-white towel hanging beside the washbasin. Then he thought better of it. He hung the towel up again, climbed out of the tub, and marched naked and dripping down the dark corridor, past the bedroom and into the kitchen. He opened the fridge and took out a bottle of mineral water, intending to rinse himself. As he held the pleasantly cool bottle with its slightly nobbly surface in his hand, he looked out of the kitchen window and tried to forecast the weather. The sky was a regular shade of concrete grey. Grey sky, grey trees, grey horizon. Even the leaves somehow looked grey. A morning like a bin bag. Leon let his gaze move slowly over the toolshed, the two straggly blackcurrant bushes, the blue and gold garden fence . . . Suddenly he had such a shock that he felt it in his fingers like physical pain, and quickly put the bottle down on the window sill. There was the drowned woman just beyond the fence – in one of the marshy pools. She was up to her belly in the mud, and her skin was so white that it shone. Long black hair fell over the upper part of her body. When she shook the hair back over her shoulders, Leon realised that he was mistaken. This woman was much fatter than the corpse. She had round arms and large, pendulous breasts, but she too was naked – or what he could see of her, anyway. She was not alone. A smooth skull was moving between the rosy islands of her knees. It was difficult to make out whether it belonged to an animal or a very small human being, particularly when you didn't have your glasses on. The creature noticed that it was being observed. Its head swivelled round and looked towards the house. Now the woman too saw the naked man behind the kitchen window. She quickly slipped further down, until the mud was up to her throat. Laughing, she put a dirty hand in front of her mouth. Leon ran into the bedroom.

'My glasses!' he cried. 'Where are my glasses?'

He snatched his black jeans off the chair, got his legs all tangled up in them, tugged at the zip, and at the same time shoved his feet into his trainers and stumbled round the bed looking for his glasses. He kept frantically pulling the flowered curtains aside to stare at the marshy pool. The woman climbed out. The rest of her, previously hidden from view, was naked too. The creature with her had either run away or dived under the water.

'What's up?' murmured Martina, without opening her eyes.

Leon's glasses were marking his place in a book about bullfighting which lay under the bed. He fiddled with the earpieces until he got them on, and then took another look out of the bedroom window. The woman had gone. He rushed along the corridor. When he tried to wrench the front door open it was locked. He lost more valuable seconds falling over the laces of his trainers.

The dog Noah was sleeping on his quilt, which now had a pink cover on it and lay inside a large crate. Leon had sawn the front of the crate away. The mattress had begun to smell in the damp, and Leon had had to take it to a recycling tip quite a long way off.

Noah raised his head in surprise as Leon rushed out of the door and raced past him. He felt briefly tempted to run after the man and join in chasing whatever it was. Then he decided that Leon's hunt was none of his business. The dog let his head fall heavily to the quilt, smacked his lips a couple of times to get his tongue back into place, and dozed off again.

When Leon had run round the garden fence, he spotted the naked woman just disappearing into the dead undergrowth. The wobbling flesh of her fat, mud-smeared buttocks was the last part of her to vanish. He ran after her so fast that water splashed up at him from the puddles. The keen morning air filled his lungs. His civilised, complex, sophisticated personality had shrunk to the primitive, panting *I want* of the male animal in pursuit. *I want, I want*; that was all he knew. A few strides took him into the drowned wood. Without slowing his pace, he forced his way through the trees. They were slimy, and black as coal. Dead branches scratched his naked torso. He leaped over fallen trunks and roots which wound their way like snakes before his feet. At every step and every jump, moisture oozed from the spongy carpet of moss. Before he knew it, he was up to his knees in water. Leon stopped and looked round. His heart was thumping. He was standing in a pond overgrown with marsh marigolds, his ankles garlanded by frogspawn. Naturally the woman had disappeared from sight long ago. The wood ended on the far side of the pond, and Leon could make out a dark shape beyond the trees: the Schlei house. He splashed his way to the edge of the wood. There were smells everywhere: rich, rank, wet jungle smells of growth and decay. Leon stopped in the shelter of a stout tree trunk and looked ahead. His shoes squelched, and a flock of crows squabbled overhead.

The villa the estate agent had kept quiet about was even larger than it looked from a distance, and had ivy all over it, including the tower and a large part of the roof. It dated from an ornate architectural past when people must have enjoyed adding borders of crochet work in wood to every nook and cranny of their houses. Above the entrance, which looked like a small church porch with its arched doorway and two columns, stone dragons' heads looked out through the leaves. Water probably ran from their open mouths when it was raining. The building stood in a wild meadow surrounded by bushes varying in height and spread, which might once have been part of a neatly clipped hedge but were now growing unchecked in all directions. There was a fountain in the meadow, and several life-size stone statues: a fat man with a cornucopia under his arm had two women dancing round him; further on, a gigantic centaur was galloping after a nymph; and quite close to Leon there was a faun, which he took at first for a youth wearing outsize trousers. The faun was wrestling with a he-goat which had reared up on its hind legs. The horns of the two figures were locked in combat, and in fairness to his opponent the faun had linked his arms behind his back. All the statues were damaged in some way, with an arm or half a head missing. The moss growing on them, depending on whether it spread over the centaur's back or something more human, looked like either a piece of left-over winter coat or a nasty skin rash. Leon did not share the taste of the Schlei ladies. And what ridiculous behaviour, skinny-dipping in front of his window! For Leon assumed that the fat woman bathing in the muddy pool must be one of the Schlei sisters. As she had probably been back in the house for some time now, and Leon no longer expected to see her or the strange creature with her – perhaps it had been nothing but a large round sponge – he retraced his steps. This time he avoided the treacherous floating carpet of waterweed, and picked his way over the tree trunks. He was exhausted, his wet trouser legs chafed his calves, and the water in his shoes sloshed back and forth at every step. However, he made his way through the flooded wood without slipping. When the last tree was behind him, he realised that even here the going was not entirely safe. He was surprised to remember how fast and sure-footed he had been as he ran this way before. Now he carefully tested the ground before venturing on to it. Cautiously, his feet felt their way from one mossy tussock to the next. He made extremely slow progress. Although, or perhaps because, he was concentrating so hard on what lay before his feet, he noticed only tiny details: a yellow snail shell on a blade of grass, a delicate cobweb full of dewdrops, plants which looked like little cotton-wool balls. It was when Leon was back near his garden, feeling safe again, that it happened: he shifted his weight from his back foot to his front foot, and the patch of grass which had looked so trustworthy suddenly broke up. Leon's left leg sank up to the knee in mud. He smiled in astonishment. He was unable to pull his leg out again at once, and now he tried to use his right leg to get closer to the marshy pool. In the process he recklessly put weight on his left leg again. This time he sank in up to his hip. He now realised that the situation was serious, and dropped on his stomach to distribute his weight as evenly as possible. Trembling, he lay with his face and hands in the mud, silently praying that he would sink no further, that he wouldn't have to die yet, not now, not for such a ridiculous reason. Finally he dared to raise his head and look over the top of his filthy glasses for a large rock or a bush to help him haul himself out. No rock in sight anywhere. A bush three metres away – right out of reach. When Leon tried to move his leg he could feel the cold mire clinging to him, refusing to let him go. He even thought he felt it sucking him down. Leon groped about for firm ground. Around his head, the imprints of his hands in the mud at once filled with dark water again, but the closer his hands came to his hips the less yielding was the surface beneath them. And the ground seemed surprisingly firm just beyond the place where his left leg was stuck. Slowly, Leon rolled his body around the axis of his submerged leg, at the same time turning over on his back. When he felt a firm, resistant surface he waited, breathing hard, until his right leg, still free, stopped trembling. Then he dug his heel into the ground and pushed backwards. The marshes released Leon's leg with a subterranean squelch, pulling the trainer off his foot at the same time. Still gasping, Leon kneeled down, put his arm into the viscous mud and felt about for his shoe. It was an expensive trainer. A Nike. Even though Leon had just feared for his life, he wanted it back. It couldn't have sunk straight down again. A shoe like that weighed next to nothing. Leon felt further and further down, in wider and wider circles and figures of eight, but all he could feel was dampness and plant fibres. The trainer was swallowed up for ever. It had become a part of some immeasurable entity.

The rain set in that afternoon, thin strands of it falling from the sky. Martina put all available pans and buckets outside the door to collect rainwater, since the water from the pipes was still running brown, and Leon had used the last crate of sparkling mineral water to wash off the mud encrusting him like the carapace of an armadillo when he hobbled in that morning. He was now sitting in his study, brooding over the best way to describe the full extent of the injustice done to the eight-year-old Benno Pfitzner by one of his teachers at school. The daylight filtering in through the little window was the dim, vague light of rainy weather. He couldn't concentrate. His thoughts kept wandering back to his adventure that morning. Not that it mattered. In spite of moving house, and then all the repairs he had had to do, he was well within his delivery deadline. He had sketched out the rough synopsis of the book before leaving Hamburg, and over these last two rainy weeks he had made such good progress that he expected to be able to send Pfitzner the opening chapters in four to six weeks' time. He had known he could write better here than anywhere else. He had only to sit at his desk, look out at the wide expanse of the marshes, and inspiration unfolded its wings with a loud flap. Leon always pictured inspiration as some kind of giant bat. He tilted the window a little way open, and the distant metallic drumming of raindrops falling into the pans came in from outside. The washing machine with his muddy jeans inside it was churning away in the kitchen. Washing black trousers in brown water might not matter. He hadn't told Martina about the naked woman and the peculiar creature; instead he said he had fallen into a boggy pool in the marshes while he was jogging. How could he have explained why he ran after the fat, naked lady? Martina had just been surprised to find him suddenly deciding to take exercise.

The tinny patter in the pots and pans gradually changed to a gurgling, splashing sound. And another noise mingled with it – the sound of a car engine. The postman didn't call as late in the day as this.

Harry, thought Leon, jumping up. He was avid for company, any company so long as it wasn't Martina or the postman. He had even caught himself wishing their neighbours would drop in to say hello. But Harry would be particularly welcome.

The shopkeeper Kerbel's white Ford Transit was drawing up. Martina was already on the veranda when Leon came out to join her. The dog was out on the prowl again in spite of the rain. Kerbel got out of the van. He was even shorter than Leon, and wore an olive-green parka and black gumboots. He put up a large, dark umbrella, opened the back of the van and took out a small cardboard box, holding the umbrella carefully over it. He was waving to Leon even before he came through the garden gate.

'Oh, my God,' said Leon under his breath, automatically

stepping back. Kerbel stopped outside the veranda and offered his right hand, juggling the box and the umbrella with his left. Leon had never seen him at such close quarters before. He had once waited in the car outside Kerbel's shop while Martina was stocking up, and had looked at the stack of foodstuffs piled high in the shop window, all of them, unless he was much mistaken, from the Aldi range – Aldi biscuits, Aldi noodles, River brand cola – and beside them a pyramid of jigsaw puzzles, with the lids of their boxes faded. Then Kerbel's grinning head had suddenly appeared in the display window, nodding to him. Even at a distance it was a shock. That great expanse of gum. Now here was Kerbel right in front of him. As long as he didn't grin the display of gums wasn't so bad. The man had doughy skin, a great many little golden-blond curls, jowly cheeks, and a lower jaw the shape of a shovel. The rain was performing a nimble tap dance on his umbrella.

'Hi. We meet at last,' said Kerbel. 'I already know your lady wife.'

'Ulbricht,' said Leon, introducing himself very formally and withdrawing his hand.

'Exactly!' said Kerbel, drawing in his breath with a whinnying sound as his torso jerked with merriment. Leon raised his eyebrows and turned back towards the door of the house. Kerbel stopped laughing at once and assumed a contrite expression, as if he were about to fling himself into a puddle and cover his head with mud.

'I was on my way to your neighbours,' he said rapidly. 'I always deliver shopping to the ladies, so I thought I'd bring the books you ordered at the same time. Save you having to go out in this weather. You'd think it might finally stop raining, wouldn't you?'

'What books?'

'For me,' said Martina. 'Herr Kerbel was kind enough to get me some books from the library. For Noah.'

'A pleasure,' said Kerbel. 'I drive into Freyenow almost every day. If there's anything I can bring you too . . . maybe from the discount store? I'll be in Freyenow again tomorrow.'

'No, thank you,' said Leon, putting his head on one side and inspecting the box Kerbel was pressing into Martina's hand. He read the titles of the two books on top: *The Misunderstood Dog* and *The Secret Life of Dogs*.

'You're a writer too, I hear,' said Kerbel. 'What kind of books do you write, then?'

Leon cast Martina a reproachful glance.

'You're not the only writer among us, oh no. There's another one here. Erich Harksen. Maybe you know him. He writes poetry, sells his books in my shop. The latest is called *Will o' the Wisp*. I can display your books in the shop too if you like.'

'Thanks, that's very kind of you. But the Schleis will be waiting for their delivery. I wouldn't like to keep you.'

'Do go carefully,' said Martina. 'My husband fell into a boggy pool in the marshes today.'

'What?' Kerbel's brow furrowed into mastiff-like folds of concern. 'You went out in the marshes? You don't want to do that, you know. You have to know your way around here. You have to be born here. The marshes are treacherous. One false step and you're gone. If you want to go for a walk, you'd better drive to Freyenow. There's a lovely forest there.'

Leon looked furiously at the shopkeeper.

'I live here. I can go for a walk here if I like. Or are you telling me I'm virtually living on an island and I can't leave my property without drowning?'

'Suffocating,' said Kerbel. 'You suffocate in a bog. That's a hundred times nastier than drowning. Well, wait till it isn't so wet, anyway.' He turned his eyes to the sky. 'Right now the marshes are even more unpredictable than usual. And take a long stick with you to test the ground ahead. Shall I bring you some bamboos from the discount store?'

'Thanks,' said Leon, 'but if there's one thing I have in abundance in my toolshed it's bamboos. I can manage for myself, thank you.'

'Oh well, then . . .' Kerbel looked at the round toecaps of his boots, disappointed.

'Have a nice evening,' added Leon, taking Martina by the elbow and drawing her into the house. From the doorway, they watched Kerbel taking a large box out of the Transit van and clutching it firmly to his chest with his right arm, while he held the umbrella in his left hand. He steered a zigzag course through the puddles.

'How does his wife stand it?' Martina wondered.

Leon pursed his top lip, thrust his upper jaw forward, and looked as if he were aiming for her mouth.

'Kissy kissy!' he mumbled, putting out his arms to her. Giggling, Martina fled into the living room with her box of books and barricaded herself behind the coffee table. A coffee table was not an item Leon had ever intended to possess. The quintessence of bourgeois style. Now, however, he simply found it useful. You could put things down on it. Martina dropped the books on the table and took refuge behind the sofa. *The Dog-Lover's Encyclopaedia*, Leon read on the back of one ancient volume. He stopped chasing Martina, picked up the encyclopaedia and leafed through it. It was yellow with age, and had been much read. Leon sneezed. He liked books to be new, and never bought from second-hand bookshops. He always suspected that long-extinct diseases were preserved in the pages of old books, and that snot a century old clung to them. 'If you ask me, that dog's not normal,' said Leon. 'A normal dog sticks close to its masters.'

Noah came to be fed at irregular intervals – there was a fifty-kilo bag of dry dog food in the kitchen – but persistently refused to come into the house or let them put a collar on him.

'Noah's probably turned feral,' said Martina.

'Turned what?'

'I read it in the book Kerbel brought me last time. When . . .'

'So you've ordered books before?'

'Yes, and the book said that if puppies aged three to seven weeks don't mix with human beings they get fixated only on dogs, and never want contact with people, and they're feral.'

'He enjoys his dinner, all the same,' said Leon. He put the book back in the box and went out on the veranda again to bring Noah's quilt in to dry. The pans of rainwater were already brimming over. Leon carried them into the bathroom, tipped the water into the bath, which had the plug in, and placed the pans outside the house again. Once he almost slipped, and when he looked down at the ground he saw that he had trodden on a brown slug. Its back half was squashed flat. When he touched the slug, it turned rust-coloured and a globule of transparent fluid welled out of its front end. He threw it into a flower bed. When he came back into the living room and hung Noah's pink quilt over the radiator, Martina was lying on the sofa reading.

'We ought to have asked Kerbel to bring us some large

containers,' said Leon. 'We have to collect water in some-thing.'

'Oh, the pans!' cried Martina, jumping up.

'Done it already,' said Leon, frowning. 'But perhaps you could at least look out for Kerbel to come back. Tell him we need two twenty-litre containers – no, three. I want to get a few hours' work done in peace.'

But when Kerbel did come back Martina was just looking at a picture of a large schnauzer gazing up adoringly at his fat, beer-swilling master. Whereas when she patted Noah he looked as wary as if she were about to apply leeches to him. He really came in only to eat. Greed and indifference. Some-times that dog reminded her only too much of a certain kind of man. None the less, he had recently given her hand a brief lick, and he had once come into the passage when she was fetching his dog food from the kitchen. So there was some progress. She mustn't give up.

When Kerbel started his van Martina leaped up and ran to the door of the house. Too late. Kerbel was already driving down the muddy path and couldn't see her.

Late that evening they had more visitors. The doorbell rang. It was such an unusual sound in this house that instead of going to open the door, Martina came into Leon's study and looked at him with a distraught expression.

Harry, thought Leon. 'Well go on, answer it!' he said. 'I'll just switch the computer off.'

He didn't want Harry seeing any of Pfitzner's biography before it was finished. Martina made her way out into the dark corridor. Why couldn't Leon manage such simple jobs as getting the light to work? When she had finally found the door handle, Leon joined her. Outside stood two women, one of them so tall that her head nearly touched the top of the door frame. That was all Leon and Martina could see in the dark, and they recognised the tall figure as a woman only when she said, 'Good evening.'

'Good evening,' said the second woman too. She was considerably shorter, and rather plump. 'We're your neighbours. My name's Isadora Schlei, and this is my sister Kay.'

The brimming pots and pans gurgled behind them.

'Well, come on in before you drown,' said Leon. He was disappointed. Disappointed but at the same time excited. Martina placed herself in the rectangular patch of light that fell from the living room.

'I'm sorry, but the light here isn't working. Do come in.'

The women followed her into the living room. Leon stood back against the wall to let them go first. They were not wearing coats, and before he could relieve the plump sister of the umbrella and plastic bag she was holding she had marched past him. The tall sister wore green dungarees, the kind you get in specialist workwear shops, over a man's grey shirt. She had stout boots on her feet. Her short brown hair was shaved at the nape of her neck, and a few unruly strands fell over her forehead. Her face was curiously regular – oval eyes under straight brows, a nose that might have been drawn with a ruler, thin lips. Leon did not think her attractive. Well, yes, she was slim, and as far as he could see with her dungarees on she was narrow-hipped. But her shoulders were broader than his own, and her breasts were pathetic: practically non-existent. And she was really tall, at least one metre ninety. Her sister was the exact opposite. Everything about her seemed soft and voluptuous. She wore a green velvet skirt so long that it trailed on the ground, and the hem was sopping wet. A blue silk tunic with a Chinese pattern stretched over her opulent breasts, and several gold chains hung over those breasts too. She also wore showy gold rings with coloured stones on her short fingers.

Laurel and Hardy, thought Leon, offering Isadora Schlei his hand. Isadora stuck the umbrella and bag under her armpit, took his hand in her two plump paws, and pressed it warmly. He looked into her face, to see if she would show any embarrassment under his gaze. Water was dripping from her nose. He was pretty well sure she was the woman he had surprised in the marshy pool that morning, but she showed no awareness of it. She had piled her long black hair up in a geisha style, with two gold pins stuck into it. But if the rest of her resembled anything Japanese, it was probably a sumo wrestler. Kay Schlei held Martina's hand a little too long, staring at her.

'I'll make tea,' said Martina, withdrawing her hand rather awkwardly. 'Or would anyone rather have coffee?'

'Coffee,' said Leon, and Kay chimed in. 'Coffee . . . please.'

'Tea would be lovely. How kind of you!' said the fat Schlei sister, dropping to the sofa with a thump, still with the folded umbrella and plastic bag under her arm. Martina disappeared in the direction of the kitchen, and Leon invited the Amazon to sit down too. What a pitiably ugly creature! The fat one wasn't his type either, but at least he could make use of her as a sparring partner, to see if he still had his old effect on women. Leon pulled up his favourite armchair, and as he sat down he looked at her with an expectant smile. She responded with a similar smile, showing no trace of embarrassment. Perhaps she wasn't quite right in the head. The tall sister sat awkwardly in her corner of the sofa, like a dustman invited into a drawing room. She appeared to be interested in the interior decoration, inspecting each individual item of furniture with ridiculous thoroughness, letting her gaze wander up to the ceiling, and then staring at her feet. Isadora Schlei was still smiling. She had a pretty face, with a small nose, a full mouth, and eyes as black as cherries, but the beginnings of a double chin lent her an amphibian look. Leon realised that he would have to bring up heavier artillery if he wanted to embarrass her. And he definitely did.

'Haven't we met somewhere?' he asked.

'Yes, this morning, I think. But I wouldn't exactly call it meeting.'

Leon was surprised by the composure with which she acknowledged that he had seen her naked. After all, she was distinctly fat.

'I'm sorry I startled you. I didn't mean to,' he said.

'Oh, you didn't startle me at all.'

'You ran off pretty fast, though.'

Isadora Schlei giggled, putting her hand in front of her mouth like a schoolgirl. She was probably only in her mid-thirties. He had thought her older that morning because she was so fat. It was harder to guess her sister's age, but he put her in her late twenties.

'And if you didn't mean to startle me you ran after me pretty fast too,' said Isadora.

Kay Schlei looked from Leon to her sister, and snorted scornfully. Martina came back, put the teapot and coffee pot and a plate of biscuits on the table, and sat down on the sofa beside Kay, who moved ostentatiously aside and then went rigid as a telegraph pole.

'I brought you something,' said Isadora, handing Leon the wet plastic bag. He took it, looked inside, and was disconcerted. It was a dirty shoe. He carefully took it by the heel and held it up to the light. A few bits of dried mud crumbled off and fell on the coffee table. 'My shoe?' asked Leon, looking blankly at Isadora.

'I thought you might like it back, said Isadora. 'Wash it and it'll be as good as new.'

Leon drew his eyebrows together with suspicion.

'Where did you find it? And how do you know it's mine?'

'Oh, it was just lying around,' said Isadora, waving a hand vaguely in the air. 'And who else would it belong too?'

'But I don't understand . . .' Leon began again.

'I thought your trainer sank in the bog,' said Martina.

'So did I,' said Leon, 'unless it didn't get stuck after all when I pulled my leg out . . . I almost sank into a boggy patch in the marshes this morning, you know.'

'How dreadful,' said Isadora, without a trace of sympathy in her voice.

'I mean,' Leon continued, 'unless the shoe didn't get stuck, unless it flew off when I pulled my leg out, and I just didn't notice.'

'That'll have been it,' said Kay quickly, holding her cup out to Martina.

'I do hope the coffee's all right,' said Martina. 'I have to admit that we're cooking with rainwater. I boil the water for longer, but it's been raining for days, so it can't be too dirty.'

'What kind of animal was that?' asked Leon suddenly, looking hard at Isadora.

'I don't know what you mean,' smiled Isadora.

'Oh yes, you do,' said Leon, irritated, scratching his shoe with his fingernails.

Martina looked at Leon in surprise, and quickly said, 'By the way, we have a brown dog here. He just walked in. Is he yours, by any chance?'

'No, not ours. He belonged to the man who lived here before you. I expect he left him behind. Nice dog. Rather self-willed, maybe. Be kind to him!'

'For self-willed read bloody-minded,' commented Kay.

Leon said nothing. He decided to question Isadora Schlei again when he met her on her own. Martina saw from his face that it was not the dog Leon had meant. She remembered the salamander.

'What kind of water creatures live in these marshes?' she asked Kay. 'Look at that mark on my husband's hand.'

Leon held out his hand, showing the red and still weeping mark.

'It was some kind of giant amphibian, at least half a metre long. A salamander or something. It spat on my hand.'

'We don't have anything like that here. Maybe they do in Asia,' said Isadora. 'And we certainly don't have poisonous salamanders. That's just mediaeval prejudice. You could be allergic to whatever it was. People are allergic to all kinds of things these days. Or perhaps you just touched a poisonous shrub.'

'It really was enormous,' Martina confirmed. Leon rubbed the mark. Isadora took a large gulp of her tea.

'Tea made with rainwater tastes good,' she said.

'What happened to your tap-water?' asked Kay, and then answered her own question. 'I bet it runs brown. That's what I thought the moment I noticed the smell in here. You've got an awful lot of work ahead of you.'

'What do you mean?' asked Leon, offended. 'What kind of smell?'

'Damp . . . musty . . . mouldy. It smells as if you could grow mushrooms here, no problem.'

'You're quite right,' Martina agreed with her.

'Yes, but that's only because it's so long since anyone lived here. It'll soon wear off,' said Leon.

Kay cast him a pitying glance.

'No, it won't. It's only just getting into its stride. If you don't do something pretty quick the whole house will soak up water like a sponge.'

'Oh, do stop being such a doom merchant!' Isadora Schlei stuck the sharp end of her umbrella in her sister's side. 'I think it smells really nice and fresh in here. I don't like dry rooms. They give you allergies. A bit of water never hurt anyone. Anyway, no one asked your opinion.'

Kay rose to her feet.

'Come along, I'll show you.'

Isadora rolled her eyes and reached for the biscuits. Kay went over to the living room window, crouched down and knocked on the wall beneath it. Then she impatiently beackoned Leon over.

'Stop showing off, do! Sit down and drink your tea with the rest of us,' said the fat Schlei sister crossly. But Leon rose and crouched down beside Kay, who rolled up her shirt-sleeves. Her lower arms were incredible. Like a weightlifter's. She knocked on the wall again.

'Hear that?'

'What?'

'It's full of water.'

'Sounds perfectly normal to me.'

'Then come this way.'

Kay and Leon went to the bathroom, followed by Martina. Only Isadora remained behind. Rain was beating against the bathroom window. Kay knelt down and put her ear to he wall. Then she knocked again. Leon stood beside her with his back bent, hands propped on his knees, holding his breath and listening. Martina had stopped at the door, where she wouldn't be in the way and couldn't do anything wrong. Tap, tap, tap went Kay's knuckles on the wall.

'Now do you hear it? There's even more water in here because this side of the house is closer to the marshes. It was only ordinary rainwater in your living room, coming through the cracks in the plaster. But the water here is coming up from the ground. The same water that's flooded the well.'

Leon couldn't hear any difference. Kay stood up again, and they went back to the living room, where Isadora Schlei was just stuffing the last of the biscuits into her mouth. Nervously, Leon brushed some non-existent hair back from his forehead and sank into an armchair. He wondered whether the fat woman was mentally disturbed. She ate like a pig. The plate now held only a single chocolate biscuit, which she'd squashed with her short, fat fingers.

'So what does all that mean?' he asked Kay.

'Well, you can forget about insulation with walls like that, of course.'

'So we'll just have to turn the heat up higher?'

'I'm afraid that's not all.' Kay's initial hesitancy had disappeared. She calmly held her coffee cup out to Martina to be refilled. 'Think what'll happen when it freezes and the water in the stones turns to ice. It's almost up to the windows already. Get a hard frost and the whole wall will collapse. Break up like aerated chocolate.'

'Then what can I do?' asked Leon, in tones of resignation.

'Hm,' said Kay, draping one arm over the armrest of the sofa. 'Zaven – that's the man who lived here before you – he exposed the outside of the foundations and we painted it with bitumen. That did the trick for a while, but there's probably just too much water in the ground now.'

'There can never be too much water in the ground,' said Isadora. 'Water is life. Water is fun.'

'The really dangerous thing,' said Kay, 'is that only half the house has a cellar. That means it could break in half down the middle. In the worst-case scenario. You ought really to install a groundwater tank. But that'd be horribly expensive. Your best plan is to sue whoever sold you the house.'

Leon tried to inject an assertive and confident note into his voice.

'Aren't there any other possibilities? Something that doesn't cost money?'

'The next best thing would be to wrap the foundations in some kind of foil. Or perhaps just draining the site properly would work. All you need for that is a drainage spade. Even an ordinary spade would do the job.'

Leon, who had been seeing his house, himself, and his dream of a dignified and peaceful writer's life disappear into the brown maw of the marshes, tried to pull himself together.

'I'll lend a hand,' said Kay, and looked at Martina. 'To start with, anyway. I can come over with a spade tomorrow if you like.'

'That's extremely kind' – Leon too cast a brief and fleeting glance at Martina – 'but I think I only need you to show me how to get started. Then I can do the draining myself.'

'We'll see,' said Kay. 'Anyway, I'll come over tomorrow. It's going to be a lot of work, and I'd be happy to help. What time shall I arrive?'

'Whenever it suits you. Around ten? But then I'll do the work on my own.'

Isadora pushed away her teacup in annoyance.

'Time we were going,' she said. 'And you don't want to take what my sister says too seriously. She doesn't really know anything about the land. You ought to take a look at our garden!'

She brushed the crumbs off her skirt and stood up.

When Leon opened the front door, Noah was lying in his bare crate, looking cross. The Schlei sisters said goodnight and walked off under the umbrella. Martina went back into the living room and fetched the dog's dry, warm quilt.

'What do you make of them?' she asked Leon as they watched Noah snuggling his wet, dirty coat into the quilt.

'Arms like clubs, legs like columns,' said Leon. 'I wonder what on earth they live on.'

'That shorter one really is seriously overweight,' said Martina.

'And the other one fancies you, did you notice?'

'Yes, I did. And did you see the fat one stuffing herself with biscuits? I never saw anyone eat so fast.'

They stood leaning against each other, breathing in the clear night air, listening to the rain.

'Arms like clubs, legs like columns,' murmured Leon. The dog had gone to sleep.

4

Skies heavily overcast, widespread rain. Highest temperatures 18 degrees. Moderate winds veering from east to south.

'Fucking Wessi!'

A clod of earth landed right beside the plastic bucket at Leon's feet. He looked up. Two little boys were standing at the gate. They wore bright red raincoats with matching sou'westers and gumboots, and looked like miniature American firefighters. The smaller boy bent to pick up a piece of mud which had fallen out of the tread of a tractor tyre, and threw it in Leon's direction too.

'Fucking Wessi!' he too shrilled.

They must have walked through the rain for at least half an hour in order to tell him what they thought of him to his face – all the way along the gravel track from Priesnitz to the manor house, and then the rest of the way to the maize field and up the path to the house. Leon hoped they would catch colds. He shifted his weight from his left to his right foot. Kerbel had brought him and Martina gumboots from the discount store. They were black and too large. 'Sizes 41 and 42,' Leon had specified. 'Better get a size bigger. You always need a size bigger with gumboots,' Kerbel said, and Leon nodded, although he had already calculated for a larger size. Even through the thick soles of the gumboots, he thought he could feel the ground below the matted, mossy grass wobbling back and forth like a gigantic water-bed. The moisture obstinately lingered in the soil, trickling only with reluctance into the system of open ditches which he and Kay Schlei had dug in the garden: a main collecting ditch with the others arranged in a fishbone pattern running into it. Some water, if not much, had flowed into the collecting ditch. But if the weather didn't change, all the ditches would soon be so full of rainwater alone that – purely theoretically – the miniature firefighters could drown in them. He looked at the boys again. They were still standing in the same spot, holding hands, glowering at him from under their sou'westers.

'Well? Got nothing better to do?' said Leon, taking a step towards them.

'Shithead! Shithead!' yelled the larger child. Then they both turned and ran back down the path.

Leon cast them a brief glance, then turned away and listened to hear if that horrible noise was still coming from his garden. Had it finally gone, or was the rain just drowning it out? It had been tormenting him for days: a gentle rasping, rustling sound. Slugs!

He was an expert on slugs by now. He had read all about them, he knew their little ways. They rolled their sack-like bodies through his garden, hauling themselves up the stems of the delphiniums, lupins and roses which had already suffered from the rain, grabbing the edge of a leaf in their little lips and pressing it against their upper jaws with a spiked, spoon-shaped tongue. That was what made the curious rustling sound. It was audible only because there were hundreds of these stupid, shapeless, brick-red creatures doing it at the same time. One gardening book claimed that slugs preferred stocks, dahlias and cucumbers to other plants, but Leon's slugs ate anything they could get their jaws into. The garden looked as if some madman had gone round punching tiny holes in all the plants up to the height of a metre above the ground. Rain penetrated the leaves, which fell off and dropped to the ground. The grass and flower beds were covered with perforated foliage. Any flowers were choked by slime.

Leon and Martina had tried all kinds of different methods of slug control: they had filled yoghurt pots with beer and sunk them in the ground, they had wrapped quantities of rags round the plants most worth protecting, they had put out lettuce leaves as a peace offering. The slugs had eaten the lettuce leaves *and* the roses. There were just too many of them. Once Leon had leaned over one of the bubbling heaps of slime and saw that one slug, obviously using something resembling a penis to have sex with another as a male, was simultaneously being penetrated as a female by a third. This non-stop procreation was more than he could take. In helpless embitterment, he had boiled a bucketful of his prisoners of war and poured the stinking result over the last intact rose bush. But even this cruel act protected the rose only until the pouring rain washed away the slug broth, which it did in about half an hour.

Finally Leon had decided to collect the slugs, picking their brown bellies one by one off the wet leaves and stems, and raking them out of the grass with his fingers until his hands were covered with gloves of slime. The bucket at his feet was the fifth he had filled. Four more stood outside the front door, covered with paving stones from the toolshed. Leon had only five buckets. But the rustling really had died away.

He went to the veranda, sat down heavily on a step, undid the hood of his black anorak, and looked at his booty. A red-brown mass devouring itself. A worm which had somehow got in with the slugs was twisting and turning in the middle. Leon's back hurt. First digging ditches for days on end, now bending over to collect slugs. He fished out the worm and put it down beside the wooden steps. The worm wriggled into the nearest puddle, where it immediately drowned. Leon wiped the slime off his hands on the grass and his gumboots.

The door opened and Martina came out, with Noah walking stiff-legged beside her. He yawned, braced his back legs on the floor, put his head almost right down on the wooden planks of the veranda, and stretched, tail erect. Then he raised his head and lowered his hips to stretch his backbone and hind legs. He sat down beside Leon.

Ah, at last, thought Leon. Finally the stupid dog had realised where he was supposed to sit. That was dogs for you. However much fuss Martina made of him, Noah had ultimately opted for the master of the house. Dogs were pets for men. Cats were pets for women.

Leon patted Noah's head, and Noah immediately stood up, trotted over to the far side of the veranda and lay down. Martina took the paving stone off one of the buckets.

'That's the most disgusting thing I've ever seen. What are you going to do with them?'

'Pour Domestos on them and bury them. I can't really flush them down the loo.'

'Oh no!' cried Martina. 'Don't do that! That's terrible. Can't you let them go free somewhere in the marshes?'

'What, and have them knocking at the door again tomorrow morning? No fear. I'm not collecting slugs till my back's all bent just to let them go for a nice walk.'

'You could take them somewhere in the car,' suggested Martina. 'Drive a few kilometres and tip them out in a wood. They wouldn't come back then. Oh, please! Don't set up a torture camp here!'

'They don't feel anything,' muttered Leon, but he was already taking the car key out of his trouser pocket.

He removed the paving stones from the buckets, carried the slugs to the car and loaded them into the boot. Martina brought him plastic bags to cover them up. Leon got in and wound his way down the muddy path in the Mercedes. Rain drummed down on the roof. At the end of the drive, Leon let the car drift round the bend in the muddy silt and nearly ran into the letter box. A bucket promptly fell over. Leon stopped to take a look, but the slugs were sticking to each other; none of them had fallen out. He had only to stand the bucket up again and cover it with the plastic bag. The idea of letting them go on feeding at their leisure somewhere else made him feel quite ill. He might have summoned up some pity for a single slug . . . but a thick, brown mass like this?

Steam was rising from Leon's clothes. He drove past the beet fields and willows. Even the horse and the calves were not outside now. This place was no good. He couldn't simply dump five buckets of slugs in the farmer's field. What a stupid idea, finding the creatures a new home after he'd spent hours collecting them. They had to be withdrawn from circulation entirely. He'd tip them out in a heap and then drive the car over them. No need to tell Martina what he'd done.

Leon reached the main road and drove to the nearest lay-by. Two trucks of gravel were standing there side by side, the drivers talking to each other through the open windows of their cabs. Leon immediately drove on again. Witnesses he could do without. No luck at the next lay-by either. Although there were not many people out and about, there seemed to be cars and lorries parked everywhere. He wished he had Kay with him. She always knew what to do in tricky situations. She had been the soul of calm when they found more than fifty distended tins of food on the point of exploding down in Leon's cellar, and had to take them to the recycling centre. He liked Kay. Yes, he definitely liked her. Her unfeminine manner mitigated his desire for male company, although obviously she could not replace it.

Leon suddenly knew where to go. The ideal place when you wanted to get rid of something. He drove on through Freyenow.

As he had expected, there were no cars in this lay-by. Leon parked next to the boarded-up snacks van, which would give him a little cover if anyone did pull in here. It was pouring with rain. Leon opened the boot, took the plastic bags off the buckets, picked off some of the slugs which had made their way up to the rim and threw them back. He seized three buckets at once, ran off with them, bending low, and tipped the slugs out on the wet asphalt. They made quite a large pile. Leon shoved them together with his feet. Then he went for the other two buckets, but as he tried to lift them out of the boot he suddenly felt a stabbing pain around his lumbar vertebrae. He put the buckets down again, stood there bent double, and breathed out, wheezing. At that moment a cattle truck, its load area covered with blue tarpaulins, pulled in and made straight for the heap of slugs, hardly slowing down at all. Leon stood there rooted to the spot. The truck driver, whose name was Edgar according to an illuminated name-plate behind the windscreen, now saw the obstacle and braked. Unfortunately, however, he did not brake until the vehicle had already reached the slugs. A fountain of brown scraps of slug and bits of slime rose and came down on Leon's anorak, splashing his face and hair. The truck swerved to one side and skidded towards the Mercedes. With two strides, Leon took refuge behind the snacks van. The pain in his back had suddenly gone away again. The driver of the cattle truck got it under control again and steered the other way. Leon heard a great deal of thudding under the tarpaulin as the consignment of calves or whatever it was carrying were flung about inside. The truck came to a halt thirty metres away. Leon went over to it, clambered up on the running-board and opened the cab door.

'You all right?'

The driver switched off the engine and mopped his brow. He had a scanty Genghis Khan beard.

'Yeah, yeah, sure, mate,' he said. Then he looked at Leon in alarm. Leon was not a pretty sight. Brick-red bits of slug were stuck all over his face and his jacket. A piece of black slug intestine hung from his right eyebrow, and small channels of reddish-brown liquid were running out of his hair and over his forehead.

'Christ, it got you! Keep calm! Here, come in. You can lie down on the bed. I have a bed in the cab. I'll call for help.'

He reached for his mobile phone, which was lying on the dashboard next to a thermos flask on its side and a green cattle halter.

'It's OK. Nothing to worry about,' said Leon, wiping the worst of the mess off his face. 'It's not my blood.'

'But what was it? What was that – that heap of something?'

'Slugs.'

The driver stared at him blankly.

'They migrate at this time of the year,' said Leon. 'You ran straight into a slug migration.'

'What?'

'A slug migration. You have to watch out for them in this kind of weather. Particularly near water.'

'*What?*'

'And especially in July, that's when you have to look out for them most of all. They're on the way to their spawning grounds. Imagine if you'd run into those slugs in the middle of a major road at full speed.'

The driver narrowed his eyes suspiciously.

'Oh yeah? Is that right?'

'Yes,' said Leon firmly, jumping down from the running-board. 'Don't you want to take a look at your load?' he asked, trying to move the blue tarpaulin aside. 'I wouldn't be surprised if something's happened in there.'

'Take your hands off that!' bellowed the driver, leaping down from his seat. He pushed Leon away and snatched the tarpaulin from his hand. Leon saw two rusty barrels on the loading area.

'This is my truck! Go wipe your paws somewhere else!' the driver snapped at him.

'OK, OK, Edgar,' said Leon. 'I don't know what you're planning to dump in this protected nature reserve, but it's none of my business.'

The driver snorted, climbed back into his cab, started the engine with a hiss and a roar, and drove out of the lay-by.

Leon went back to the heap of slugs. It was a positive massacre, a vast expanse of slush, little clouds of reddish-brown sauce spreading in the water of the puddles. The few survivors were moving away from the scene of the accident very slowly, their feelers testing the lie of the land in all directions. They appeared to be in shock. Leon touched the pool of squashed slugs with the toe of his boot. He had to get rid of it before anyone else skidded on it. Fetching one of the empty buckets, he scooped up the mess from the tarmac. He had to scrape the last remains off with his hands. He tipped the stuff down the slope, and then fetched the buckets still in the boot. Some of the slugs had already climbed out and were stuck to the outside of the plastic like little handles. Leon shook the bucket vigorously over the slope, and then knocked it against a wooden post, but a few of the slugs stuck persistently to the bottom and had to be picked out with his fingers. He flung the empty buckets back in the boot and closed it.

Filthy as he was, he got behind the steering wheel. By now the Mercedes looked very different from when he had been given it. Leon started the car. The fan whirred. The windscreen wipers refused to move. Cursing, Leon drove the Mercedes back into the road. He wondered whether to drive to the filling station in Freyenow, and decided against it. He could scarcely make out anything through the streaks of water on the windscreen. Letting the side window down, he leaned out. Just before the filling station he saw the shopkeeper's white Transit coming towards him. Leon flashed it briefly, but Kerbel did not seem to notice him.

Guido Kerbel was driving very fast. He had an erection as stiff as a board and an hour and a half to spare. That was the time it usually took him to go and buy something from the discount store. He had told his wife he was off to stock up with sets of screwdrivers, and if he was any longer she would start asking questions. But he wouldn't need any longer. He never did. Kerbel indicated, automatically glanced round to make sure no one was watching him, and drove into the lay-by. The sight of his boarded-up camper van had been depressing him for some time. He had bought it directly after reunification and converted it himself, but there seemed to be a hex on it. No one stopped in this lay-by, no one wanted to buy his sausages. Last year he had taken out the grill and the deep-fat fryer and advertised them for sale. Kerbel parked, kneaded his penis briefly, and got out. Rain-drops left spots on his grey overall. He looked round again before opening up the camper van. It was comfortable inside. A full-length mirror, a clothes rail on castors, a sofa, a small make-up table. It looked a little like an actor's dressing room. The box with the sets of screwdrivers stood behind the mirror. Kerbel double-locked the door and undressed. He let himself drop naked on to the sofa, opened the drawer of the make-up table, and took out a small bottle. The label said 'Nail Sensation'. Kerbel unscrewed it and painted his thumb-nail. Great stuff, this. If he painted it on his nails before applying the nail varnish then he could peel the entire layer off later like foil, saving himself at least ten minutes. He painted quick-drying aubergine nail varnish over the base layer. Kerbel leaned back and kept an eye on the time until three minutes were up. Then he grabbed his prick and got going. It was great to see his aubergine-coloured fingernails moving up and down. Just before he was about to come, Kerbel stopped and went to the clothes rail. He took a dark blue bra and matching knickers from their hanger, put both of them on, and looked at his reflection in the mirror. The knickers were baggy and tent-like, and had the price label still attached. Kerbel liked new things. He couldn't under-stand why some men fancied used knickers. That was dis-gusting. Perverted. Second-hand *dresses* were something else.

This one was anyway. He took it reverently off the hanger. He had found it a few weeks ago. A beautiful dress. Aubergine, square-necked, cut straight and very simple. He had just gone for a pee in the bushes and there was the dress caught in the branches, perfectly clean and almost as good as new. A gift, and it had fitted too. Quivering with excitement, Kerbel put the dress on. Even before he had finished pulling up the zip, he came in his knickers.

When Leon stopped outside the garden gate with its gold-painted spikes and circles the rain had slackened slightly. Martina and Kay were on the veranda, with Noah on a folding table between them. Martina must somehow have persuaded him to climb up on it. She was doing something to his back. It looked as if she were going to bath him and was just rubbing in shampoo. Noah had grown fatter. His coat shone. He turned his head to Leon, but it was clear that he had no intention of running to meet him. He had folded his legs under his body, which gave him a plump and baggy look. Nothing but a torso. He didn't look like a dog at all to Leon. A dog had legs. This was a giant slug, the queen of all slugs, who had set her horrible offspring on him. All it needed was the feelers. Leon got out of the car and strolled towards the house, hands in his trouser pockets.

'You've been gone for ages,' said Martina. She took a fold of fat on Noah's hips between her fingers and rolled it along his back towards the neck. Noah sighed. His large eyes were fixed on the horizon. A half-hearted wag of his tail expressed moderate pleasure at seeing Leon again.

'He's enjoying this,' said Kay. She was holding an open book in her hand and watching Martina manipulate the fat at the back of Noah's neck.

'What's all this about?' asked Leon, annoyed.

'What next?' asked Martina, turning to Kay. Kay ran her finger down the page.

'Next you're supposed to take a fold of skin and roll it along his back.'

'I just did that. And the next thing too. Read me the next but one!'

'Keeping your fingertips level with the root of the nose . . .'

'Oh yes, I remember.'

Leon took the book from Kay's hand and read the title: *How to Massage Your Pet.*

'You two must be crazy! Did Kerbel get you that as well?'

He handed the book back to Kay.

'I bought it with my own money,' said Martina. 'Don't upset me. That would transfer to Noah immediately.'

She ran her fingertips from the top of Noah's skull over his head, neck and back and down to his tail. The dog closed his eyes, but opened them again at once when Leon snapped at Martina.

'Just why does that fat dog have to be massaged, can you tell me?'

'Because it's the only way to get closer to him. You know he doesn't like being petted. Well, now I've found a way of touching him that he does like. He's got nothing against being touched, you see, he just doesn't like being stroked and patted.'

'It's perverted, if you ask me,' said Leon. 'I wouldn't be surprised if he has a hard-on.'

The way Noah was lying on the table meant that this eventuality could not be checked.

'Suppose he does,' said Kay. 'Let the poor dog have a bit of fun.'

Martina smiled at Kay. When she turned back to Leon, her face darkened. 'You can be just so horrible,' she said.

Leon pushed himself away from the balustrade of the veranda and clicked his tongue.

'Come on, Noah,' he called. 'Come on, good boy, come on, Noah! Let's go round the garden and check to see if there are any slugs left.'

He slapped his leg with the flat of his hand, and Noah did indeed jump up, claws grating and scratching on the plastic as he slipped off the table top. Master and dog disappeared round the corner. Leon was whistling to himself. Sighing, Martina folded up the table and leaned it against the wall of the house.

'Never mind,' said Kay. 'Noah may have gone off with Leon, but that doesn't mean he likes him better than you; just that Leon has more authority.'

'I don't care. The dog can do as he likes as far as I'm concerned.'

'Hey, don't be sad,' said Kay. 'Noah loves you. Adores you. You don't know what he was like before. He was the most peculiar dog I ever saw. He never used to like anyone, couldn't even stand his own master, although Zaven was always nice to him. This is the first time I ever saw him willingly let anyone touch him for hours like that.'

'It was only quarter of an hour. Would you like a coffee?'

'Sure,' said Kay.

Leon and the dog came back round the corner.

'Hey, Kay,' called Leon, 'before I forget, could you come and take a look at the car? The windscreen wipers have packed up again.'

'Sure.'

She went over to the Mercedes with him. Leon gave her the

car key. Kay sat in the driver's seat and started the engine. Then she reached forward to the front of the windscreen and gave the blade of one wiper a tug. The windscreen wipers instantly began to work again.

'Good,' said Leon. 'I'll remember that.'

'If that's not it, then the trouble's usually the fuse, and you just have to change it.'

Leon nodded. Kay went back to the house, and Leon went round the garden with Noah beside him. At the fence between the garden and the marshes he stopped and listened. He could hear nothing but the never-ending rain falling on the roof of his house and the new satellite dish, the grass, the boggy pools in the marshes, the freshly dug ditches. Leon picked up a stick and threw it out into the marshland.

'Go on, Noah, fetch! Fetch!'

Noah did not move. It might sometimes look as if he were obeying Leon, but in fact he obeyed only the higher laws of his own canine nature. Leon did not press the point. He looked out at his marshes, beautiful even in the rain, looked at the melancholy, unfathomable pools of water. Then he saw them: brown, reddish-brown and grey, fifteen centimetres long and two centimetres wide, damp and glossy and naked. He could count ten straight off. They were crawling over the moss and the mud, their breathing holes twitched when blades of grass touched their backs, and their heads moved forward in the direction of the garden. Fifteen, eighteen. No, Nature was not charming. Nature was malevolent, undisciplined and dirty, and hostile on principle to Leon and his hopes and endeavours. Nature wanted to wear him down and humiliate him. There were over twenty of them. Two were nibbling a mouldy mushroom with their fluted semicircular upper jaws, but they didn't fool Leon. The squashy mushroom was only a starter, an appetiser, a canapé, an *amuse-gueule*; they were planning to eat their fill in his garden. Leon clambered over the fence and kneeled down in the wet grass, which immediately soaked his trouser legs. He picked them up. He collected all of them within a radius of three metres around his garden. There weren't too many. Two handfuls. Leon threw them into the main ditch, and then went back to the house. Noah, unnoticed, had left him and was back in his basket. Leon was about to go into the house, but just as he was pressing down the door handle he saw another slug. It was sitting on top of the folded plastic table. It was not brick-red or brown like the slugs he had just collected. It was yellowish-white and exuding milky slime. It had crawled up the side of the table and was now trying to reach the wall, which was not easy, since its wrinkled and much-elongated lower body seemed to be full of eggs. The white slug reared up like a performing animal in a circus, waved the front of its body about in the air, and spread its feelers in a 'V' shape.

'V' for Victory.

5

Showers dying down. Fog likely in the evening, particularly in low-lying areas. Highest temperatures will remain rather cool at around 16 degrees.

Guido Kerbel left his shop and backed the delivery van out of the entrance. It was just after five. Kerbel wanted to visit Karli's Bargain Basement before closing time to look at various cheap and cheerful items and perhaps stock up with them. The insulating tape and screwdrivers were going well, and he'd sold four of the little trolls with brightly coloured hair. The windows of the van were steamed up. Kerbel wound down the side window and leaned half his torso out so as to keep the two dustcarts in sight. His shovel-shaped lower jaw jutted with concentration. Someone hooted. A sound like a cry of rage. Kerbel's foot slipped off the clutch and the engine flooded. It was a car he didn't know, a red Mercedes with a spoiler and the broadest tyres Kerbel had ever seen on a private car. The man behind the wheel looked furious. He had long grey hair. His jacket was grey too, so that for a moment Kerbel thought the man had such long hair, and so much of it, that he could wrap himself in it. A younger man with an impassive expression sat beside him. He signalled to Kerbel to get out of the way. Kerbel made haste to move over to the right-hand side of the road.

He'd guessed as much – once one person from the West moved here, others were bound to follow. And then they'd have to buy things. The neighbourhood was coming up in the world. A little patience, that was all you needed. He raised a hand, half in greeting, half in apology. The man at the wheel of the other car automatically raised his hand too, but then at the last moment let it drop with a dismissive gesture. Kerbel saw a white dog sitting on the back seat. The dog was slit-eyed and had a head like a fat cucumber split lengthways. It was slobbering all over the window. Kerbel watched the car in his rear-view mirror until it had disappeared round the next bend.

As the red Mercedes made its laborious way along the tractor ruts, Leon was kneeling beside Noah on the veranda, picking slugs out of the dog's bowl. Not for the first time. These field slugs loved dog food. The red car braked outside the garden gate and parked next to the black Mercedes.

'It's Harry,' Leon shouted into the house. He threw the slugs down on the grass and stood up. He could scarcely remember when he had last talked to another man – really talked. Conversations with the shopkeeper didn't count.

Martina came out. She was wearing a yellow dress made of the same fabric as the new cushion in Noah's basket. Noah yawned, opened his jaws wide and let his tongue loll. Then he crossed his forepaws on the cushion and laid his muzzle on them. He watched, unmoved, as Pfitzner and Harry got out. Only when a bull terrier followed them did his head shoot up, while an uncontrollable, half-stifled growl emerged from his throat. Maybe it was Leon and Martina's business if other human beings set foot in this garden, but when a dog appeared it was very much Noah's affair. The bull terrier had noticed the large brown dog himself, and was making for him, but no sooner had he taken the first step in Noah's direction than Harry shouted: 'Rocky! No!'

The bull terrier immediately flung himself on his back. Harry grunted approval and fixed a lead to Rocky's studded black collar. He had bought the dog from Albanian Roy a month ago, because Albanian Roy wanted a real fighting dog instead, a pit bull. Harry wasn't interested in dogfighting; he wanted the bull terrier for himself. Even a character like Harry needs something to love. Rocky was still young, and a fast learner. In fact everyone learned fast with Harry, girls and dogs alike. He told the whores he'd break their fingers if they ever dared touch his dog. And the bull terrier soon realised that he would get a beating if he ran to greet the whores or indeed anyone else. The only time he couldn't control himself was when he saw another dog.

'Harry,' cried Leon, running to meet him. He grasped his friend's lower arm and pressed his hand. 'Benno,' he said, still beaming, although it struck him at the same moment that he would probably have done better to greet Pfitzner first.

'So these are the beauties of nature you were carrying on about?' asked Harry. 'This isn't nature, not this. I've been through the Grand Canyon on a motorbike – now that's nature for you! Goes on for ever. Las Vegas. Rodeos and that.'

Noah rose from his cushion, the hairs on his back bristling, took three stiff-legged steps towards the bull terrier on its leash, and lay flat on his front on the ground. Martina was not sure if she ought to go out into the rain to welcome Leon's friends, or fetch Noah back, or simply wait under the veranda roof. The bull terrier looked at the brown dog, eyes wide, and whined to itself. Noah leaped to his feet and ran over to him. The hairs on both dogs' backs were bristling now. Rocky lowered his nose to Noah's belly, and Noah uttered a deep growl. At the same moment Martina grabbed his collar and placed herself between the two animals. She bent down to give Rocky a soothing pat on the nose.

'Don't touch him!' Harry snapped at her. 'He can't stand women.'

But in any case Rocky had turned away. He had not forgotten that whores were out of bounds, and as far as he knew all women were whores – a view which he shared with his master. Harry did not go to the trouble of greeting Martina. He walked past her and tied his bull terrier to the veranda.

'Take your dog indoors. I'll leave Rocky out here, or he'll tear him to bits like an old rag.'

Martina was about to say something about Noah's dislike of being in the house, but Leon was already dragging him along by his collar. She bit her lip.

'This your girlie, is it?' asked Pfitzner. He took Martina's hand and held it tight, bringing his broad nose much too close to her face. 'Pretty thing. I like her. You got taste, Blacky.'

He finally let Martina's hand go. She swiftly withdrew it, placed her other hand protectively over it, and glanced at Leon for help. He avoided her eyes. Nor did he put his arm round her as they followed Pfitzner into the house, as he usually did when they were coming in from outside. For one thing he had to haul the dog after him, and for another he didn't want Harry and Pfitzner thinking he was love-stricken. And now of all times, of course, Kay had to turn up. She was strolling past the fence, and waved. Martina waved back from the doorway. Leon pretended not to see Kay, silently praying that she wouldn't take it into her head to pay a visit now.

'What on earth's that?' asked Harry. 'Not a bloke, is it?'

'No idea,' replied Leon, with a nervous laugh. 'I guess she isn't too sure herself.'

He quickly closed the door. Pfitzner turned back to Martina.

'Hey, she's made you comfortable in here,' he said, nodding appreciatively in the direction of the living room. 'You're a real little sugar-pie, aren't you? Think you could rustle us up something to eat as well?'

'I'll go and look,' said Martina, feeling daunted, and went into the kitchen.

'Get the frozen steaks out and thaw them in the microwave,' said Leon in a tone he had never used to her before.

She stood in the kitchen, staring at the closed cupboard doors. It was dawning on her that she didn't really know much about Leon, or what mattered to him. The way he looked at that old brute! As if he were God Almighty! Mechanically, she opened the freezer, took the frozen meat out, unwrapped it, put it on a plate and put the plate in the microwave. Then she leaned her hands on the window sill, looked out at the thin rain, and wished herself back in the city. She felt like throwing up, but this house wasn't soundproof, so she would have to wait until she was alone again.

Pfitzner dropped into the armchair where Leon sat when he was reading, undid the laces of his ankle boots, took his feet half out of them and stretched his legs. He put a cigar in his mouth and lit it with a gold Dupont lighter, filling the air with its odour. Leon let go of Noah's collar and sat down on the sofa. The dog trotted back to the door and waited, dour and motionless, for someone to let him out. Harry had stationed himself in front of the bookshelves, legs spread wide, his back to Pfitzner and Leon. He took book after book out and then put them back without opening any of them.

Meanwhile Pfitzner was inspecting the signet ring on his fat middle finger with close attention. Leon shifted uncomfortably on the sofa.

'Nice Mercedes . . . your new one, I mean,' he said, for the sake of saying something, 'and your old one's pretty good too. It's a great help to me here. Fantastic car. Honestly. I'm really grateful.'

Pfitzner scratched his signet ring with his thumbnail, then looked up and stared right through Leon, without expression and in silence. Leon cleared his throat.

'I thought you were planning to buy a Porsche. Isn't that what you said?'

He knew perfectly well that Pfitzner had never planned to buy a Porsche, but he couldn't stand the silence any longer. He had not been mistaken.

'A Porsche?' growled Pfitzner. 'A Porsche looks like a dog crapping.'

Noah came back in. When no one was looking, he went over to the fireplace and lay down on the rug. From this position he watched the three men, trying to work out their ranking order. Noah sensed the tall, grey-haired man's clarity of mind and overwhelming determination, the kind of determination possessed only by a male dog absolutely certain of his strength. It was good to have a dog like that in the pack. But if the grey-haired man was not part of Leon's pack, he must be driven away as quickly as possible, because by comparison Leon was just a yapping little dog, outranked even by the man beside the bookshelves. The man by the bookshelves was not to be trusted. He was the kind who would bite and attack without warning. There was a quiet threat in the eyes of the grey-haired man – not aggression, just a threat. But it looked as if Leon had seen it too and was conducting himself appropriately. That reassured Noah. A respectful display of his own low rank would secure Leon's membership of the pack and spare everyone trouble.

'Porsche,' snorted Pfitzner. Then he looked straight at Leon, and Harry opened one of the books and appeared to be immersed in it.

'How come you've not been to see me? If you never phone I can at least expect you to come and see me, bring me up to date. What d'you think I gave you the car for?'

Leon struggled to retain his composure.

'I . . . er . . . I did try to call you. I bought a mobile specially. And I've sent you the manuscript – the first half of it. I didn't want to show you anything before I'd got it to a state where I was really happy with it. That always takes me quite a long time. That's the way I work. And I'd have called this week anyway, because I now have two publishers showing an interest. I didn't want to agree to anything before clearing it with you first. And then I was going to ask you about the royalties from the book. I'd be getting around ten per cent, and I don't know how we're going to work that out with your hundred thousand . . .'

'Peanuts,' said Pfitzner. 'I'm not interested in your ten per cent. If I like the book you can keep it. Just make sure I do like the book.'

He fixed his gaze on Leon again. His eyelids were at half-mast.

'And what's all that shit in aid of?' he added suddenly.

'What . . . er . . . ?' asked Leon.

'What you sent me. What makes you think I'm bothered about my mother having so many men? That's her business. I like to think my mother had a good time. How come you write that kind of shit? What's the idea? And all that about school . . . look, I told you how it was. So how come you write it all wrong? What's the matter with you?'

'I . . .' Leon began.

'You'll have to write it all again,' said Pfitzner. 'Write it the way I told you. And don't start inventing anything extra. Have you got that clear?'

Leon looked from Pfitzner to Harry, who still appeared to be deep in his book. Martina came in with the meal and put two plates on the table.

'Ah, just what we need,' said Pfitzner, slipping his shoes on again. He went over to the table and sat down in front of one of the plates, which held a sizzling steak. There were onion rings on top of the steak, and chips and bright green peas beside it.

'Looks delicious,' said Pfitzner, beginning to saw at the meat. Harry finally tore himself away from the bookshelves and sat down too. Martina brought in the other two plates.

'Aren't you going to join us, Leon?' she asked. He rose, went over to the table as if sleepwalking, and sat down in front of his food without touching the cutlery. Noah sniffed. He didn't beg; he never begged.

'Delicious,' said Pfitzner again. 'so she can cook too. You're a lucky bastard, Blacky.'

He speared a pea, an onion ring, a chip and a piece of meat on his fork one by one, and put them all in his mouth together.

'It never stops raining here,' said Harry, chewing. 'Next time we'll bring you an inflatable dinghy.'

Pfitzner sawed off another piece of meat, put it on his fork and dipped it in its bloody juices. Leon felt as if he himself were that piece of meat, and the fork was Pfitzner, who had grabbed hold of him and was holding his head in a puddle.

'About the book . . .' Leon began.

'Not now, not while we're eating,' said Pfitzner, sawing away, shovelling up peas, carrying chips to his mouth. A small drop of meat juice spurted out between his lips and on to his chin. Harry bent close to his plate. Martina gave Leon a cool, searching glance. Leon jumped. Her gaze obliged him to contradict Pfitzner, even if he'd rather not.

'Yes,' he said, 'yes, we must talk about it now. I have to explain something to you. I have to explain what writing's like. I'm sure you'll see things differently then.'

Noah moved his head uneasily on his forepaws. What had got into Leon? As long as a dog knew and accepted his place, he needn't fear attack from higher-ranking males. But the way Leon was behaving, he was putting himself and thus the pack in danger.

'You have to trust me over one thing,' said Leon, avoiding looking at Pfitzner as he spoke. 'I can write. I know what I'm doing. A person who's never done it finds it difficult to get a real idea of why some things have to be expressed in exactly one way and no other. Most people think a writer is someone who . . .'

'Don't you start telling me what a writer is. I know what a writer is,' said Pfitzner. 'A writer's a man who can't shit because he spends the whole day sitting at his keyboard and never moves from the spot. But instead of getting up and running round the block a few times, he just sits there writing about how he can't shit.'

'Not a bad way of putting it,' said Leon, forcing a smile, 'but all the same I must ask you not to tell me how to do my job. You have to accept that I simply know more about writing than you. After all, it'll be my name on the book. I'll be responsible for what's in it.'

'Shut up,' said Pfitzner, looking out of the window. 'I'll send you a list of the parts you're to change. I've rewritten some of them myself. I'll be docking part of your fee for that. You just stick to what I've done and carry on the same way. And you're to send me ten new pages every week! Well, I'm off. Harry will get everything else straight with you.'

'No, I . . .' Leon objected, and fell silent when he met a penetrating, imploring and angry glance from Harry, who was slowly and almost imperceptibly shaking his head. Noah was looking at him too. He could smell the fear in Leon's sweat, and he saw that Leon was not acting appropriately for someone who felt that fear.

'Why don't you just give him his money back?' said Martina, who had kept silent up to this point. She almost added that she could give it to him herself, but bit the remark back just in time.

'Tell your sweetie to go powder her nose,' said Pfitzner.

'Why don't you just take your money back and leave us alone?' Martina's voice was shrill and unsteady. She was trembling.

'Go away, please,' said Leon, between his teeth. Martina rose. It was obvious to her that she had done something wrong. Yet again.

'OK,' said Pfitzner, when she had closed the door behind her. 'What was that you said?'

Harry moved away from the table. There was perspiration on his forehead.

'Look, Leon . . .' he began.

A happy yapping came from outside. Noah ran to the window and put his forepaws up on the sill. Leon pretended to be interested too. Rocky the bull terrier had wriggled his head out of the studded collar and was now strolling across the garden, sniffing Noah's scent markings and lifting his own leg over them. Noah's scent markings were quite high up, because he was a large dog, but Rocky succeeded in leaving his even higher by dint of contorting himself so that he was almost standing on his head. Noah jumped down from the window sill and ran to the door, barking. He came back, barked, jumped up on the window sill again, saw Rocky pissing in his garden while he was unable to do anything about it, howled hysterically, pricked up his drooping ears as far as he possibly could, whined, yowled, despaired, ran back and forth, his claws scraping on the floor whenever he ran over part of it not covered by the rug.

'You'll do it the way I tell you. Is that clear?' Pfitzner looked at Leon. Leon went on pretending to watch Rocky, pretending not to hear. He was frightened. Frightened of Pfitzner. And worst of all, he was frightened of Harry too. At the same time he was afraid to say 'Yes' and look like a weakling to them ever after. Rocky was pissing against the toolshed. Noah howled. His entire body was shaking with helpless rage. He began to bark non-stop.

'Shut your gob,' shouted Pfitzner, kicking him in the side. Noah fell to the floor with a pitiful squeal. Martina flung the door open.

'Don't you touch that dog!'

Her eyes were blazing, her face was white as a sheet.

'And you shut your mouth too, cunt,' said Pfitzner. Martina ran to Noah, kneeled down beside him and said in a toneless voice, 'Get out! Get out of our house at once!'

She waited for Leon to say something too, and when he said nothing she shouted, hysterically: 'Out! Get out of here! Go away!'

Pfitzner glanced at Harry, who went over to Martina,

grabbed her by the hair and jerked her head to one side. She screamed with pain, and then immediately fell silent.

'Look here . . .' said Leon, taking a step forward, at the same time seeing and hearing himself and his pitiful 'Look here'. He did not know what to do. But Noah did. He jumped up and bit Harry in the leg. Harry swore, and kicked out at him with his other foot, but Noah clung on, and Harry had to let go of Martina. Pfitzner pushed Leon aside, marched down the corridor to the front door, opened it and called to Rocky. The bull terrier came racing up, and pushed his way between Pfitzner's legs and into the house. Unhesitatingly, he made for Noah and jumped at him. He caught him full on, swung him round with the force of his attack, and buried his teeth in Noah's neck. Noah snapped wildly around him, but Rocky was faster. His jaws kept working, always close to the other dog's muzzle or the soft, loose skin of his chest. When Noah finally managed to scramble to his feet, Rocky attacked from underneath, this time getting him by the neck. Noah realised that this was serious, really serious, a matter of life and death, and he couldn't win. He flung himself on his back and showed his vulnerable throat. A display of his own low-ranking position would pacify the attacker. But Rocky was not interested in his opponent's surrender. He was going to kill this brown dog. Howling, Noah jumped aside at the last moment, and only just managed to pull his neck out of those foaming jaws, while his coat was slit from chin to ribcage. Harry seized the bull terrier's throat and picked him up, in effect lifting two dogs in the air. Rocky had sunk his teeth into Noah's face with such force that the other dog, almost twice his size, was still hanging from his muzzle.

'Let go,' shouted Harry, hitting Rocky's head with his fist. Rocky just clung on even more tightly.

'Get me something to use as a lever,' said Harry, turning to Leon. But it was Pfitzner who handed him a fork. Harry thrust the fork into Rocky's mouth, prongs first, and worked it around, while all the time Noah hung from Rocky's teeth, squealing. Finally the bull terrier gave way and let him drop, sneezed and shook his head. Noah fell to the floor like an old sack and lay there motionless. Martina ran to him and raised his head. The brown, marble-like eyes looked dully through her.

'He has to see the vet,' she cried. 'We must get him to the vet at once. He's bleeding to death. Leon, you'd better bring the car round to the door.'

'That fucking animal isn't going in my car, not bleeding like that,' said Pfitzner.

Martina tried to lift Noah.

'I said: not in my car!' Pfitzner repeated. Then Martina realised, and so did Leon, that he meant the black Mercedes. Leon's Mercedes.

'I'll be off now,' said Pfitzner, turning to Harry. 'You follow me with the other car. And don't you dare let that mongrel in it.'

'What?' said Leon.

'Blacky never drives to Hamburg anyway, so he won't be needing the car any more.'

Pfitzner went out, slamming the door behind him. Harry put his bull terrier under his arm and gestured to Leon to follow him. It had stopped raining. There were clouds of mist over the maize field. Pfitzner backed out along the tractor ruts. Harry and Leon were left standing outside the garden gate.

'Give me the keys and the papers,' said Harry.

'You wouldn't do a thing like that, would you? You're not really going to do it?'

'Christ, Leon, pull yourself together,' said Harry. 'I have to, don't I? Sure, you're my friend, but if you act like that I can't help you any more.'

'You know he gave me the car. You know he did!'

'You never stop talking bullshit, do you?' said Harry. 'Why would Pfitzner give you a car like that? Any idea what it cost?'

'But he did give it to me. He can't just take it away again.'

'If it was new that car would cost at least 80,000. You think Pfitzner would give you 80,000 marks, just like that, for the sake of your pretty face?'

Leon spread his arms and barred Harry's way. 'Don't you touch my car!'

'Christ, Leon, that Mercedes belongs to Pfitzner and he can take it back any time he likes. Or did he actually say: here, I'm making you a present of this car, from now on it's yours? Well, did he? No, he didn't, right? If you'd got your act together a bit better you could have gone on driving it indefinitely.'

Leon let his arms fall again. They hung limply from his shoulders. He stepped aside.

'OK, now give me the key,' said Harry.

Leon handed it to him.

'And the papers.'

'In the glove compartment.'

Harry unlocked the car and put Rocky on the back seat. He took a jacket of Martina's and an opened bag of sweets from the ledge behind the seat and passed them to Leon. Then he put a hand on his shoulder.

'Don't take it so hard. You got by without a car before. And don't forget I'm your friend. You can rely on me any time. Call me if you need anything, OK?'

Before Leon could answer he turned away, got into the black Mercedes and drove off. The bull terrier was barking and slavering against the side window. Leon turned and went back into the house.

Noah was now lying in a pile of bloodstained bedding. Martina was kneeling beside him. She looked at Leon. His face was grey, but she did not feel sorry for him.

'Bloody hell,' said Leon, with a difficult grin, 'and I could have sworn Pfitzner gave me that car.'

'Never mind your damn car,' said Martina, 'we have to get Noah to a vet, or he'll bleed to death.'

This was an exaggeration. Noah had stopped bleeding some time ago.

'I'll call Kerbel,' said Leon, taking the mobile out of his pocket. 'That'll be quicker than calling a taxi. A taxi would have to get here first. Do you know his number? Where's the phone book?'

They were in luck. Kerbel was there and said he'd come round. Then they waited.

'Is he all right?' asked Leon.

'Of course not. You can see he isn't all right.'

Martina stroked Noah's nose, put her fingers in a bowl of water and held them under his muzzle. Noah gently licked the water off her fingers, and Martina began to weep. Leon went into the bathroom. He turned the tap on and looked at himself in the mirror. The repulsive and pitiful face of a failure. He had not protected Martina. He had let them humiliate him in his own house. He was nothing, nobody. And he was still afraid. Afraid of Pfitzner. Afraid of what would happen if he didn't write that bloody book, if he didn't write it the way Pfitzner wanted. Christ, the man hadn't the faintest idea about literature! Pfitzner would force him to write a trashy novel. Suppose he just threw his money back at him? Why didn't Martina come in now and ask if he wanted her money? She just had no sensitivity in these things. Too stupid, the silly cow! But still, it would have been crazy to give back the 50,000 marks. Pfitzner could have what he wanted. It would be clear to everyone that he had written this pathetic stuff just for the stupid pimp, no one would throw it up at him, quite the opposite: people would laugh with him because he was such a wily fox. Leon involuntarily smiled at his reflection in the glass.

A vehicle drove up. Leon and Martina went out. Kerbel's van: the shopkeeper jumped out. Kay was with him.

'We tried to reach the vet in Freyenow,' said Kay. 'He's out with a sick sheep at the moment, but he'll be back in half an hour, an hour at the latest. If we start now we'll be there about the same time as him. Otherwise we'll just have to go on to Behnsen and straight to the animal hospital.'

'Oh, Kay, I'm so glad you're here,' said Martina. The three of them went back to the living room. Kay bent down and picked up the large, blood-encrusted dog, bedding and all. Leon was going to help her, but Kay said, 'No, don't; it'll be better if I hold him on my own.'

She carried Noah out to the van. Kerbel held the back doors open.

'This kind of thing always happens when your car's off the road, doesn't it?' he said to Leon. Kay and Martina got in the back to look after Noah. No one asked Leon if he wanted to come too. He was a man nobody needed, a man without a car, a man who hadn't defended his wife, a man who didn't know how to pick up an injured dog.

Kerbel turned in the maize field. Leon put his hands in his trouser pockets and walked round the house. He went to the end of the garden and stood on the large plank he had brought down from the attic, so that there would be at least one place where you could stand on the lawn without getting your feet wet. He wished he was a smoker. Just then he would have liked to light a cigarette and blow dry smoke into the misty air. It would have been a suitable and comforting gesture. The air was so damp that he had to keep removing his glasses to wipe the little drops of moisture off the lenses with a handkerchief. The marshes were wrapped in ghostly cotton wool which swallowed up the light, lying so close to the ground that only the tips of the long reeds emerged from it. Leon liked that. He would have liked to wade about in it, but he was afraid of falling into another bog. *A man who dared not leave his own garden.* Leon climbed over the fence and took a couple of steps. The cloud of mist rolled towards him, half a metre above the ground. Then he saw the light. It was not more than twenty metres away. Someone was waving a torch or something similar. He narrowed his eyes. A shadow on a tree stump. Leon thought of everything he had ever heard about will o' the wisps. Well, he had not actually heard anything about will o' the wisps, but he still felt uncomfortable.

'Who's there?' he called.

'It's me – Isadora,' the reply came out of the mist.

'Where are you?'

'Here,' she replied, 'here!'

And the light swayed back and forth.

The vet in Freyenow was a giant. Everything about Dr Brunswick was enormous, his hands the size of frying pans, the muddy size 50 gumboots which he had not taken off since seeing to the sick sheep, the white coat which fluttered around him like a sail, and his large skull, with a few stiff bristles left on its bald patch.

'Bring him in here. Looks like an Ikea shelving unit after its third move,' he said to Kay, and marched into the consulting room, where there was no light on. He pushed the switch down with his elbow, went over to the washbasin and soaped his hands and arms as far as his rolled-up shirtsleeves.

'Tie my coat at the back, would you?' he told Martina. She pulled the edges of the white sail together and tied the tapes into a decorative bow behind the gigantic vet's back.

'Right then, let's take a look at your boy.'

Dr Brunswick turned to Noah, whom Kay had placed on the examination table.

'Good Lord, who or what did that to him? Playing games with a crocodile, was he?'

'A dog bit him,' said Martina. Dr Brunswick picked up one paw after the other and moved them carefully to and fro.

'Not just once, either. What kind of a dog was it?'

'I don't know. It looked like a pig with a fat nose – as if a bee had stung it.'

'Oh, one of those. Nice dogs really. It's a shame what people turn them into. Yours is tough too, though. I'll sew him up and then you can take him home again. He can stand up to quite a lot. Just let him sleep it off for a week and he'll be almost like new. And you can be grateful you've got a proper dog. A Peke wouldn't have survived.'

He examined Noah's left ear, which was hanging on by a piece of skin the width of a finger, thought briefly, and then without comment cut it off with an ordinary pair of scissors. Noah squealed faintly.

'Want to keep it as a souvenir?'

He offered Kay the ear and then dropped it in a bucket. Finally he gave Noah two injections, bandaged one paw, put a plaster where his ear had been, and stitched up the long tear on his throat and chest and the three bites to his head.

'At least yours is a big dog,' he muttered under his breath. 'How I hate all those small animals. But you can't tell people that, you have to treat them all the same. Yesterday a man came in with a birdcage, two canaries in it, one of them sick. Buy a new one, why don't you? I told the man. They only cost fifty pfennigs. And he says yes, he knows, but he can't say that to his wife, so please will I treat her little birdie. I try to reach into the cage, but I can't get my hand straight in. I swear I almost couldn't get it through the door of that cage. Then I grab hold of one of the birds, and of course it's the wrong one, the healthy one, and before I know it the bird's died of fright. Nothing but trouble, working with small animals. I only wish I could give it up entirely.'

He painted violet-coloured disinfectant on parts of Noah.

'There we are. I haven't made him any prettier, but it's the best I can do.'

Leon had made his way cautiously towards the light. He was relieved to see that it really was Isadora Schlei sitting there on a tree stump, waving a torch about. Yet again Isadora was wearing long velvet skirts, green and brown and blue, in several layers on top of each other, soaked with moisture and dirty at the hem. Her hair fell in loose tangles over her shoulders, and was full of leaves and bits of bark. She wore quantities of gold bangles on her fat white arms.

'What are you doing here, for heaven's sake?'

'I'm not doing anything for heaven's sake,' replied Isadora in a languid manner. 'I'm sitting here waiting for you, on purpose and for my own personal pleasure.'

She lowered her arms with a clinking sound and crossed

them in her large, shimmering green lap. The torch rolled into the hollow between her two mighty thighs.

'You'll catch your death,' said Leon. 'Or at least pyelitis.' Then, as if he had only just heard what she said: 'Waiting for me? Why? And what made you think I'd be coming here?' He grinned, 'You were lucky I went out in the garden then.'

'Not lucky,' said Isadora. 'Patient. You think this is the first time I've waited for you here?'

She removed a small twig from her hair, and began combing through it with her long, green-lacquered nails. Leon pictured Isadora coming out here in the pouring rain every day for the last few weeks, waiting for him in the mist twenty metres from his house. He thought about what he had been doing on those days . . . watching television, working, making love to Martina, fixing the waste pipe . . .

'Really every day?' he asked.

'No,' said Isadora, 'what makes you think that? I've sat out here two or three times, and now here you are. Come on!'

She put out her hand, which was round and soft as a baby's. Leon shook his head, amused.

What might be going on inside her head? What made her think he could feel attracted to someone who looked like her?

'No, Isadora, sorry. No, really.'

He turned round. The lights of his house shone dimly through the veil of mist. The empty living room would smell of cigars, violence, and the fear he had felt. Leon did not particularly fancy the idea of waiting alone there for Martina to come back and call him a coward or, even worse, say nothing at all.

'Come on,' Isadora repeated, stretching her hand out to him again. Her obesity and elemental sluttishness intrigued him. What on earth did the ridiculous woman think she was up to?

'You want me to fuck you?' asked Leon.

'It's not the expression I'd use, but I guess we mean the same thing,' Isadora replied.

'Right,' said Leon. 'Let's go to your place, then.'

He grasped that warm, plump hand, pulled Isadora to her feet and went a couple of paces ahead of her, drawing her after him. Then he thought better of it, and stopped.

'You go first. You know the way. At least, I hope so.'

'I know the marshes as well as the frogs and toads do.'

The tall blades of grass had bowed beneath the burden of the rain, and brushed against Isadora and Leon's hips. There was a sound of crawling and rustling around them. All the amphibians of the fen seemed to be on the move, making their noisy way through the grass or plopping into puddles. When the curtain of mist parted, Isadora's torch was reflected in the water. Once there was a dead, hairless rat drifting in the reddish liquid into which Leon trod. He thought of the replies he should have made to Pfitzner, what he ought to have said and done if he'd been a real man. Glugging, squelching, gurgling sounds accompanied him and Isadora through the lifeless wood. Suddenly the Schlei sisters' villa emerged before them, tall and threatening. Although Leon was already wet through, it seemed to him that the house exuded additional moisture. Isadora opened the front door and propelled Leon ahead of her into a dark hall. She stumbled on the threshold. Her large breasts pressed against his back, soft and warm.

She giggled. Then she told him: 'Turn left and up the stairs.'

Leon groped his way ahead of her over a musty-smelling stair carpet, holding on to the banisters. Isadora opened a door on the first floor and switched on the light. Leon found himself in her bedroom. It was dry. It was comfortable. A place that had nothing to do with the weather outside. Rather untidy, perhaps a touch vulgar. The light hung like a birdcage from a curved brass stand, and had a red velvet shade which cast a pink hue. The wallpaper bore a pattern of hummingbirds in flight with ribbons in their beaks, and tiny baskets of flowers. The bed was large and bizarre. A four-poster with its uprights made of gnarled, untreated tree trunks; even the bark was still on them, as if the bed itself was a plant and its green canopy would grow to the ceiling one day. White sheets, which did at least look clean. On a sky-blue chest of drawers lay a jumble of necklaces and earrings, coloured stones, dried roses and postcards, and the floor was strewn with pieces of clothing. Leon's gaze lingered on Isadora's enormous bra dangling from the back of a chair, its cups looking like a pair of cornucopias. He cleared his throat.

'Have you got a drink?'

'Yes, of course, darling,' said Isadora. 'Just get undressed and I'll be right back.'

Leon wondered why he had come with her. What was he doing here? She was so incredibly fat. She couldn't have had a man for years. Not here in the back of beyond. That meant that she'd be grateful, anyway, and he could probably do anything he liked with her. A picture emerged before his mind's eye of Isadora afterwards – when he had finished with her – cowering in the sticky sheets, looking up at him with tear-filled eyes and stammering uncomprehendingly, 'Why? Why?'

Why? Well, hadn't she invited him herself, hadn't she wanted just that – wanted him to give her a good seeing to? Leon hung his wet black jacket over the bra and sat down on the edge of the bed. He couldn't help thinking of Pfitzner and Harry. He sighed, troubled, and let himself fall back on the bed, his lower arm over his eyes. Isadora came back, balancing a teapot and two cups on a tray. She was now wearing a shiny black kimono with pagodas, junks and Chinese coolies harvesting rice embroidered on it in red and gold thread.

'I was really thinking of something stronger,' said Leon, sitting up again, but Isadora only answered, 'This'll warm you up and relax you. You need it.' She poured him a cup. The spout of the curiously crooked teapot was much too wide, and the tea splashed uncontrollably into the cup, filling the saucer too and running over on to the floor, but Isadora paid no attention at all. She handed Leon the dripping cup and poured herself one, yet again causing a small deluge in the process. Leon spluttered into his tea and looked at Isadora sitting on an unfortunate chair in front of him. She looked like a big warm cushion full of comfort and love and yielding softness. Leon stood up, put down his teacup, went over to Isadora, took her by the chin, turned her face up to his and kissed her. He began slowly and tenderly, then put a hand round behind her head, drew her firmly towards him and kissed her harder, letting her feel his teeth, pushing his tongue deep into her mouth. When he moved back from her again, his head a little way from hers, Isadora's hair was hanging over her face like tendrils, her lips were half open, wet with saliva and a little blood. He felt better already. Isadora lowered her face, smiling, and took a small sip from the teacup she had been balancing in one hand all the time – there was blood on the rim of the cup too.

'Put that stupid tea down,' he said hoarsely. With a melancholy expression, Isadora took another sip and then rose too. Leon pulled the bow of her kimono sash. The kimono parted, fell away on both sides and exposed Isadora's large breasts, which hung heavily down to her belly as if full of sand. Isadora slipped out of her Chinese landscapes. She went over to the gnarled four-poster and lay down on the pillows on her stomach, turning her head and looking invitingly at Leon. Leon looked at her bottom, working out whether Martina's would fit into it twice or three times over. He could think of no comparison for that pale-pink, shapeless moon. It was a repulsive sight, but in the darkest corner of his subconscious mind, where no ray of civilised light had ever fallen, he wanted this woman. Isadora could not have missed seeing his expression. He was waiting for her to blush and pull the covers modestly over her huge body, so that he could comfort her, assure her that he liked her in spite of her size, and would still sleep with her.

'What's the matter?' said Isadora. 'Seen enough? Come on, don't keep me waiting any longer.'

Leon sat down on the bed beside her. Isadora propped herself on her elbows, wriggling towards him, placed her head with all its black hair on his chest and bit one of his shirt buttons off. Leon grasped one of her breasts, weighed it in his hand and then dropped it, like something not worth holding on to, and watched it dangle.

'Ouch,' said Isadora. 'Rather clumsy, aren't you? Looks like I'll have to teach you everything.'

Leon laughed.

'What makes you so sure I want to sleep with you? Perhaps I don't. Perhaps you're too fat for me.'

'Is that your way of saying you can't get it up?'

Leon took off his glasses, pulled his black shirt over his head, unbuttoned his black jeans, and stepped out of his underpants.

'Wow!' said Isadora.

He lay on top of her. She felt extraordinarily soft. Well, of course she felt soft, but he hadn't expected her to be quite so soft. There was almost no resistance in her body. It was like porridge, like uncooked cake. Heavens, when did he last run his finger round a bowl of uncooked cake? It must have been when he was a child. He burrowed in. This was the first time he'd ever slept with a fat woman. It was good. She was so . . . so soft. There was so much of her. It was liking sleeping with the whole of the marshes. As if the bogs and the peat and the rotten leaves, the pimply fungi and the soaking-wet bark, and all the little creeping creatures living there, the common frogs and marsh frogs, the various species of toads, fire-bellied toads, newts and salamanders and everything else crawling and excreting and procreating, the tadpoles and the spawn and not least of all the rain, the endless rain dissolving everything, caught and held in the marshes – as if all of that had become a single woman. The voluptuous curves of her toad-like thighs, the little folds on her ribs, the vast cushion of her buttocks. It was not too easy to make his way into all this. Isadora's legs clung together so plumply that he twice thought he was inside her before realising that his prick was simply enclosed by the fat of her thighs. She had to help him, take it and put it in its place, make it compliant to her will. His thrusts sent movements running through her body, waves of trembling, quivering flesh rolling towards him. She gave off great heat. A film of sweat formed between his skin and hers. He couldn't lie on top of her without beginning to slide or sink in immediately. She enveloped him like the warm mist of the marshes, ran down him like rainwater, gave way beneath him like soft ground, rose again like the green sap of a plant. Leon dug his hands into her hair, bit the soft white flesh, grasped her and thrust again. She seemed to be enjoying it. She responded to every bite with a harder one and scratched his back with her long green fingernails. Her thighs clung around his hips, he felt one of her heels, soft as a baby's, kicking at his buttocks, urging him to thrust harder and harder, and more than once preventing him from slipping out of her.

He came only a moment or so after Isadora had clung to him, twitching and moaning, and when he came it was like falling off a fairground ride. Her big, hot body drank him up, absorbed his fluids into itself. Leon offered no more resistance and let himself sink into the white flesh of her breasts, where he simply lay for a few minutes, breathing heavily. Then he rolled off Isadora and looked at her sideways. All that flesh. Gulliver in Brobdingnag. What he felt now was definitely not satisfaction. Leon looked away, in search of his clothes. It had always been like that before he married Martina. He encountered women with firmness and they left him soft – and wanting to be alone again. Leon fished for his underpants. He got dressed quietly, as if vanquished. I ought to shower, he thought, so that Martina won't smell anything. But he wanted to get away from here as fast as possible. Isadora's fingers caressed his arm.

'What's the hurry?' she murmured. 'You can't get home without me anyway.'

He knew she was right; he didn't dare to wander through the marshes on his own, in the mist too. He had a terrible idea that she could force him to stay here if she felt like it.

'Get dressed,' said Leon. 'I might still get back before Martina comes home with the dog.'

'Oh, how unloving,' complained Isadora, stretching on her back like a fat cat and releasing a cloud of sexual odour from between her thighs. Three hundred million sperm cells on their way through the vaginal fluid to the egg.

He ought to have asked if she was taking precautions. That was par for the course too: he always thought of that question too late. The idea that Isadora might have his child nauseated him. She was probably much too fat to get pregnant, but you couldn't be sure. Leon picked up the kimono and dropped it over Isadora's pudenda without looking at her. She stood up, sighed, and wobbled out, the crumpled kimono in her hand. Leon put his shirt on.

Half an hour later they were on their way back side by side through the sodden wood, Isadora humming, splashing along, in the best of humour, Leon in silence. So he'd had her. That was no comfort; she was easy. Wasn't it always easy to get a woman into bed? Leon thought of the brown, sweating bodies of Pfitzner and the young Turk boxing, and compared them with the quivering, soft flesh he had just possessed. A body without any muscles, like a white slug. Isadora was a particularly bad example, but all women were like that really, or not much better anyway, not even Martina. Those limp extremities – nothing by comparison with men's legs and arms. That odourless body – except for the stink between their legs. And most of all the female genitals – hairy, wrinkly, a deep red hole – and the way they felt like boiled noodles afterwards.

Outside his garden fence Isadora put her arms round his neck and clamped her mouth to his. Leon felt slightly dizzy.

'You can come and see me any time you like,' said Isadora, 'and I'll show you shiny salamanders and bright blue frogs.'

That reminded him.

'I've been meaning to ask you all this time . . . when you were sitting in that waterhole outside my window – that creature with you, that skull thing – what was it?'

'There wasn't anything there. No animal, no one else. I was naked, after all.'

She darted away with agility, became a spot of green, brown and blue velvet dissolving into the mist. Leon wondered whether to believe her. It would make things simpler. But he didn't. He knew what he had seen.

Leon climbed over the garden fence and went towards his house. Looking through the living room window, he saw the dog lying on the floor, painted a peculiar shade of purple and covered with bandages, like a comic figure in a cartoon after being caught in a scrap metal press. Only the little starburst round his head was missing. Martina was asleep on the sofa with her head in Kay's lap. Kay was awake, sitting bolt upright and stroking Martina's hair. This was all Leon needed. He felt dampness penetrating the seams of his anorak. Leon stamped his feet loudly on the veranda and went indoors.

'Oh, there you are,' said Kay. 'We were worried.' She was standing up with her hands in her trouser pockets, looking nervous. On the sofa, Martina rubbed her eyes sleepily. She didn't look as if she had been worried at all. Leon wished she'd ask him where he had been, so that he'd have to lie to her. He could live with feeling he'd been unfaithful. That wasn't so bad. It was bad having to feel a failure and a coward. But she didn't ask.

'I went for a bit of a walk,' said Leon. 'I met Isadora.'

Martina went over to Noah and patted the intact parts of his head. Noah went on sleeping.

'You poor brave boy,' said Martina. She didn't even look at Leon.

6

Cloudy, very wet. Winds north-north-west, changeable.
Daytime temperatures up to 18 degrees.

Leon moved his mobile to his left hand and wiped his damp
right palm on his trousers. His face was grey and distorted
with stress. Small drops of sweat had formed on his upper lip.

'I'm afraid I can't do that. I need at least another week.
Five days – at the very least,' he said.

'You send those pages off tomorrow, is that clear?' replied
Pfitzner's voice.

'Yes . . . if . . .' said Leon, but Pfitzner had rung off. Slowly,
Leon put the mobile down on his desk, picked up his brass
paperknife instead, and absently fondled the handle, a lion's
head with its jaws open. He looked out of the window – rain.
The luxuriant, soggy vegetation in his garden was bent over.
Leon, unlike the plants, felt drained and dry. He put the
paperknife down on the desk and went into the living room.
Martina was sitting on the sofa. She wore white trousers and
her outsize FIT FOR LIFE sweatshirt, and was leafing through
a magazine with headlines such as 'Clever Poodles', 'The
Prejudice Against Fighting Dogs' and 'Your Dog's Horo-
scope'. Noah was lying in front of the sofa, noisily chewing
a marrowbone. The bone was so big it might have been a

dinosaur's vertebra. Noah put his head on one side and tried in vain to crack it with his molars. Saliva from his open jaws dribbled on to the rug. He stuffed his tongue into the hollows inside the bone, sucking and slurping. He took no notice at all of Leon. Martina looked up from her dog magazine. At first it seemed that she was going to ignore the sight of Leon entirely – twisted face, bloodshot eyes, drooping shoulders, dragging gait. Then she did say something.

'Listen,' she said, closing the magazine but leaving one finger between the pages, 'listen, this can't go on. We'll manage without that man's money. I'll ask my father. And I'm not suggesting you take anything from me as a present. I'll lend it to you, right? I'll give you credit and you can pay me back some other time.'

'Don't be stupid,' said Leon, trying to look supercilious and thereby distorting his face even more, 'I'd be a fool to borrow a sum of that size. I'll write what he wants and that'll be the end of it. It's his book. What do I care if it turns out to be the worst bullshit of all time?'

'But you're not writing at all. I mean, what have you written these last few days? He keeps on phoning! And why do you look like your own corpse when you talk to him? He's getting you down!'

'Don't worry your little head about it, I'll cope,' said Leon, wrinkling his brow as he turned to the noisily chewing and sucking dog. Martina began to shed tears. Now, of course, she had to cry! Oh how Leon hated that! The emotional blackmail of it all, weeping every time she ran out of arguments. He scrutinised Noah with exaggerated interest, as if the dog might be about to explode any moment.

'It's not just you,' Martina sobbed. 'I'm scared too. I don't want that man coming back here. I don't want to be jumping with fright every time I hear a car drive up, praying it's the shopkeeper and not one of your marvellous friends. Just give him his money back and then he'll leave us in peace.'

'Shut up,' hissed Leon furiously, 'you've got no idea what this is all about. You think I wouldn't have tried doing that long ago? You think I like having that idiot interfering with my manuscript? Pfitzner doesn't want his money back. He insists on my writing the book. And I bloody well will write the fucking book. Exactly the way Pfitzner wants it.'

The veins on his neck stood out. He was breathing heavily.

'But suppose you just don't?' said Martina. 'Have you asked him what would happen if you just didn't do it?'

'No, I have not asked him. Because I don't want to know. Because I fucking do not want to know what happens if I don't write his book, or if he doesn't like it.'

Noah got up and began scraping at the rug with his forepaws, as if digging a hole in the middle of the living room. His claws caught on the looped wool, and red fluff and particles of dust rose into the air.

'Stop that!' roared Leon, taking a step towards him. The dog stood over his bone, one paw placed protectively over it. He growled at Leon.

'That'll do! Give it here! Come on!'

Arm outstretched, Leon tried to snatch the bone, which was dripping with saliva. Noah's jaws snapped.

'Fucking brute!'

Leon jumped back, his bitten hand dangling, and swung a foot in the dog's direction. The bite didn't hurt much, but he had been frightened. Noah shook his head, his remaining ear flying. He put his other forepaw over the bone too, and a growl issued from deep in his throat.

'Don't you touch that dog,' cried Martina, jumping up from the sofa. 'He hasn't done anything to you!'

'The filthy brute bit me!'

'Why don't you leave him alone, then? What's his bone to do with you?'

'I'm getting him out of this house! I don't want to see the filthy creature any more! How come he's still lounging around here? The whole place stinks of wet dog!'

'You're so mean! I'm glad Noah bit you. You're rotten all through. A dog can sense that kind of thing.'

'Oh, really? It can, can it? Well, I'm sure that's good to know!'

Leon turned, strode into the hall, put on his black anorak and over-large gumboots, opened the front door and closed it behind him. Furious, he stalked off into the garden. The unmown wet grass brushed his boots. The rain welcomed him like a familiar friend, clapped him on the shoulders, patted his cheeks. Leon put the anorak hood over his head and went to the toolshed. The wood was swollen, and the blue and white paint was coming away in great leprous flakes. When he opened the door the garden hose fell out and unrolled itself. Leon bent to pick it up and knocked into the bamboo canes in the process. They fell on top of him, clattering, like a huge game of spillikins.

'Shit, shit, shit!' he bellowed, kicking and hitting the bamboos. He grabbed the spade and shovel and a rake. The shed door refused to shut properly, so he kicked it several times until it came off its hinges. He looked around him with murder in his eyes. A horde of yellowish-white slugs, moving in a 'V' shape like a formation of migratory birds, was crawling extremely slowly over a flower bed where everything had been eaten long ago. Leon dropped the shovel, took the spade in both hands and brought it down on the slugs like a man possessed, hacking at them until they lay writhing before him in bits and bloody bubbles. Then he threw the spade aside and jumped into the middle of the slushy mixture of mud, slime and fragments of mollusc, stamped around on it, gasping and uttering inarticulate sounds, and performed a mad tap dance on them until his right gumboot looked like coming off his foot. His efforts to pull the boot up again gradually calmed him down. Leon collected his spade and shovel and jumped into one of the side ditches passing through his garden. In many places, the spoil from the ditch was piled so high that he couldn't see over the top of it. The water in the ditch came up to his ankles and was full of frogs. Countless thin brown frogs, no bigger than Leon's thumbnail, much too small to be any threat to the slugs. Some of them still had the stumps of their tadpole tails. They were tirelessly attempting to climb up the side of the ditch, struggling through the mud, diving head first into the murky brew to save themselves from the blows of Leon's spade. They circled around him with tiny swimming strokes, staring up at him with goggle eyes scarcely the size of a pinhead. Leon cut earth away from the sides of the ditch, scooped it up from the water with the shovel and flung it out. Once again he felt the muscles in his arms, felt himself getting fit. He'd dig for another hour. Then he'd be able to go back to his desk and revise Chapter Four. After that he'd put it straight into an envelope addressed to Pfitzner without reading it through again. He drove the spade into the moist red earth, drove it in again, slashed through worms, dug out stones, scooped, shovelled out soil, water, sand, mud, frogs, stones; drove the spade in again while the rain came steadily down on him. At some point he heard feet splashing through puddles. Kay was standing on the edge of the ditch, looking down at him the way you look at a coffin which has been lowered into the grave. She was wearing a green waxed jacket and a black baseball cap. She mopped the rain off her nose.

'Hi, Leon! I'll come and help you dig your swimming pool in a minute if you like. Just looking in on Martina first.'

'You do that,' said Leon, without interrupting his work, and shovelled some mud in her direction, so that she had to jump back. 'Go and amuse yourself with Martina. Have a few dainty cakes, tell each other about the latest crochet patterns while I'm drowning out here.'

Kay disappeared. Half an hour later she came back and stationed herself on the edge of the ditch, arms akimbo.

'You're in dead trouble.'

Leon did not reply, but went on shovelling harder than ever. Kay jumped down to join him, took the spade and cut away more soil, while Leon picked it up with his shovel and flung it out. They went on working together in silence. Not a word, just the crunch of metal in the earth, the patter of the rain, and the thin, chirping croaks of the miniature frogs. Mud sprayed all over Kay and Leon's boots, trousers and jackets. The rain made channels through it. After over an hour of silent digging, shovelling and loud sniffing, Kay said suddenly, 'Pfitzner's one up on you for the simple reason that he's not afraid of the consequences of what he does. It's no good putting your faith in the criminal code if you're planning to tackle Pfitzner.'

'What ought I to do, then?' said Leon, propping himself on his shovel like a monument to the working classes. 'You think I ought to shoot him?'

'Well, it might not be a bad idea to get yourself a pistol or something like that.'

'Are you out of your mind?' said Leon. 'Why would I shoot Pfitzner? I mean, he's not done me any harm. And what's more, then I'd have his whole gang coming down on me. I'll write him his book and that'll be the end of it.'

'Who said anything about shooting him? But it's not your job to let the man dictate books to you either.'

'Oh yes it is. I'm writing the book the way Pfitzner wants, and then I'll collect my money and I'll be perfectly happy.'

'I don't believe you. I'm sure you're feeling lousy, and I think it would be a good idea to get yourself a pistol.'

'You must be crazy! Mind your own business!' said Leon, digging his spade into the side of the ditch. He hit a stone. Leon dug the spade in a couple more times to find out how large the stone was, then levered it out and slung the stone and some mud out of the ditch in a high arc. When he bent down again the agony hit him like an electric shock. A hot, overwhelming pain ran up and down his backbone, a red-hot wire bored through his marrow and his nervous system, reached his brain, ravaged his lumbar vertebrae, and twitched in his left leg at the same time. Leon did the obvious thing: he let out such a shrill scream that Kay dropped the spade in alarm. Then he doubled up and rolled over on his side, and lay in the water groaning. Kay bent over him.

'Don't touch me,' whispered Leon, 'don't touch me.'

Kay put a hand on Leon's shoulder.

'Don't touch me!' screamed Leon, and Kay stepped back, crossing her arms. Leon rolled about in the water, eyes narrowed, lips twisted. He was breathing heavily. Then his breath gradually calmed down and came more slowly.

'It'll be gone in a minute. Just don't touch me,' he whispered, lowering his head until the whole of the right half of his face was beneath the surface of the water. He stared straight ahead blindly, observed what was going on inside him, and tried, in slow motion, to find a physical position in which the pain would be bearable. One of the little frogs came paddling up, perched on Leon's glasses to take a short rest, and swam on. Leon rolled over on his stomach and began straightening up. He got as far as propping himself on his elbows, then screamed again and let himself drop back.

'You'll have to help me,' he told Kay, 'it's the only way I can get up. I'll have to pull myself up holding on to you, but I must do it by myself. You mustn't move.'

Kay crouched down beside him and cautiously placed an arm round his back. Leon put his own arm round her shoulders and Kay slowly straightened herself, bringing him with her. 'No,' cried Leon, 'no, no, stop, I can't!'

But Kay continued pulling him upright, while Leon screamed and clung to her.

'Lumbago,' said Kay, 'it'll be lumbago. I'm just wondering how we're going to get you out of the ditch.'

She positioned him with his face to the side of the ditch so that he could rest his hands on it, and left him there. Leon waited, staring through glasses with brown streaks running down them at the muddy red earth which kept oozing more water. Water, water, water! And the rain still coming down. Very likely the frogs pissed in the ditch too. What did he think he'd been trying to do? It was pointless. Draining this land was totally impossible. He might just as well try baling out Lake Constance with a nylon stocking. He ought to have left long ago. For somewhere where there wasn't much rain. Spain, or Eritrea.

'Leon, what's the matter? Is it bad?'

Martina's voice. She sounded concerned, but at the same time somehow as if she wasn't concentrating on his plight. Slowly and cautiously, he raised his head.

'Could be lumbago.'

'Oh you poor thing! Wait a moment.'

She came back with a piece of cardboard which she placed on the muddy spoil from the ditch before kneeling on it in her pale trousers. She reached her arm down and brushed Leon's cheek with the back of her hand.

'Don't touch me! I'm in terrible pain.'

Martina removed her hand and looked at him helplessly.

'Where's Kay?' asked Leon.

'She's phoning Kerbel, so we can get you to a doctor.'

'Kerbel's about the last person I want to see right now.'

'Wait a moment,' added Martina, 'I'll be right back. I've got to take a look at Noah. He was retching in such a funny way.'

Leon stared at the side of the ditch again. Martina was gone rather a long time. He considered that she had her priorities wrong. When she came back she was wearing her yellow rainproof jacket, and had a handkerchief to clean his glasses. Kay hauled up the stout plank which had been acting as a path over the swampy lawn. She lowered it lengthways into the ditch and jumped down to Leon, placed herself behind him, took him round the waist, and thus heaved him on to the plank and out of the ditch. A step . . . and another step – a scream . . . and another scream.

Kerbel's van drove along the path and stopped outside the garden gate. The shopkeeper leaned out of the wound-down side window, and bared his gums. A violet blouson with diagonal white stripes adorned his torso.

'What a terrible thing!' he cried. 'I told my wife she had to mind the shop by herself. Being a good neighbour comes first. I was really supposed to be getting kohlrabi and cherries in stock today, but of course this is an emergency.'

'Thanks,' grunted Leon, limping to the van with Kay's help and tipping himself sideways on to the back seat. He tried to work himself into a comfortable position, but the friction of his wet clothes on the upholstery slowed him down. Leon kicked out, and had to sit halfway up and work his way forward with his hands, screaming twice, before he was lying in a position he could bear.

'Would you mind going with him?' Martina asked Kay. 'I can't leave the dog alone. He's just been sick and he's still retching. A bit of the bone could have stuck in his throat.'

'Of course,' said Kay. 'We can manage on our own, can't we, Leon?'

He didn't reply, but lay motionless on the back seat, breathing hard in his pain. Kay got into the front passenger seat, and Kerbel turned the key in the ignition.

'I don't want money,' he told Martina. 'After all, this is an emergency.'

She stared blankly at him for a moment as the rain pattered down on her stiff yellow rainhood. Then she understood.

'But of course, we must pay you!'

Martina ran back to the house through a series of puddles. 'Wait a moment,' she called from the veranda.

'No, no! I really don't want money.'

'Wait,' cried Martina, disappearing into the house. She came back to the car with her purse in her hand.

'No, honestly,' said Kerbel, 'I don't mind you paying me for the dog, taking him to the vet, I mean, but your husband – well, your husband is my neighbour. I can't take anything for that.'

Martina thrust a fifty-mark note through the window and placed it on the dashboard.

'For the petrol.'

'Oh, well . . .' said Kerbel, and put the van into gear. The Transit turned and made its way down the path again. Martina heard Leon screaming. His screams were distant and muted, but they rose above the sound of the engine. Slowly she turned, walked a few steps over the soggy ground, suddenly quickened her pace, and by the time she reached the veranda she was almost running. At last! At last she was alone again and could finish what Kay's arrival and then Leon's lumbago had interrupted. She took off her gumboots, the yellow rainproof jacket, and her sweatshirt. Noah came out of the living room with the bone in his mouth, happily wagging his tail. Martina took a towelling hair scrunch out of her trouser pocket and tied her hair back with it. She went into the bathroom, put up the lavatory lid and seat, washed her hands, sighed and knelt down. Noah dropped his bone and pushed the bathroom door open with his nose. There she was, crouching on the floor. Off she went again! He gave Martina a comforting lick on her back, licking the bare skin below her bra. She pushed him away.

'Get out! Go away!'

She rose, dragged him out by the skin at the nape of his neck, and slammed the door in his face. Noah picked up his bone, wandered into the living room, and began to gnaw it listlessly.

Martina washed her hands once again, looked at her face in the mirror, squeezed an imaginary pimple, washed her hands for the third time and knelt down again. She bent her head over the lavatory bowl. *Father, I have sinned.*

Kerbel was leaning forward with his face close to the windscreen, but none the less he thumped into every pothole. Leon groaned.

'Further left,' said Kay, pointing to where the track was more even.

'Shame you don't have your car any more,' said Kerbel. 'I

know about these leasing arrangements. First you think: hey, that's cheap, and you get this great limousine outside your door, just for a few thousand marks. Then a year later they suddenly want all the money at once or they take it away again. The car's gone, your money's gone, and you think it wasn't really so cheap after all, because now you've got nothing left.'

Leon groaned again. He was seeing the world at an upward slanting angle: the flattened blond curls on the back of Kerbel's head, the shaved nape of Kay's neck, the manor house with the satellite dishes, the roofs of the cottages along the road. It all looked strange. Leon felt alone in the world: gravely ill and entirely alone.

Kerbel stopped outside his shop and hooted. Someone came out. Small footsteps, clattering heels. Kerbel wound the window down and said, 'Back in a couple of hours.'

A face like a full moon appeared in the window above Leon's head and stared silently down at him. So that was what Kerbel's wife looked like. She had a broad nose and a big mouth, and she looked dim-witted, stupid, slow. Her hair was bleached blonde, felted together like candyfloss. Two other similar female faces in their mid-fifties pressed close to the window. Kerbel's wife whispered something to them.

'This is Herr Ulbricht,' said Kerbel. 'Not *the* Ulbricht, of course, ha ha!'

The women looked down at Leon. The one wearing dark glasses did at least give him a nod. Leon nodded back. Well, if they'd quite finished staring at him, the van could drive on. Why didn't the silly cows move off? What was there to gawp at? Another hot pain shot down his back, and he twisted his face like a baby about to start howling.

'I hope it's not too serious,' said one of the women. 'Well, get better soon!'

At last Kerbel drove off. The faces retreated. Leon saw treetops and grey sky with black clouds in front of it. He was floating on a carpet of dull pain, listening to the sound of the tyres on the wet road, the patter of rain on the roof of the van, and staring at the scratched artificial leather of the back seat, adorned with a sticker from a Duplo collectable series, showing Asterix with his biceps swelling just after he's drunk the magic potion, and another from a wrestling series called 'The Undertaker'. The Undertaker was holding a small urn aloft.

In Freyenow, Kerbel took a map out of the glove compartment and drew in at a bus stop to consult it. The windscreen wipers swished regularly. The van started off again. When they stopped next time they were in a street of private houses. Kay helped Leon to his feet. Fine needles shot through his skull. Intending to be helpful too, Kerbel took his other arm, whereupon Leon screamed so loud that a man in pyjama trousers and a vest came out of his house on the opposite side of the street.

'Don't touch me,' whispered Leon, 'you meant well, but please don't touch me.'

Kerbel looked annoyed and got back into the Transit. Leaning on Kay, Leon limped through a garden gate under the suspicious gaze of the man in pyjama trousers. Kay rang the bell at a door with a decorative black grille and yellow glazing. There was a purring sound, and they pushed the door open. Kay led Leon to a semicircular white counter behind which two nurse receptionists were busy with a card index. One of them looked up. She was pretty. Dark hair pinned up on her head, with a couple of strands left loose to fall over her face, a classical nose. She was young. Robust and big-bosomed. The white coat suited her. Eyebrows raised, she inspected the two mud-encrusted figures before her.

'It's an emergency,' Leon got out. 'I'm in terrible pain.'

'Have you been to us before?' she inquired. The other girl was entering something on the computer. She too was dark-haired and strikingly pretty – as if the doctor recruited his receptionists at modelling competitions.

'No,' said Leon, 'this is the first time.'

'Can I have your health insurance certificate, please?'

'I forgot it. I'll bring it in later.'

She began asking his details and typing them in. When he mentioned his surname, she stopped in surprise, as he expected.

'Ulbricht? Really?'

Leon pulled himself together and patiently answered all her questions, trying to distract himself from the pain by observing his surroundings: the walls, which were painted yellow, the calendar of Tuscan scenes, the poster of cats, the life-size poster of a flayed man consisting mainly of nerves and sinews, a glass-fronted cupboard full of medicines, a pair of blue crutches in a corner, and a plastic notice for the doctor's absence: 'On holiday from . . . to . . .'. Beside this wording was a caricature of a doctor playing tennis with a stethoscope round his neck. Leon clung to the counter and tried to steady himself. Kay yawned beside him.

'Please take a seat in the waiting room,' said the pretty receptionist at last.

'I can't. I'm in pain. Terrible pain. I must see the doctor at once.'

She smiled gently and put one of the intentionally untidy strands of hair back behind her ear.

'I'm sorry, but almost all our patients are in terrible pain today. One of them has been in terrible pain for four years. If you can stand and walk, I'm afraid I must ask you to take a seat in the waiting room.'

She was patronising him, the cow! Young, healthy little bitch! He normally threw women like her off balance with a single well-judged improper remark. A small and charming liberty – half compliment, half coarse but amusing insult – and they began stammering and stumbling and fell straight into his bed. But he didn't feel up to it just now. He felt more like bursting into tears. Without resisting, he let Kay lead him to the waiting room. He was relieved to see most of the chairs there empty. There were only four patients before him, sitting as far away from each other as possible. At one end of the room, by the window, sprawled a young man with an amputated leg and crutches painted in a black and yellow jungle animal pattern. The trouser leg of his jeans had been cut off and turned up, and was held together with a clothes peg. A bent old lady whose chin seemed to have grown into her breastbone had just managed to get to the first chair by the door. On the other two sides of the room two middle-aged women sat halfway between the amputee and the old lady; at first glance it was difficult to guess what was wrong with them. They were leafing through *Ambiente* and *Madame* magazines. The young man was reading the sports pages of a newspaper. The doddery old lady was entertaining herself by opening and closing her lips. None of them appeared to be in pain.

'Good afternoon,' said Kay. Leon was too furious to wish anyone a good anything.

'Afternoon,' said two voices from behind *Ambiente* and *Madame*.

Kay had to help Leon out of his anorak and gumboots like

a toddler while he clutched the wall, in the process almost tearing down a framed photograph of an Indian tomb. There were mediocre photographs of Indian scenes hanging on all the walls: large high-gloss prints of dancers with nose chains and men in baggy trousers wearing make-up, mutilated beggars, begging monkeys, ostentatious elephant processions, phallic jungle plants, children bathing, and a stocky man with abnormally long arms posing in a white linen suit in front of a ruined temple – all very colourful and mounted in metal frames. Kay kept her jacket and boots on and sat down beside the old lady, muddy as she was. Leon stood there in his socks, watching the reception area. As soon as the doctor appeared he would accost him. A doctor would immediately see how serious his condition was. Kay picked up an issue of *Peter Moosleiter's Interesting Magazine* and immersed herself in a story about UFO landings. The doctor did not appear. Instead, the old lady's name was called, she tottered out, and a little under ten minutes later reappeared at the counter, where the receptionists shovelled medicines into a plastic bag for her, helped her into her coat and escorted her to the door. Next the one-legged man swung himself out on his patterned crutches, and duly reappeared at the counter a prompt ten minutes later. Ten minutes! No one could expect Leon to believe that this youth or the cemetery-fodder who preceded him had been in as much pain as he was.

'I'm just going out for a minute,' said Kay, and she rose and disappeared. Everyone was letting him down. The dog mattered more to Martina, and now Kay had to go out for a cigarette, even though he was in such a bad way. The big-breasted receptionist put her head into the waiting room.

'Herr Ulbricht, please.'

The women leafing through their magazines looked crossly

at him. Leon stared triumphantly back and dragged himself out.

Dr Pollack was dressed in white and completely bald. He had short legs and arms as long as a monkey's, and seemed to be made entirely of muscle. He spoke rapidly, in a kind of telegraphese. Leon registered, with hostility, that Pollack wanted to be finished with him quickly so as to go on to the next patient, and then the next, and then the next . . . Of course a man like that needed money. Lots of money for tennis lessons, trips to take photographs in exotic foreign lands, and ridiculous white linen summer suits.

'Hurts in the small of your back, right? Nature of pain? Stabbing? Tearing? Bend to your left! Can't? Forward! To your right! That OK? Ah, I see. Could be one of your legs is shorter than the other. Looks a bit like it. Try standing up perfectly straight!'

Dr Pollack perched on the edge of the examination couch and told Leon to place himself in front of him.

'Stand here, back towards me.'

He drew him even closer with his powerful arms, so close that Leon could feel the doctor's ribcage touching his back, and something soft, presumably the doctor's genitals, brushing his behind. What was the idea? Uncomfortably, Leon tried to take a step forward, but Dr Pollack had already wrapped his short legs around Leon's hips and locked his perforated healthy-living shoes in front of Leon's stomach. He was clinging to him like a hobgoblin who would never let him go. A gay hobgoblin who intended to penetrate him. Leon gasped for air. Dr Pollack took hold of Leon's shoulders. With an unexpected movement he pulled the right shoulder back, at the same time pushing the left shoulder

145

forward. Leon thought appalling agony would tear through his backbone, and opened his mouth to scream. Ever since the pain first hit him in the ditch he had been moving in slow motion. But the pain did not materialise. He felt rather than heard a slight click somewhere near his coccyx, as if a wooden door had gently closed. Dr Pollack's hands grasped his shoulders again. Leon went rigid, expecting the next movement in the opposite direction. Dr Pollack waited. Leon turned his head to look at him, smiled, and at that moment the doctor wrenched Leon's torso round to the other side. He unwrapped his legs, and Leon staggered a step forward.

'Now bend forward again. Right. And again. And left. Right. OK? Does it still hurt?'

It did not. Or at least, hardly at all. Leon could scarcely believe it. With his thumbnail, Pollack scraped at the particles of mud transferred from Leon's dirty jeans to his own white cotton trousers, and told Leon to lie down on his front on the couch. He managed that almost painlessly as well. Pollack gave him two injections in his buttocks and advised: 'Exercises! And touch your toes under the shower! Like this.' He touched the floor with his fingertips, not difficult for a man of his proportions with short legs and orang-utan arms. 'And plenty of good hot water on your back while you're doing it.'

Leon thought of the boggy brown water which trickled from his pipes. Never mind. He was better again already. He was the happiest man in the world.

When Kay took her cigarettes out of her jacket pocket under the porch of the doctor's surgery they were wet through, a sodden packet oozing yellow liquid. It must have happened when she was kneeling in the water in the ditch to help Leon out. Bloody ditch! Bloody rain! There was no rubbish bin.

She had to wring the water out of the packet of cigarettes and put it back in her pocket. Kay went over to the Transit van to cadge a cigarette from Kerbel. Kerbel wound his window down a little way and held a gold cigarette packet out to her. Benson and Hedges was a strange brand for a village shop-keeper to smoke, thought Kay, but there had always been something strange about Kerbel. She took a cigarette, let him give her a light, and walked a little way along the pavement to avoid having to discuss Kerbel's purchases and projects with him. His latest half-baked idea was to open a coffee bar in his shop. It was still drizzling. Three girls came down the street. They were about fifteen, wore no jackets, had trainers with ludicrously thick soles, and were huddling together under a blue umbrella bearing the legend FUCKING AWFUL WEATHER. When they saw Kay in the distance they suddenly adopted a dainty tripping gait, whispering and giggling to each other in embarrassment. Then, when they were close enough to see their mistake, they burst into raucous laughter, laughed so hard that they had to lean against each other, merging into spluttering Siamese triplets beneath the umbrella. As they passed Kay they stared at her face and were overcome by yet another fit of mirth. Kay inhaled cigarette smoke and blew it out through her nostrils. The door of the surgery opened. Leon came out. Hardly quarter of an hour had passed since she had left him in the waiting room. Kay went towards him, but Leon was standing perfectly upright, and obviously needed no help.

'What happened?' asked Kay. 'A miracle cure?'

'It was just a displaced vertebra. It's back where it belongs now, that's all.'

He got into the passenger seat beside Kerbel. Kay sat on the back seat and threw her cigarette end out of the window.

'Am I ever glad for you!' said Kerbel, starting the Transit and turning on the radio: he got a report on unemployment in eastern Germany. He pushed the next knob and tuned into a classical music station. Mozart's *Requiem.* He pushed another knob, and there was a frightful hissing and crackling. Kerbel turned the radio off again. Leon leaned back, feeling the vibration of the van in his backbone. But it was nothing by comparison with what he had had to endure earlier. Once again the trees, houses, sky and clouds passed him – but now he could look at them all from an upright position. He felt fine. He'd just have to take care of himself a bit.

'The drainage system will have to wait for now,' he told Kay. 'I don't think I ought to touch a shovel again this week.'

Kerbel seemed to have been waiting for this cue.

'You need a burner to dry the site off,' he said. 'It's the only thing that'll work, believe you me! No offence to Frau Schlei here, but you won't really get anywhere by digging drainage ditches. I'll get hold of a burner for you if you like. My brother runs a drainage firm. He doesn't really hire out burners, but I'm sure I could fix it for him to make an exception for you.'

'I don't even want to think about that fucking muddy garden before the end of the week,' said Leon.

Kay tapped him on the shoulder, and when he turned round she rolled her eyes to indicate what she thought of Kerbel's proposition.

This time they drove right through Priesnitz without stopping. Leon saw the woman who had hoped he would get better soon standing in her garden picking up green cherries. The cherries were not ripening this year; they began to rot before they could turn red and then fell from the tree.

Leon waved to the woman, but she was deep in her own thoughts and did not wave back. He told himself he ought really to go to Priesnitz more often. Take an interest in the lives of the people who lived there. After all, this was his home now.

The Transit rattled up the path to Leon's house, with Kerbel scrupulously driving into all the potholes he had hit on the way out. Leon felt the jolts in his back. When he saw Martina standing on the veranda with Noah it struck him yet again that his wife had stayed with the dog rather than go with him. Not that it mattered. After all, it hadn't been anything serious. Kerbel stopped, and Leon immediately opened the door and leaped lightly out. There it was again, that thin, hot wire. Not so strong a pain this time, and thinner, but it was there, boring through the marrow of his spine and up to his brain. Leon grimaced, and clung to the bonnet of the van. Well, he'd better not go jumping about for a while, then.

'Are you feeling better?' Martina, standing in front of him, was about to embrace him, but hesitated at the last moment. 'Can we touch you again?'

Leon put an arm around her shoulders. Martina had changed her clothes, and was now wearing a short skirt and close-fitting white blouse which was turning translucent where the rain hit it. She looked sexy.

'Yes, of course,' he said. 'But you'll have to nurse me now. I suppose I might as well go and lie down beside Noah. Then you'll have only one trip to make.'

Kerbel turned the van. Leon went over to him, opened the driver's door and shook hands. The raindrops falling into the car left little black marks on the dusty dashboard.

'Thanks. I don't know what I'd have done without you. My regards to your wife.'

'You're welcome. Of course. Any time,' said Kerbel, effusively.

Kay had climbed out of the back and got into the passenger seat.

'Aren't you getting out here?' asked Leon.

'No, I'm going on to the supermarket. The parking stand on my bike needs welding.'

They rattled away. Leon went into the house with Martina. While he showered with that day's pale brown water she brought: warmed towels and his jogging suit to the bathroom. Then she made him up a bed on the couch, put a sofa cushion under his back and fetched his pillow from the bedroom, to prop him up higher so that he could see the TV better. Leon zapped through the channels. Now and then he asked for a beer or a sandwich. The dog was out, presumably off for a walk somewhere in the marshes. Leon stayed on the sofa until it began to get dark, leafing through an old sports magazine and an even older copy of *Stern*. Then he rose and went into his study, and once again tackled the chapter in which the seventeen-year-old Pfitzner made his girlfriend go on the game. Leon slowly read the first sentences out loud to himself:

It troubled him to see her stumbling down the road, turning to look back at him again and again, as if she were hoping he might yet change his mind, hoping he would say: Come back, it was only a joke, I wanted to find out how much you love me. But Benno said nothing, even though he felt icy cold with grief. He knew this was his only chance of getting rich, he knew he had no chance of ever making real money by working. Not with his education. Not in this area. Not with those parents. If he had weakened now, then they would have married, had children, he'd have ended up working in a factory and so would she. They'd have lived in a two-room flat, shouting at each other, and they would have hated one another. Benno decided that if he was going to be unhappy anyway then at least he wanted to be unhappy and rich.

What garbage! No wonder Pfitzner had crossed out the whole page. Sentimental crap, all of it. Leon cut the bit about *grief*, and changed the last sentence:

Benno decided that it was enough for one of them to be unhappy, and that one wasn't going to be him.

Leon grinned. If he remembered correctly, this was one of the passages which had annoyed Pfitzner most. And Pfitzner was right, really. Perhaps he was a pretty good editor in his own way. Leon went on to the next pages. It was simple enough. Cut, change, cut. He shifted in his chair to avoid a faint, nagging pain in his back. There, he'd take it straight to the post tomorrow. He rose and stretched, enjoying every movement he was able to make, feeling well. Liberated. Pfitzner couldn't complain, Pfitzner had no reason to turn up here again. His unwelcome visit two weeks ago suddenly seemed to have as little to do with Leon as if he had merely heard about it from someone – and after all, nothing much had really happened. OK, so Leon already knew the way Pfitzner spoke to women. And Harry wasn't exactly squeamish. But if Martina hadn't interfered nothing else would have happened. And then there wouldn't be this stupid tension between him and Harry now. Always the same. If you didn't take bloody good care women could wreck any male friendship. He didn't understand now how he could have been so scared. Had he really been scared at all?

Leon went into the living room, where the heat from the fireplace met him. The fire was humming, hissing, smoking, casting flickering light on the sleeping dog. In his dreams, Noah was hunting something large. He snorted gently and twitched his paws. Martina reached out an arm to Leon from the sofa, and he took it and laid his face on the palm of her hand.

'That wood you're burning is too wet,' he said, looking up again. 'It's smoking too much.' Leon stood in front of the fireplace, enjoying the dry, burning heat of the fire through his jogging trousers. Hot and dry. The only way to fight back against the rain. With a sudden decisive movement, he went to the coffee table, picked up the mobile and tapped a number in.

'Sorry to disturb you so late,' said Leon. 'It's about the burner. I've been thinking . . .'

'You're not disturbing me at all,' shouted Kerbel down the phone, and Leon pictured his bared gums. 'I'm going to see my brother this evening. You can get going with the drainage next week.'

'No, wait a moment,' said Leon, 'there's no great hurry. I have to get the foundation walls exposed first. That is . . . I was going to ask if you knew anyone who could do the job for me at a reasonable price, seeing I'm out of action for the moment?'

'I can do it myself. I'll be with you tomorrow and we'll fix a price then.'

'No,' said Leon, suddenly irritated, 'I have to know now how much it will cost.'

'Let's say 300, and I'll start tomorrow.'

When Leon had put the mobile down, Martina asked, 'Do you think getting that old gossip to come up here is a good idea?'

'Why not?' said Leon. 'What is there here for him to gossip

about? Anyway, he'll be working outside. You don't have to say a word to him all the time he's here if you don't want to.'

'And supposing Pfitzner and Harry come back?'

'What do you mean? They won't. Even if they do, I don't think I need feel ashamed of myself because of Harry.'

'Oh, let's go to bed,' said Martina, resigned.

At the same time Harry was standing on the shore of the Elbe outside Hamburg, waiting for the last people still walking about to go home. It was not raining, but it was too wet for him to sit on a bench. He lit another cigarette. Now and then a ship passed, a stout tug or a launch, a cutter with long lines, or a huge freighter with greenish lights and an exotic name, its engine thudding dully, its bow waves slapping on the dirty sand. Not far away a beach party was in progress. Thin girls in short dresses. Boys in drooping baggy trousers much too large for them. The music floated over to him. Of course the police had put in an appearance – and gone away again – and the droning basses had been turned down for twenty minutes but were now thumping away at their previous volume. Harry went over to his Camaro, which he had parked close to the beach. He opened the boot to see if Rocky had come round. But the bull terrier was still lying on the floor of the boot, limp as a hot-water bottle cover. Harry had hit him hard. Even unconscious, Rocky seemed to be smiling. Smiling as only a bull terrier can smile. Beside him lay a roll of florist's wire and a decorative stone which Harry had bought at a garden centre, a miniature version of a millstone. It was so heavy that Harry could hardly get it into the car. He glanced at the partying ravers. The boys and girls were probably too busy with their twitching limbs and modern drugs to notice him at all, but an elderly couple in blue waxed jackets was coming straight towards him. Harry quickly closed the boot and sat in his car. He sat there for some time, smoking and listening in case Rocky began to whine, and once Melanie called him. She wanted a day off next week to go and see her sister.

'You just make sure the dough's right,' said Harry. 'If the dough's right, that's OK by me. And if it's OK by me, I'll take you to Mauritius again.'

'Does that mean no? Look, I only want a day off to go and see my sister. Just one day. I'll work longer hours on the other days to make up for it.'

'Oh, forget your sister! Now, hang up and get your fat arse out on the street.'

Finally darkness fell and the beach emptied. Harry opened the boot, put the wire in his pocket and took Rocky out. He had come round now, leaving a dark patch of urine beneath him.

'Filthy brute,' said Harry.

Rocky was so weak that he could hardly stand. Harry carried him round the car and put him on the bonnet. Taking the wire out of his jacket pocket, he wound it round Rocky's forepaws with rapid circular movements, passed it on to the back paws, bound them together in the same way and then fastened the two sets of paws together, passed the wire from the paws on to Rocky's head and wound it round his muzzle. He let the dog's collar out two holes and pushed a couple of flat stones which he had found near the car between the collar and Rocky's neck. He didn't need the millstone now. He would give it to Leon next time he visited him – for the garden.

'You stupid old bastard,' said Harry, patting the top of Rocky's head. He had taken his eyes off the dog for just two minutes that morning. They'd been in the park, and Harry had gone to buy ice cream. Strawberry and vanilla for himself, chocolate for Rocky. The bull terrier loved chocolate ice cream. When Harry turned round, Rocky was chasing a cocker spaniel. He didn't find him again for half an hour, and by then it had happened. There was a pram tipped over, a screaming woman bending over a bloodstained bundle on the footpath, and beside them Rocky with his teeth sunk into a briefcase which a man had swung at him trying to drive him off.

Harry could do without any trouble. He had been involved in two court cases. There were state prosecutors just waiting to throw the book at him for some stupid little thing, simply because they couldn't get him for what really mattered. But first they'd have to prove it had been his dog. Luckily he hadn't bought a dog licence. He didn't have a dog at all. He'd never had a dog. Rocky's food and water bowls, throttle collar, spare leash and eleven cans of dog food were lying in someone else's dustbin in a distant part of town.

Harry made sure no one was watching him, and carried Rocky down to the Elbe. A large, sparsely lit container vessel was making its slow way upstream. The engine throbbed with a hollow sound, like a gigantic heartbeat. There was no one on deck. Harry put his bull terrier down in the sand and undressed except for his underpants. Then he picked Rocky up again like a baby and waded into the Elbe. It was very cold. When the water was up to his navel he let Rocky go. The bundle of dog sank at once and was carried away by the current. The bow waves of the container ship reached Harry and sent the cold, stinking waters of the Elbe slapping against his chest. He waded back. From the bank, he watched the navigation lights of the freighter. A ship at night was the finest sight in the world. Harry walked a little way along the beach, making sure Rocky had not been washed straight back on shore. Then he put his clothes on, got into the car, turned and drove back to Hamburg. The avenue beside the Elbe was empty. He could step on the gas. He had not been indifferent to the dog. Rocky had meant more to him than most human beings. More than his father, more than his mother (of course), more than his stepbrothers, more than his girlfriends (of course). But Harry would never let weakness allow him to make a mistake. He could give up anything, any time, if he had to. Now he was going to buy a new bull terrier. One with a monocle this time, that funny dark patch over the eye. He would train the dog himself from a puppy, and then there'd be no unpleasant surprises later. He and his new bull terrier would have fun together. Endless fun.

Leon stared at the ceiling of the room. This had happened to him only twice before in his life. The first time he was still very young, not yet eighteen, and it was obviously the woman's fault. A silly girl, she kept talking to him about her five previous lovers. On the second occasion he'd been so drunk he couldn't even get his head up, let alone anything else. And now it had just happened for the third time. Well, no reason to stare at the ceiling. He'd had a hard day, that was all. In fact it had been a stupid idea even to try, with his bad back. But he'd really fancied Martina. Odd. But not a tragedy. He and Martina had been able to laugh together about it. Now she was asleep, her narrow shoulders rising and falling. Had she sighed? Was she still awake after all? No, she was asleep. And if it didn't bother her then why should it bother him? Leon got out of bed, went to the kitchen, took the milk out of the fridge, and drank greedily straight from the flabby cardboard carton. The milk ran down over his chin. He wiped it away with the back of his hand, threw the empty carton into the sink, and went to his study. He sat down at the desk and set to work on the next chapter. Enveloped by the soft rhythm of the rain, he began reading Pfitzner's 'corrections'. Not everything written in ballpoint pen above and between the lines was useless. However, Pfitzner had also cut some of Leon's best sentences right out. Well, so what? Leon would be able to write a hundred more books of his own, just the way he wanted. He stretched, fidgeted in his chair . . . The pain was even worse than it had been when it first felled him in the ditch. Not a wire boring into him this time, more like a screwdriver stuck between his vertebrae. Red flashes of light danced in front of his eyes. He couldn't even scream, just whimper hoarsely. When would it stop? He had to get out of this chair. At once. He had to lie down. But the moment he moved everything became even worse. A violent shivering fit shook his body. How much could a man endure before he finally fainted? Leon had no choice. If he was going to lie down he had to throw himself through the pain as you might throw yourself through a burning wall. He let himself fall from the chair.

Martina found him the next morning. When she opened the door of the study, Leon was lying on his stomach in front of the desk, his hands clutching the rug. His face was tear-stained and swollen. His lips were twitching. He had shouted half the night without managing to wake Martina up.

'Please,' whimpered Leon, 'don't touch me. Just please don't touch me.'

7

Mainly cloudy but dry. Occasional bright periods. Temperatures rising to 26 to 29 degrees. Very humid.

Leon lay strapped to a stretcher which was not much more than a padded plank covered with black plastic. The plank was propped at an angle of about forty-five degrees to the linoleum floor, and Leon was hanging head down on it. The strap prevented him from sliding off, for not only was he hanging at quite a steep angle, he was also being shaken as if he were racing over cobblestones in a badly sprung car. He coughed. The strange device shook mucus out of his lungs, and when he let his chin drop his teeth chattered as if he were shivering. In addition, the peristaltic movement of his gut was greatly stimulated. And as Leon coughed and suppressed farts, he turned his head aside and read, for the twelfth time and with increasing bitterness, the newspaper cutting fixed to the wall: *Help At Last! No More Pain!* – and similar encomiums which seemed as antiquated as the machine itself.

After being shaken about on the vibrating device he went to the sun-lamp room. By now Leon knew the way in his sleep. When he passed the open door of the waiting room he saw the bent old lady. She watched Leon putting one foot in front of the other with sympathetic interest.

'Well, Frau Hillmer,' shouted the receptionist with ghastly cheerfulness, 'do you remember what it was like when you could only walk that way yourself?'

'Oh yes, oh yes,' croaked the old granny, turning to watch Leon go, as far as her worn cartilage would allow.

The sun-lamp room was tiny. It must originally have been a store room, and its equipment consisted of a horribly hot infra-red lamp on an occasional table and a horribly uncomfortable kitchen chair in front of it, which made Leon's back feel worse to at least the same extent as the infra-red radiation might make it feel better. The receptionist shoved the chair behind his knees, adjusted the timer of the lamp, and left Leon to himself and his thoughts.

This had been going on for four weeks. Four weeks – twenty-eight endless days of pain – 672 hours of purgatory – 40,320 bloody awful minutes of his life. He could have dispensed with them without the faintest regret. Howling and roaring, he had been delivered back to Dr Pollack's surgery by Martina and Kerbel. This time he did not have to wait. He was permitted to drag himself into the consulting room at once, and was put on a stretcher with a foam cube under his knees. There had been no question on this occasion of wrenching his back into place again. Pollack had X-rayed him and then held the pictures up to the light, baffled.

'Can't see a thing,' he had said almost reproachfully. 'All the symptoms suggest a slipped disc, but nothing shows on the X-ray.'

He had hung the photograph of Leon's lumbar vertebrae up on a lighted screen, and tapped a spot on it with his forefinger.

'But here – see that, there?'

Instead of answering, Leon had groaned. He was supposed to be looking at a disc worn down on one side.

'That's because your legs aren't the same length. It's worn much too much for a man of your age.'

Since then Leon had had injections twice a week, along with the infra-red and vibration treatments. Over the first few days his condition had indeed improved. He could soon make his way from the sofa to the lavatory without help again, he could dress himself (except for his socks), even though his underpants alone took five minutes, and if they escaped him and dropped to the floor he could haul them up again with a pair of kitchen tongs. But after that – for the last twenty days – there had been no further improvement. Leon still could not climb stairs, sit up straight, or stand for more than two minutes. He couldn't scratch an itchy foot or climb into the shower. Of course he couldn't sleep with Martina, that was out of the question. And he couldn't finish writing Pfitzner's bloody book. He'd tried. It was no use, not even lying down. He could just about hold a slim volume or a magazine, or fill in a crossword puzzle.

The timer of the infra-red lamp went off. Leon, who had got into a half-lying position on the kitchen chair, hauled himself painfully to his feet. Dr Pollack overtook him in the corridor. Pollack nodded to him, pushed the door of the consulting room open with one hand, never slackening his brisk pace, and with the other hand picked Leon's case notes out of the basket beside the door. While he skimmed through the papers, he pointed to the couch with his outstretched forefinger.

'On your front, please! Trousers open, pull them down a bit.'

Leon clambered up on the couch like a toad making its

way up a high kerb. He remained on his hands and knees, turned his head to the stocky man standing beside him with a dripping syringe at the ready, and said, crossly, 'What about trying something else? These injections stop the pain for exactly three hours and then it's back to square one. How about massage? Or why don't you just prescribe a course of treatment at a health resort?'

Dr Pollack snorted.

'What you have is an inflammation – massage won't help that. If the pain isn't gone next time, we'll inject you again, and if it still doesn't go away we'll just give you a higher dose.'

Leon let his head sink on his arms. Dr Pollack disinfected an area for the injection, pressed air out of the syringe once more, and pushed the thin needle smoothly into the flesh. He injected the fluid under the fatty tissue of Leon's buttocks, withdrew the needle again, and massaged the spot once more with his thumb.

'What's it got in it?' asked Leon.

'Something for the pain and something for the inflammation. I mix it myself from three different medicinal drugs.'

'I'm getting fatter,' said Leon. 'I'm getting fatter very fast. Look at me! I've put on at least ten kilos.'

Dr Pollack looked at the broad white buttocks before him. 'Yes, well, there's a bit of cortisone in it too. But only a very little. Shouldn't really be that. You just have to eat less! I mean, obviously while you can't take exercise you ought to eat less.'

'I don't eat much! I hardly eat anything. And ten kilos in three weeks . . . that can't be normal!'

'Good God,' said Dr Pollack, 'in my student days I myself weighed eighteen kilos less that I do today. I lived entirely on black bread and peanut butter. Three slices of black bread and peanut butter a day – there's everything you need in that. But I think ten kilos is exaggerating. Have you weighed yourself?'

Leon straightened up. The pain had ebbed sufficiently for him to do so quite quickly.

'There, you see?' said Dr Pollack. 'You're feeling better already! The injections are doing you good.'

Leon felt helpless. The doctor was a fool, a tennis-playing quack, not a person to be taken seriously, but the nearest orthopaedic specialist lived twice as far away. And he could hardly ask Kerbel to go that far twice a week.

'And rest,' said Dr Pollack. 'When you get home lie down and don't move. Put something under your knees to take the strain off your back. And don't do anything, you hear me? Don't do anything at all.'

Kerbel was waiting in the Transit van, reading *Bild-Zeitung*. When he saw Leon coming he scuttled out and opened the passenger door. He was wearing red mechanic's overalls and sweating profusely. Leon clung to the door frame and tried to bend at the waist. Getting into the van was always the most difficult part of the whole business. When he had clambered into the seat tears were running down his face – in spite of Dr Pollack's cocktail of drugs. Leon had tipped the seat so far back that he was lying rather than sitting in it. That helped to some extent. He had also begun to sweat, and the perspiration from his forehead flowed down to his chin along with his tears. It was incredibly sultry. Leon ought really to have been pleased: it wasn't raining. It hadn't rained for nine days now. A miracle. Somewhere in Germany there must be one right-eous man for whose sake the Lord had desisted at the last minute from his plan to wash away the whole horrible human race in a new Deluge. None the less, it was not really dry. The sky lowered over the countryside like a scratchy grey woollen blanket beneath which you had to breathe in the stale exhalations of the damp and spongy earth, and the air was so thick that it seemed visible and thread-like. The insects could hardly believe their luck. They emerged from under roof tiles, bark and other damp hiding places in their millions, crawling, fluttering, reeling past one another with stiff legs and crumpled wings, tried to pollinate a few flowers or suck some vertebrate blood, and they copulated at every available opportunity. Quick, quick! Before the rain begins again. In places like Schlangisburg it might have been almost endurable, but around Leon's house the air, thick enough anyway, was saturated with swarms of gnats, fruit flies and all kinds of tiny living creatures which got into your nose and mouth, staging a major spectacle day and night, along with their larger relatives. Bumblebees, honey bees and hornets buzzed like lawn mowers, beetles clapped their wings, and crickets almost sawed through their back legs in their enthusiasm. During the day they got musical backing from the local birds. By night the croaking of frogs and toads chimed in; the lavish supply of available food had helped them to develop resonators like car horns. In the dark they got together and croaked as loud as they could. Now that it had stopped raining even the fish leaped out of the water. Leon was presumably the only living creature who did not join in this general frenzy of enthusiasm. He hardly went out of doors anyway.

'What terrible luck you're having,' said Kerbel, as the trees lining the road passed them by. 'Specially now it's turned fine and there's so much to be done on your house.'

A wretched-looking cat crossed the road. It was tabby with white paws and extremely thin, unless that was the damp. Kerbel trod hard on his brakes. The five sacks of gravel in the back slid up to the back seat. Leon was flung forward in his seat belt. He groaned. The shopkeeper was worse than the vibrating machine. And in practice, Leon was at the mercy of his driving and his conversation all the way there and back.

'We want to build up some kind of economy here at home,' said Kerbel. 'No point in everyone moving away.'

Leon was dozing; he had simply switched off the sound to his brain, until Kerbel went into a particularly deep pothole just past the Priesnitz manor house.

'Hell,' said Kerbel, as Leon uttered a shrill scream, 'I just can't seem to notice. When I come by next time this'll be the first hole to fill up.'

Incredible. The man drove even worse than Martina.

'But as I was saying,' continued Kerbel, picking up some conversational thread, Leon knew not what, 'as I was saying, that's what you want to write about – what's happened to the GDR. First the politicians said: yes, well, there are good ideas in the GDR too, it wasn't all bad, we might even take over the green arrow on the traffic lights ourselves, and then . . .'

Leon could not muster much real interest in Kerbel's second favourite subject either. What did he care about the way the world was going when he couldn't go anywhere himself? He switched off again, and did not wake up until the van came to a halt outside his garden. By now it looked like the site of an archaeological excavation. A kind of moat running round Leon's house had been added to the drainage ditches. Kerbel had exposed the foundation walls to lay a dampcourse of gravel to enable him to work with the burner.

While the shopkeeper clambered up on the loading area of the Transit, Leon was dragging himself towards the veranda.

'I can do it myself,' called Kerbel. 'Better not try lifting anything with your bad back.'

Leon had had no intention of lifting anything. Patches of sweat spread under the arms of his black T-shirt, a swarm of gnats hovered above his head like an aerial wig. Kerbel tried to raise one of the sacks by putting both arms round it and clutching it to his chest, but he had to put it down again at once. He jumped down from the loading area and went to get the wheelbarrow out of the toolshed. Leon waited on the plank put across the moat for him. He wanted to watch Kerbel lay the dampcourse. Small hymenoptera crawled over Leon's glasses and kept patting the rims of his eyes with their probosces. Kerbel opened the first sack of gravel, tipped the wheelbarrow, and the gravel went into the ditch and lay there in a tiny heap on the bottom. Like a handful of grain scattered for a small bird. Five sacks would never be enough to lay a good gravel dampcourse round the foundations. Five hundred would be more like it. Leon brushed the insects off his face.

'I don't think we need fill it all in with gravel,' said Kerbel. 'The wet bit here by the cellar, that's the main thing. We can fill in the rest with earth. That'll do it; the coat of paint will be enough. Just wanted to dry the walls out first.'

He clambered over the ditch, stretched, and picked up the multijet burner and protective goggles from the veranda. He slung the bottle of propane gas over his back, took hold of the burner pipe, put the goggles on, and jumped down into the ditch. A furnace-like bubbling and hissing began. Kerbel bared his gums, directed the jet of flame at the house, and heated the foundation walls. He marched along the wall with the implement, which resembled a flame-thrower, waving it up and down.

'Too fast,' shouted Leon. 'You're going much too fast.'

Kerbel looked up and turned the regulating valve until the jet of fire was reduced to a thin, translucent tongue of flame making no more noise than an angry viper.

'What?' he yelled back.

'I don't think the wall's dry yet,' said Leon. 'You have to work on one part of it for longer. Much longer!'

'I'll be going over it all again,' said Kerbel in injured tones. 'I'll be going over it once or twice more. Everyone knows it doesn't dry right out first time.'

Leon raised a hand in apology. 'OK,' he said. 'You can leave the burner in the toolshed afterwards. Frau Schlei mended the door.'

The shopkeeper nodded and turned the valve. Accompanied by his cloud of insects, Leon hobbled into the house. He closed the door behind him, and cast an anxious glance at the dish on top of the shoe cupboard where Martina always put his post. Only a leaflet: a collection of signatures for a petition against turning the manor house into a residential centre for asylum seekers. Nothing from Pfitzner. Leon breathed a sigh of relief and went into the living room. It smelled of dog and shaving cream. Martina was lying on her stomach on a blue towel on the floor. She wore jeans, her top half was naked, and depilatory cream emerged from under her armpits. The dog lay beside her. He looked briefly at Leon, then turned his head away again, looking bored, and went on licking the chemical foam off Martina's ribs. Leon's mouth narrowed to a thin line. It was disgusting. It was perverse. But did he have to get worked up about it? No – he, Leon Ulbricht, did not have to get worked up about it. He had to be careful of himself. That was the only thing he had to do. Let his wife do whatever she fancied, with his blessing – have it off with dogs or pigs if she wanted. He was going to put his feet up now. Everything else was of secondary importance. Martina stood up and greeted him with a fleeting kiss on the mouth.

'Well, what did he say? Did you get anything but those injections this time?'

Leon gave a couple of grunts. This answer seemed to satisfy Martina fully. She knealed down in front of him without further questions and took his shoes off. Her small, firm breasts did not change shape even when she bent forward. Leon would have liked to say something to her now, something along the lines of: *Look, while you're down there, how about doing me a little favour?* But his desire to lie down was more pressing. Anyway, his back probably wouldn't have stood up to it. He couldn't even sneeze without yelling with pain afterwards.

'Kay said the whole house will collapse if the foundation walls are exposed much longer,' said Martina.

'I'm sure Kay knows best.'

'She says the walls will bulge out now, so the cellar will subside and then the foundations will break up.'

Leon shrugged his shoulders, so far as his back allowed.

'It's rather late for that now.'

He simply no longer felt strong enough to get worked up. So the house was going to collapse, was it? Well, great!

Martina stood up and went into the bathroom to wash off the cream. The dog kept close on her heels. Leon dragged himself to his bed on the floor. Even the slight sagging of a mattress was torture to his back, which had to have a firm, hard surface under it, something to support it. Leon lay down in front of the sofa so that he could put his calves and feet on the seat, pressing his thighs against the front of the sofa. Martina came back in a sleeveless pink T-shirt, carrying a scratched, grey plastic bucket.

'Noah and I are going to collect slugs,' she said, and disappeared again. Leon heard the patter and scrape of the dog's paws in the hall, and then the door closing. *Noah and I* . . . it couldn't be true. That stupid dog had come between them. Everything revolved around Noah. And the dog was wrong in the head too. If only Martina would at least slip into his sickbed with him now and then. But he dared not ask. The last time he'd tried to sleep with her . . . how long ago was it? Four weeks? Yes, four weeks ago! He hadn't been able to manage it last time, he'd failed, he couldn't get it up. Not an incident to be repeated, not in any circumstances. And now the pain in his back! His body was no longer an instrument which brought him pleasure and satisfaction, no longer a friend who stood by him. His body was just an irritating appendage, burdensome as a rucksack full of stones. The risk of disappointing her again, of not being able to do it, was just too great. What had Dr Pollack said? Don't do anything. Don't do anything at all.

So Leon did nothing. That is, despite the heat he got himself a second blanket, wrapped himself and his sweat-soaked clothing in it, and picked up the newspaper which Martina had left ready for him, along with a plate of biscuits and some chocolate, and a thermos flask full of coffee. He used the politics and economics section as a fan to keep off the heat and flies, bending his mind exclusively to the back page. Local and miscellaneous news and curious facts were about all his back could cope with. He shoved two biscuits into his mouth. Runaway cattle causing an accident on the main road. Fancy that! Record failure of tomato harvest. Yes, well, even plants of the Solanaceae or nightshade family need a bit of sun now and then. Latest news of the plague of slugs: it was no use collecting slugs, because the next generation would only increase and multiply all the faster if they didn't find enough slimy trails left by older members of their species. A girl had disappeared, daughter of a former high-up functionary. Leon looked at the photo. Yes, the girl had long dark hair – how long you couldn't see in the head-and-shoulders photo taken when she was alive. But that didn't mean anything. It wasn't necessarily the corpse he had found. Leon ate a piece of chocolate. What other news was there? Men were emigrating. It said here that it was mainly men who emigrated to West Germany to seek their fortunes and look for work. Women stayed here in the East. Women and Kerbel. One day all the women of the former GDR would belong to Kerbel. And he, Leon, had gone and moved here. How could he have done it? You didn't move to the GDR, you moved away from it. Always assuming you could move at all, that is. He ate another piece of chocolate and put the newspaper down. Cautiously, he stretched his torso and felt his fingernails. If they'd been a little longer he could have rolled them up. He'd have to ask Pollack about that next time. His nails were getting softer every day, even though he kept munching calcium tablets.

Martina's return interrupted Leon's sullen reflections. Clutching the dirty bucket to her breast with dirty bare arms, she came into the living room and showed Leon her booty. He looked into the bucket, simultaneously disgusted and fascinated. By now there were almost as many of the white slugs as the brown ones.

'You can go and tip them straight back into the garden,' he

said, showing her the page of the newspaper with the report about the effect of insufficient slime trails on slug posterity.

'No!' cried Martina, with assumed horror. She didn't even look at the paper, and put the bucket down by the fireplace. 'I'll go into the marshes with Noah and tip them out there. Far enough away for it to take them at least a week to get back. And I'll turn the bucket round ten times first, so they'll get dizzy and won't know where they came from.'

She looked for the dog. He had left her while she was shovelling handfuls of slugs into the bucket. She had thought that Leon might have pulled himself together for once and got up to let him in, but Noah was not in the house. If her luck was out he'd be on another of his solitary walks, which might last hours. And she dared not venture into the marshes on her own. According to Kerbel they were wetter and more treacherous than they had been for decades. Martina went out on the veranda.

From his bed on the floor, Leon heard her calling the dog, and then the sound of yapping and whimpering and the dog's tail knocking against the veranda surround, he heard Martina squeaking, 'Noah, oh, Noah-Noah-Noah-Noah,' in a totally half-witted voice, as if she had been searching for him in vain for a year, and he could imagine the scene that went with these sounds. He heard Martina come back into the hall and take the leash off its hook. He waited for her to fetch her bucket of slugs. But her footsteps suddenly receded, and then she was out of hearing distance. She had gone and forgotten the bucket. Typical. Leon put the newspaper over his face to keep off the tormenting flies, closed his eyes and dozed off. He listened to the soothing sound of Kerbel's flame-thrower. A clean, useful, controlled, technical sound which pleasingly drowned out the eternal chirping and buzzing of the insects. It somehow reminded him of the Montgolfier brothers.

He was woken by the ringing of his mobile phone. His legs had gone to sleep. Both of them. The newspaper had slid off his face, and squashed flies were stuck in the corners of his eyes. The mobile went on ringing. Perhaps it was Kerbel to say when he'd be back tomorrow. How late was it? Had Kerbel actually gone yet? The mobile kept ringing. Where the hell was it? Oh yes, beside the pillow. He only hoped it wasn't Pfitzner. But Leon was still too dazed by sleep to be really afraid.

It was indeed Pfitzner, and Pfitzner was furious. He began roaring at once.

'Where are the new pages?' he roared. 'I'm still waiting for them! How come you don't call? How come you don't answer when I ring? Shit, I've rung you four times already!'

'I . . . er . . . er . . .' said Leon. His legs were tingling as if hard little beetles were scuttling through his bloodstream.

'You'll send those pages off today! And don't think I'm going to keep ringing you again every time specially!'

'I'm not well,' said Leon. 'I'm very unwell indeed. Practically crippled. I can't write.'

'You really are a fucking bastard! I want to see the muck you've written. You just send it off, and send me the rest in a week! I'm fed to the teeth with you.'

Leon began shouting too now, but fear constricted his larynx and pushed his voice up to unnatural heights.

'I really am sick,' he croaked. 'You've no idea. I've got other things to worry about besides your book. You'll have it. But not now; I can't write now.'

Pfitzner abruptly stopped roaring. All of a sudden he was speaking very quietly.

'You'll do it. And you'll send the rest of it in a week's time. Is that clear?'

Leon immediately lowered his own voice.

'Absolutely impossible,' he said. 'I can make two suggestions. Either I finish writing it when I'm better again, and you'll just have to wait, because there's no way I can write it now. At the very outside I can make a few handwritten corrections. I can't work at the computer at all. Or alternatively we drop the whole idea and I give you back your money. That might be best. We aren't agreeing with each other too well anyway. It's probably best if I just give you back your money.'

'Now you listen to me,' said Pfitzner, and his voice was even calmer and even quieter. 'You don't seem to realise just who it is you're working for. You are working for me. The way my girls work for me. And if one of my girls wants to get out of the job she has to come up with hard cash. If she just makes off I'll find her. Wherever she goes.'

'But I'm offering you your cash. I'll transfer it to your account. Or give it to you in notes. Whichever you like.'

Pfitzner was roaring again. 'Fuck the money. That's no use. If you want to wriggle out of it you'll have to come up with much more than that. You will write that book!'

'I'll send you your money, I'll write a cheque,' shouted Leon, and then in his agitation he pressed a button with his thumb and the conversation was interrupted. For God's sake! Pfitzner would think he'd simply cut him off. Leon felt sick. On the other hand it might be a good idea for Pfitzner to realise he wasn't taking any more of this. The mobile rang again.

'Lick my arse, you stupid prole!' roared Leon, flinging the mobile in the direction of the fireplace. He had forgotten his back. The pain felled him even as he threw, he jerked, and the mobile landed in the bucket of slugs. Inside the bucket, it rang again. Ten times. Twenty times. Then it stopped. Silence. Only the tireless sawing of the crickets. The buzz of a single fly close to his ear. Leon's head sank to the floor – only now did he realise that he had been holding it up convulsively all this time. He stared at the ceiling. The mobile began to ring again. In a more muted tone this time, and only twice. Then it fell silent entirely. The slugs had taken it over. Oh well. Leon was tired, exhausted. Totally exhausted.

There he lay like a beetle on its back, in a hovel at the back of beyond, in such pain that he couldn't move or fuck or write, under threat from a pimp, with no car any more and a wife who'd rather care for the dog than for him, and his house looked like filling up with water, sinking into the ground or collapsing, take your pick. Anything else?

He wanted to sleep as long and as deeply as possible, and he didn't want to wake up until Pfitzner had vanished from the face of the earth.

Martina held Noah on a short leash and let him guide her forward. He led her as surely as a trained guide dog. She didn't even have to think where to put her feet. As if of their own accord, tussocks and stones and dry (or at least fairly dry) patches of ground came beneath the soles of her gumboots.

'Take it easy, fatso. We're in no great hurry.'

Panting and wheezing, Noah strained against the collar. When a large fly or butterfly came close to his nose he snapped at it and swallowed his prey. They walked on in this way for more than an hour. In fact the marshes looked much the same everywhere. Birch trees, mosses, flat water meadows overgrown with cotton grass, peaty ponds, puddles with a dull shimmer, mahogany-brown creatures scurrying in front of their feet, and clouds of vapour which looked thick as porridge from a distance but became increasingly translucent and ultimately invisible as you approached them. The union of sky and earth. It had taken the sky several months of steady rain to get the earth to this point, but finally all that water had worn it down, infiltrating it completely until it abandoned all resistance and just steamed back at the sky.

Martina stepped lightly over fathomless swampy holes, feeling happy, invulnerable, invincible; she felt like the head huntress of a matriarchal Stone Age tribe. Where were the men? Sitting in the cave threading dried mushrooms on sticks while she, the wolf-woman, went to get meat and kept a lookout for enemies. Noah had now turned towards home. There was the Schlei sisters' house, and Kay and Isadora themselves were standing by the blackened tree trunks just outside the garden. Kay was wearing dungarees and a red-check cotton shirt; she had a hammer in one hand and a toolbox in the other. Isadora's long hair was down, her billowing brown cotton dress had several layers of skirts, and her fat bare arms were encircled by gold bangles. Martina reflected that Isadora would probably have been the fertility priestess in a matriarchal Stone Age tribe.

'Hi, Kay! Hi, Isadora!'

Noah led Martina straight to the sisters, and Martina kissed them both on the cheek and unfastened the leash from Noah's collar. Noah sat down, sneezed, shook his head with its single ear, and panted hard. Swarms of gnats hovered low over the four warm-blooded mammals.

'Well,' said Isadora, pushing her gold bangles down towards her wrist and making them clink, 'so what brings you here?'

'I'm going to set the slugs free. If Leon had his way he'd

torture them to death one by one. So I always take them out into the marshes where he can't hurt them.'

'What slugs?' asked Kay.

Martina stared at her hands, at her feet, at Noah.

'Oh no! I don't believe it! I've forgotten them. I left the bucket in the living room. They're at home with Leon. He'll be furious. I must go back at once. If they crawl out . . . and Leon can't move. And he hates slugs so much.'

'They're probably crawling down the outside of your bucket this very minute,' said Isadora, with a malicious laugh.

Martina put the dog on his leash again.

'Come on, Noah, we must go back.'

'No, no, you stay here with Kay. I'll see to Leon and the slugs,' said Isadora, winking at Kay. 'I know all about slugs. And it's about time I visited poor old Leon and brewed him my famous tea for bad backs.'

'How kind of you,' said Martina, letting Noah go again, and craning her neck to peer inquisitively over the shrubs and into the garden of the villa. The stone statues only just showed above the tall grass where foxgloves and lilies grew.

'I wish I knew why all the slugs come to our garden. They've eaten almost nothing in yours.'

'Appearances are deceptive,' said Isadora, marching off right through a deep puddle in her embroidered brown velvet slippers, 'appearances are deceptive.'

'Isadora!'

Kay's voice was stern and frosty. Isadora turned to look at her with the most innocent expression in the world.

'Yes?'

'You will be sensible, won't you?'

'Huh!' said Isadora. 'Sense! You may need that sort of thing, but kindly don't bother me with it.'

She began whistling, and splashed water up on purpose as she waded through the next puddle. Martina watched her go.

'She's so kind. That's really nice of her.'

'Yes, well,' said Kay, nervously fiddling with the toolbox she was holding.

'You're even more isolated here than we are,' said Martina, trying to strike up a conversation.

'Hmmm.'

'Don't you ever feel lonely here?'

'Lonely? No, not really.'

'What about Isadora? She almost never goes out. You sometimes come over to our place or down to the village, but we never see Isadora. What does she do all day long?'

'Well . . . Isadora . . . she lives by her own rules. Watches TV all day. No idea what goes on inside her.' Kay knocked the hammer against a slimy black tree for no particular reason. A swarm of iridescent green flies immediately rose from a knot hole and made for the two women. Noah was standing by a puddle yapping at a frog.

'I've got a shutter to repair,' said Kay, when they had escaped from the flies. 'Like to lend me a hand? I'll show you how to do it.'

'Better not even try,' said Martina. 'I'll hand you the nails if you like, but don't try explaining things to me. I just can't do it. I do everything wrong.'

Kay set off along an overgrown path leading diagonally across the garden and past the fountain. It was a long time since the fountain had worked. The gargoyle from which water once spouted had crumbled out of all recognition, and over the years small pieces of zinc had collected on the bottom of the shallow basin. Noah lifted his leg and peed against the side of the fountain. Martina scolded him, but that didn't stop him peeing over the steps up to the villa as well. Kay unpacked her toolbox below a rotting shutter hanging by a single hinge, took out a screwdriver and a new hinge, and searched among the screws. She put the screwdriver into Martina's hand and said, 'Of course you can do it. It's perfectly easy.'

'No.' Martina's voice became tearful. 'You may say it's perfectly easy, but it's only easy for you. I can't do it. You just want me to do something wrong.'

She hurled the screwdriver away in a high arc. Noah ran after it, picked it up in his teeth and brought it back, wagging his tail.

'Why don't you leave me in peace?' whimpered Martina. 'I don't need to learn this sort of thing. Why would I need to?'

'Well, just in case you ever find yourself living in an isolated little house in the middle of the marshes, and your husband has a slipped disc or something like that,' said Kay. She took Martina's left hand and placed a screw between her thumb and forefinger. Then she removed the screwdriver from Noah's mouth and pressed it into Martina's right hand.

When Leon woke up for the second time it was because he had heard a noise. His sleep had been dreamless, had allowed him to forget his backbone and Pfitzner, and he resisted wakefulness, which had nothing better to offer him than gnats, flies, mosquitoes, illness, fear of Pfitzner and now quite possibly a burglar into the bargain. The door of the house was not locked. Anyone could walk in. The noise came from the corridor. Something was dragging over the floor. It sounded like a python fifteen metres long, like a heavy robe with a train at a coronation ceremony, or someone pulling along a rolled-up Persian carpet. Leon had no Persian carpets.

'Martina? Martina, is that you?'

No answer. The room was full of shadows. Shadows and mosquitoes. A dim light like that of a grotto seeped in through the windows. The insects were making a frightful noise. They seemed to have brought along small rumba rattles made especially for them. Why wasn't Martina back yet? The snaky sound was approaching the living room. Then the door flew open, and there stood Isadora on the threshold. Fat and unavoidable.

'Ugh, it's terribly hot in here.'

Painfully, Leon turned his head away. Isadora! Worse than a python and a burglar combined. She walked through the living room, took from her skirt pocket something brown the size of her hand and something which looked like a piece of white lichen, and put both on the mantelpiece.

'What are those?' asked Leon suspiciously. 'Take them away!'

'A mushroom cap and some dwarf's beard. Makes very good tea for a bad back. Unless I can think of something to do you even more good.'

She laughed. Leon hated that vulgar female laugh. The most revolting sound in the whole animal kingdom. Then Isadora noticed the bucket by the fireplace. The slugs had not liked it in there. The braver specimens among them had climbed out, and were slithering over the floor close by, or sticking to the outside of the bucket like ornamental decoration on some item of cult pottery. Isadora picked up the bucket by its handle and tiptoed through the escaped slugs. She giggled, and swung the bucket in Leon's direction.

'No!' he said. 'No! You're not going to do that!'

'Aren't I?'

He repeated once again, very slowly and very clearly: 'You . . . are . . . not . . . going . . . to . . . do . . . that!'

The contents of the bucket flowed rapidly over his lower body. Flowed? No, a brown and white chunk struck him. It was like that time at school when the medicine ball hit him in the stomach during PE. Leon sat up abruptly, yelled twice – once in alarm, the second time when pain ravaged his spine – and fell on his back again.

'Are you out of your mind? You know I've got a bad back. How could you do that, you silly cow?'

He groaned, brushed the pile of slugs off his stomach and knocked his funny-bone on the sofa leg as he did so. As if he wasn't in enough pain already. The mobile, now entirely covered in slime, clattered to the floor. Leon threw a white slug at Isadora. She picked the slug up, put it in her mouth and swallowed it.

'That's revolting,' said Leon. 'Sometimes I really fear for your reason.'

Isadora got down on all fours, crawled towards him with slow, cat-like movements and bent over him. Her large bosom, encased in brown cotton, swung in front of his face.

'Go away,' said Leon. 'I'm not going to kiss you. You just ate a slug. Anyway, Martina could come back any moment. So would you be so kind as to get up again?'

She flung one thigh over him so that he was lying between her arms and legs. Her skirt was draped like a quilt over his lower body. She looked at him mockingly. Furious, Leon felt he was at her mercy, but he assumed the expression of a man to whom emotion is foreign.

'Leave it out,' he said coldly. 'I'm not keen on repeat performances.'

Isadora put one hand under his T-shirt and placed it against his ribs.

'Ooh, how his little heart's beating! I do believe you're still afraid of me!'

She dug her fingernails into his skin and scratched his ribs and belly. Her maternal savagery made Leon feel weak. He realised that his will was stealing away from his body. A completely different person, some kind of yielding, harmless idiot, took the place of the Leon whom he knew and admired. Isadora rolled up his T-shirt and looked with satisfaction at the scratch she had given him.

'Not again,' cursed Leon. 'How am I going to explain that to Martina? Last time you left me in a state where I couldn't let her see me naked for two weeks. Not exactly easy when you're married.'

Isadora moved a little way back until she was sitting on his thighs, and fumbled with the zip of his jeans.

'What are you doing? Stop it!'

'Relax! I've got something that'll be good for your bad back.'

'No, do you hear me? I said no. Martina's out there somewhere. No!'

Isadora unzipped his flies and put her hand inside his trousers.

'Your prick says yes. See that? It says yes, quite clearly.'

She moved his penis in her hand, making it nod. It stiffened. They both stiffened: Leon and his penis.

'I couldn't care less what my prick wants,' roared Leon. 'I don't want to! Do you get the idea?'

He tried to sit up and haul himself on to the sofa. Isadora pushed him back into his original position with one hand.

'There, there, I promise to leave you alone! I'll pay attention exclusively to your prick.'

She licked her lips and bent over his trousers, like a tigress about to drag the entrails of her prey out of its stomach cavity. Leon felt helpless, wretched and ridiculous, and more excited than he had ever been in his life. She bent lower, the curtain of her black hair falling in front of her face. Leon put his hand into her hair and pulled, trying to drag Isadora away. But at the same time he moved his hips, in so far as his back would allow, pushing his sweaty prick into the middle of that hair, which resembled creeping vegetation, as if into something warm and twitching. And sure enough, behind the hair it was taken into the hot, wet pump of Isadora's mouth. He felt the elastic insides of her sucking cheeks; he felt her tongue, its soft underside and the structure of the surface, like the two different skin surfaces of a slug, he felt it winding round the shaft of his genital organ. Leon gave up. He took hold of Isadora's hair again, but this time to push her face more firmly down on his belly. She slipped out of his grasp, tossing her head aside with a laugh, and climbed on top of him. She wasn't wearing any knickers. Leon thrust into her, boring his way into that billowing body full of juices. Isadora moved forward, upwards and back, slowly rocking, let his prick slip almost the whole way out of her and then took it in again. Her head was bent forward, her mouth half open. She looked as if she were asleep, and moaned softly.

'Please . . .' whimpered Leon, '. . . please!'

Isadora did not seem to hear him. Oblivious, she continued her slow rocking, making no attempt to accelerate the tempo. And then he came. It was not the same as usual, not like a shot, an explosion or an eruption. It simply flowed out of him, slowly, softly, for an incredibly long time, flowed out like milk boiling over in a pan. It was so good that tears ran down his face. And he had been afraid he might have become impotent! Impotent? Ridiculous!

A little later he did not feel so good. Isadora's gigantic body was an uncomfortable weight on his loins, and Leon felt sweaty, smelly and sticky. The flies appreciated it. His triumph in still being able to get an erection was clouded by the painful fact that he had just been taken against his will by a stupid, fat woman. And that he had enjoyed it too.

'That wasn't funny,' hissed Leon, propping himself on his elbows. Isadora got up and simply left the room. He watched her go, her large, swinging buttocks clad in brown cotton. Isadora, his evil demon.

'Hey,' he called after her, 'how was . . . how was it for you?'

She disappeared into the dark corridor, dissolved into it. Only the sound of the door closing reassured Leon that she had in fact left the house in a perfectly normal way.

When Martina came back the slugs had crawled all over the living room. Some of them had even climbed the wallpaper. Leon was lying among his pillows and blankets in the middle of them, wiping slime off the mobile phone with a handkerchief.

'What's going on? Didn't Isadora come to see you? She promised me to look in and take the bucket out.'

Martina was beaming, as she always did when she came back from her walks with Noah. The dog made his way into the living room after her and sniffed in surprise at the slugs, which were half dried up.

'Where've you been?' said Leon. 'Where were you all this time? You think I don't worry about you?'

'Kay was showing me how to screw things together. I put a hinge on a shutter. And then we fixed some plugs in, with cement and that. And now I know what to do when the water won't stop running in the loo.'

She looked as if she were twelve years old and had just been given a pony for her birthday.

'You think it's normal just to leave me lying here like this?' asked Leon bitterly. Martina looked at the floor.

'But I have to learn things like that now you're so ill. Kay's going to teach me everything. I only have to call her whenever there's something to repair, and she'll come over and show me how to do it.'

'We don't have a telephone any more,' snapped Leon. 'The slugs climbed all over it and now it doesn't work. Do you realise I lay here for four hours – on my own and without a phone? If I'd had another relapse I could have died here.'

'I thought Isadora was going to look in,' said Martina in a small voice. Leon crossed his arms over his chest.

'You can see for yourself what came of that. I tried to pick the filthy creatures up again, but . . .'

'With your back? No, you shouldn't!'

'I couldn't anyway.'

Martina kneeled down and began picking up slugs. Leon watched her, shaking biscuit crumbs off his blanket.

'You ought to have burnt them straight away. Now we'll be slipping on slug trails for days on end.'

He slammed the mobile down on the floor and then pressed its buttons. It remained dead. Martina collected all the slugs she could find, but oddly enough the bucket ended up not nearly as full as it had been when she first put it down by the fireplace. Leon preferred to make no comment about that. She hurried out into the garden and tipped the slugs over the fence. Noah accompanied her, taking the opportunity to eat a couple of blades of grass. Then he followed Martina into the kitchen, where she rinsed out the empty bucket. She opened the kitchen cupboard, and Noah pricked up his remaining ear. Martina was hungry too. Ravenously hungry, the kind of hunger that a slice of bread wouldn't satisfy. She had to stuff herself really full, full to the brim. Perhaps if she was very quiet she could manage to throw up without Leon's hearing. In his study he couldn't hear what went on in the bathroom, but since he had taken to spending all day in the living room Martina always had to wait until he went to the doctor if she wanted to throw up. This one time she could pretend she just had a stomach upset. She put her hand on the top shelf. It was empty. Panic-stricken, she climbed on a kitchen stool and searched the cupboard. Everything was gone! Five chocolate bars, three large packets of biscuits, liquorice, jelly babies, the family pack of Mars bars . . . simply gone! She got down from the kitchen stool, opened the fridge, looked in the freezer compartment. The giant Arctic roll. Gone! She was trembling. Had Leon noticed her throwing up in secret and hidden all the sweet stuff to humiliate her? Or had he thrown it away? She opened the door of the cupboard under the sink and looked in the rubbish bin. It was brimming over with chocolate papers, foil, empty biscuit packets and a smeared ice cream packet. With her fingertips Martina fished out the black, red and gold plastic wrapper which had contained six Mars bars and took it over to Leon's bed, holding it up without a word.

'Well? I was very hungry today,' said Leon, irritated. 'And what's more, I'm in pain.'

8

Increasingly cloudy as the day goes on. Wind strengthening from various directions during the course of the morning. Showers in the evening. Temperatures of around 18 degrees.

Harry sat beside Pfitzner in the black Mercedes, staring out of the window. They were on their way to Leon's. It was nearly evening already. Muddy fields passed by, brimming ditches, wet cattle in wet meadows. A horse with a dirty coat was hanging its head. Landscapes bored Harry rigid, this one even more than most. Several large raindrops splashed on the windscreen. Harry put two fingers inside the collar of his white shirt, trying in vain to make more room for his throat. The tie constricting it was made of transparent plastic with several roulette jettons sealed into it. A present from Melanie.

'Everything OK?' asked Pfitzner. He too was wearing a white shirt, but without a tie. His long grey hair hung over his shoulders.

'Yes, why ask?' said Harry.

'Well, he's your friend, after all.'

'My best friend,' agreed Harry.

The rain increased, falling from the sky like a set of evenly arranged guitar strings. Pfitzner turned the heater on to dry the condensation off the windscreen. Harry rubbed his eyes. He always had trouble with his contact lenses when the car heater was on.

'So I can count on you, can I?' said Pfitzner.

'Sure. But I'd like to talk to him first. That OK?'

'There's been too much talking already,' said Pfitzner. They drove into the village. Priesnitz.

'Why in hell he wanted to live here . . .' said Harry. 'None of this would have happened if he'd stayed in Hamburg. I'm sure it wouldn't. No wonder he's gone peculiar. The isolation doesn't agree with him.'

Pfitzner did not reply. The Ford Transit which had barred their way last time was standing outside the corner shop. A boy was sitting on a moped under the dripping porch of the shop. A girl with short bleached hair and red cowboy boots was hanging around beside him.

Now the heavens really opened. It was raining cats and dogs.

Pfitzner turned right outside the manor house, driving fast, went on to the field of bowed and mouldering maize plants, and followed the muddy track to Blacky's house. Small, bubbling cascades flowed down the tractor ruts towards him, splashing against the spoiler. Limp maize leaves brushed the car fenders. This was one reason why Pfitzner had decided to take the old black Mercedes. He didn't want to get the new one dirty on the roads of this run-down East German state. Moreover, it could do no harm to give Blacky a sight of the car again.

Pfitzner drove to the garden gate and parked beside a puddle measuring five square metres. He switched off the engine but left the windscreen wipers running. The property looked completely devastated. Holes in the ground, mountains of mud, sheets of yellow plastic. There was a light on in the house. Pfitzner took his watch on its gold-link bracelet off his wrist and put it in the glove compartment. He picked up the pistol he had left there, thought briefly, and put it back again. Harry reached for their jackets lying on the back seat.

'We'll wait till the rain slackens off,' said Pfitzner.

Leon was sitting in his favourite armchair, a cushion in his back, his feet up on a kitchen chair. Being able to sit upright in an armchair was progress. His buttocks entirely covered the surface of the seat. The arms and back pressed him into a rectangular shape. The only pair of Leon's trousers which still fitted him, and which he therefore wore all the time, were his black jogging trousers. A black sweatshirt was stretched over his belly. Leon pushed his double chin against his chest, simultaneously gnawing a ballpoint pen and one of his soft, flaking fingernails, and looking at the puzzle magazine on his lap. There was a fire in the hearth, sending great clouds of smoke up to the ceiling of the room. Martina had used damp branches to eke out the last dry logs they had found in the toolshed. Noah, indifferent to the rising smoke, lay in front of the fire snoring slightly. Unlike Leon, he hardly ever suffered from nightmares. Martina was sitting on the sofa with a magazine, wearing jeans and a stained old shirt of Leon's. Kay's toolbox stood in front of the sofa. Earlier in the day Martina had tried fitting a new hose in the shower, and in the process had broken the ring seal fixing the old hose, which was working perfectly well, to the fittings of the bathtub. Leon had gazed, baffled, at the ruined ring seal. Solid metal. It was a mystery to him how Martina could have done it. With the help of Kay's toolbox, she was systematically destroying the few things in this hovel which had previously been in working order. Leon felt unable to stop her. A wretched sense of lethargy and hopelessness had afflicted him like a flu virus. Only crossword puzzles still interested him. Seven empty squares to fill in on the grid and he'd have completed this one.

Then he heard the noise. It had mingled imperceptibly with the sound of the rain falling and the crackling of the fire in the hearth, and for some time it had remained a disquieting but indefinable element in those sounds, until it ultimately stood out as something independent: the noise of a car engine. This was the moment Leon had always feared. For it was clearly not Kerbel's Transit van driving up. Leon bent desperately over his puzzle magazine again. If he could manage to complete the puzzle on this page without leaving a single space empty, then it *was* Kerbel after all. Kerbel with a new car. Or someone else. Martina's parents, for instance.

Rascal (Fr.), 5 letters – that was *filou*. Historic Prussian river? – Nebel? Bebel? No, of course, Memel! Felted woollen fabric – baize? Yes, why not? There. Finished.

'Leon, can't you hear it? Do put that stupid crossword down! Leon!'

Only now did he realise that Martina was trying to communicate with him. In desperation, he looked at her. She rose and went down the corridor to the front door. Noah shook himself and followed her.

'Who is it?' called Leon. His heart was beating as if fists were drumming against his ribs. Noah barked, uttering separate growls brought up from deep in his belly.

'Your black Mercedes is outside the garden gate,' Martina called back. The black Mercedes! Pfitzner's car was red. So it was just Harry coming to see him. Of course. Pfitzner wouldn't come out here himself for such a minor matter. He'd given the black Mercedes to Harry. Noah was now barking so loud that Leon couldn't hear what Martina said. She came back.

'They're not getting out. They're sitting in the car and not getting out.'

'Who?' asked Leon. 'Who's sitting in the car?'

He knew the answer already. If Harry wasn't sitting in the Mercedes alone, then the other person with him could only be Pfitzner. That meant it was all up with him. Hopelessly. Even if he could solve all the crossword puzzles in the world without leaving any empty squares.

'Who do you . . .' Martina began. The dog ran up and down the room, barking even harder.

'It's all right,' Leon tried to calm him down.

Noah went on barking.

'Tell that dog to lie down,' Leon told Martina.

'Why?'

Her question infuriated him. Why? Why the hell couldn't she just for once do as he told her?

'Tell that fucking dog to go and lie down!' Leon shouted. He instantly felt better. Felt his own personality retrieving its outlines, felt that it was not wholly impossible to stand up to Pfitzner.

'Heel, Noah,' said Martina quietly, almost without any note of command in her voice; it was more of an urgent request. Noah immediately closed his mouth and went to her side, growling. She took hold of his collar, hauled him out into the corridor again without a word, and opened the door for the second time. Water was pouring down over the edge of the gutter in long strands which hung round the veranda like a fortune-teller's bead curtain. Pfitzner and Harry were still sitting in the car. It was Leon's fault they were there. And now he was afraid, the fat pig.

Martina let Noah go and jumped over the ditch, which was half-full of water like a real moat. Kerbel had covered it with yellow tarpaulins, but they had caught and held the water, turned into yellow basins, and collapsed into the ditch after a cloudburst. Now the ditch itself was filling up. The foundation walls of the house had never been wetter. If you hung a towel on the inside of the cellar wall you could wring water out of it next day.

Noah ran after Martina. He followed her to the back of the garden, where she stopped outside the toolshed. She dragged Noah in and slammed the door in his face. He howled, jumped up against the rotten wood, and in all the agitation knocked Kerbel's high-performance burner over.

Meanwhile Leon hobbled out on to the veranda. Uncertainly, he pulled up his jogging trousers, passed a hand over his hair, cleaned his glasses on the hem of his sweatshirt and put them on again. He realised what a sight he presented. He was fat. He'd probably put on kilos and kilos. His arms and legs looked thin as a beetle's by comparison with his flabby body. His face was bloated, grey and ugly from weeks of lying about bedridden. The one thing he could do to improve his appearance was at least to meet Harry and Pfitzner standing on his feet. Martina came back, so she had only been getting the dog out of the way. He would rather she had disappeared entirely. Martina made her way into the house past him.

'Shall I make coffee?' she asked quietly.

'Yes,' said Leon. Coffee, cake – he must get Pfitzner and Harry to sit down, to start talking. Why were they still sitting in the car? Why didn't they get out? Perhaps he ought to go over to them. He imagined walking over, standing beside the Mercedes like a wet poodle, he saw Pfitzner just winding down the side window and shooting him. He saw himself lying in the big puddle, saw his blood spreading in a red cloud through the brown water, and the black Mercedes backing out and driving away.

Finally Harry and Pfitzner got out. Harry was holding a mobile phone to his ear.

'The Polonia. Stay at the Hotel Polonia. I'll pick you up there. Yup. Love you too! Ciao!' he shouted into it, put the mobile away again, and moved to stand beside Pfitzner in the mud. They walked slowly towards the house, ignoring the pouring rain. Forcing a casual gesture, Leon raised a hand in greeting. A muscle in his lower jaw was twitching.

God, he's got fat, thought Harry. That's what marriage does to you. Half a year of wedded bliss and a man's done for. Pfitzner and Harry used the plank to reach the veranda. The dog was yapping in the toolshed.

'You look a real sackful of shit, Blacky,' said Pfitzner. His lids were lowered so far in sheer contempt that his eyes were nothing but slits. Leon swallowed.

'Well, I don't feel too good,' he said, taking a deep breath. 'To be honest, I feel completely . . .'

At this moment Isadora passed the toolshed. Pfitzner and Harry glanced at her. Isadora was wearing a full-length black cape and looked like an inkwell in motion. Leon could have wept. She never, never left her house! And now of all times, just as he was about to explain everything to Pfitzner, of course she had to stroll by. She waved in a meaningful manner. Pfitzner grinned, surprised.

'You got something going with that fat tart? You do, don't you?'

'What, her?' said Leon. 'I wouldn't even have her here as a cleaning lady.'

Pfitzner and Harry laughed. Leon breathed more easily. It wasn't so bad after all. Here they were standing on the veranda talking about women. Three men at ease with each other. Leon just had to go on talking, had to keep the conversation going.

'Come on in,' he said. 'Martina's making coffee. Come into the living room and get dry. We've got a fire burning.'

He went ahead of them. God, how fat he's got, thought Harry again. All he can do is waddle.

'You're looking good, Harry,' babbled Leon. 'You too, Benno! I really must get fit again. Once I've shaken off this bad back . . .'

Martina brought the coffee in.

'Ah, coffee,' cried Leon with exaggerated enthusiasm, reaching for the dirty cup from which he had been drinking all day and holding it out. Martina ignored it. She was just as nervous as Leon. She put the coffee pot on the table and quickly went out to get the rest of the crockery. Leon put his cup down and mopped his forehead. Keep going! Coffee, biscuits, conversation – and then Pfitzner would go again in an hour's time, and Harry would stay and deal with the money side of things. Good Lord, Leon, Harry would say, is it really that bad? Leon would explain to Harry, and Harry would explain to Pfitzner, and everything would be all right again. The pain in Leon's back reached a critical level. He could no longer keep upright, and dropped with difficulty into his armchair.

'Do sit down,' he said, pointing to the sofa. Pfitzner and Harry remained standing. Small bits of earth came away from their shoes, and the drops of water running down them turned the earth into muddy slush. Pfitzner took a cigar from the inside pocket of his jacket, spent a long time removing its cellophane wrapping, and lit it. He had to click his gold lighter several times. The cigar had got damp, and did not burn at once, and when it finally did it stank and smoked almost as much as the fire in the hearth. Martina came back in and laid the cups out on the coffee table. Pfitzner went over to her with his cigar in the corner of his mouth and placed himself behind her. He put his hand on her right thigh and stroked slowly upwards and along her hip. Martina flinched, went red, and looked at Leon for help.

'Terrible rain,' said Leon. 'A couple of weeks, ago I thought it was finally drying up, but then it got worse than ever . . . !'

He too had gone red in the face, and was avoiding Martina's eyes. And when Pfitzner and Harry stared at him too he looked at the floor with an awkward grin. He must just keep cool! Had anything happened? No, nothing at all had happened yet.

Pfitzner let go of Martina, drew deeply on his cigar, and went over to the armchair where Leon was sitting. Placing his hands on the arms of the chair, he blew smoke in Leon's face.

'Hey!' said Leon, with an uneasy laugh.

'Take her off and do her,' Pfitzner told Harry, staring into Leon's face as he sat wedged between his, Pfitzner's arms. Leon had insulted him, and now Pfitzner was going to offer him the worst imaginable insult. Anyone who crossed Pfitzner was paid back for it a hundred times over. That was how he operated.

'Hey!' said Leon. He tried to stand up. Pfitzner hit him hard in the chest, and Leon fell back in the chair. His back! He screamed, but tried again. His eyes were now wide with panic. He clutched Pfitzner's wrists and tried to haul himself up by them. Pfitzner shook him off, drew his arm back, and without putting much effort into it struck him in the face with his clenched fist. Blood ran from Leon's nose. He felt for his glasses. Harry went over to Martina, took her gently by the lower arm, jerked his chin towards the door and said: 'Let's go!'

Just as he had expected, of course the silly cow started howling at once. As if things weren't bad enough for Leon already. She snuffled and begged: 'Please, don't! Please, don't do it.'

Harry heard Pfitzner's fist land in Leon's face again, heard him groan. He put one hand on Martina's neck, pushed her out into the corridor and down it ahead of him, and opened the second door. Bingo – the bedroom! A pile of ironed and folded laundry lay on the bed. Towels and shirts. Harry's feet became entangled in the legs of a zebra skin. He stumbled, almost fell, and had to let go of Martina. She ran straight to the door. He went after her, caught her in the corridor, dragged her back by the hair and flung her on the bed. She screeched, buried her face in the pillows and began weeping again. Harry took one of the towels off the pile and swept the rest of the laundry to the floor. He felt for the pipe cleaner holding his wet hair together, took it off and rubbed his head with the towel. He realised that this was some kind of a test. He wouldn't fail. He had never failed. He could do what was needed. Always. Harry undid his belt and the button of his wide grey trousers, and unzipped his flies.

'Get undressed,' he said.

Martina slowly raised her head without looking at Harry. This isn't really happening, she thought. Not in my own bedroom. Not with Leon sitting in the next room.

'Go on, get undressed, will you?' said Harry. He had taken out his prick and was manipulating it with both hands. Martina turned her back to him and undid the bottom button of her shirt. One button, then another button. As slowly as she could. As slowly as she dared. It was absurd, but suddenly she couldn't help thinking of her father, seeing his contemptuous face in her mind's eye. 'Go on, then, do as you like,' whispered that face. 'Have fun!'

'For Christ's sake get a move on!' said Harry, taking a step towards her with his trousers undone. Martina left the buttons alone. She didn't want him to touch her. Not yet. She tried to pull the shirt over her head, became entangled in it and was stuck. Sobbing hysterically, she tugged at the arms.

'Keep still,' said Harry. He put a hand carefully on her head and pulled the shirt off. He thought she was too thin. You could count all her ribs. She was too tall as well. Almost as tall as he was. And her breasts were too small. Much too small. He could see that, even before he pulled her bra off. And her fingernails were short, and unvarnished. A woman with unvarnished finger nails was not really a woman as far as he was concerned.

'Stop howling,' he said. 'Do you want Leon to hear you?'

She was naked now. It was cold in the bedroom. An unpleasant, musty smell came from Harry's wet clothes. He stank. This was not a dream. There had never been any smells in Martina's dreams. It was really happening. He took hold of her, ran a finger down the inside of her arm. He stroked her throat. She had gone rigid. Harry kissed her on the mouth. She felt sick. Wrenching her head away, she threw up beside the bed. Not much came out – she hadn't eaten all day – only a bit of yellow slime.

'You stupid cow,' shouted Harry, pushing her back on the bed. He grasped her pubic hair and pulled a tuft out.

'Spread your legs,' he shouted. 'Wider than that! Go on, wider, you cow!'

Obviously it wasn't so important to him now if Leon heard. He pulled her labia apart and stuffed his prick into her with one hand, thrusting back and forth a couple of times. This was really happening, and happening to her. It hurt. She dared not scream. She was afraid of what he would do if she didn't endure everything in silence. She heard Leon yelling in the living room. Yelling like an animal. Harry suddenly took his penis out of her and issued more instructions.

'Lie on your stomach,' he said. 'Put the pillow under you! Go on, higher!'

She did as he said. This was even worse. It was dirty, violent and vicious. This time she had to scream. This time she was afraid she wouldn't survive. It went on and on, and then it stopped, and Harry was suddenly kneeling in front of her face, holding her chin in one hand. He had a knife in the other. He pressed the tip of the knife to the skin just under her left eye.

'One wrong move and I'll cut your eye out,' he said, taking the knife away again. He stuck his prick in her mouth. She tasted blood and shit. Her own blood. Her own shit.

'Suck it,' bellowed Harry. 'Go on, suck it.'

He jerked her head towards him. She retched and coughed. He hit her on the head with the handle of the knife. She began sucking. It was like a porn film. Her body was a machine, a thing full of orifices into which a penis could be stuck, or a hand, the tip of a shoe or the handle of a knife.

Harry slowly got going. Not only did his prick become

harder and firmer, so did he. His body and whatever he meant when he said *I*. Every time he penetrated this other body he felt that *I* becoming more distinct. His mobile rang. He reached into his jacket pocket and switched it off. Then he went on.

It was happening, it was really happening. Now he was behind her again. Issuing further instructions, getting her body into position. She was to kneel, propping herself up on her elbows. His legs against her legs. The fabric of his trousers brushed along her thighs. The end of his silly tie scratched her back. Her body was a machine. She was glad her body was a machine. A machine could endure anything. A machine was nothing to do with her. She heard Noah barking out in the shed, she heard Leon screaming again, and suddenly realised that she had been keeping her eyes closed all the time. She opened them and looked round the room without moving her head. Twilight had set in. Or had it already been so dark when Harry pushed her into the bedroom? The curtains were hanging crooked. The zebra skin always rolled up at its edges, even though she tried to tread it flat every morning. By the bed lay an open newspaper with a picture of Boris Becker as a little boy holding a comparatively huge tennis racket. She had to throw up again. She pressed her head into the bedclothes, retched, and hoped Harry wouldn't notice. Harry's hands let go of her waist. What now? What would he think of next? She heard him getting up. He stood in front of her. He took a towel, wiped his prick with it, stuffed it back in his trousers and did up the zip. Martina let herself fall on her side. She pulled her legs up to her body, clasping her knees. Harry sat down beside her. He stroked her head, bent over her and kissed her tenderly on the temple. He must be completely crazy. Any moment he would stick the knife in her back. She hoped it would be quick, quicker than just now.

'You may not believe it,' said Harry, 'but I didn't want to do that.'

He was still stroking her head, and then let his hand slide over her shoulder and down to her waist.

'You're beautiful,' he said. 'Honest, you're a very beautiful woman.'

Martina did not move, scarcely breathed. She did not care in the least about being beautiful.

Kay was sitting on the grey carpet of her room on the upper floor of the Schlei villa, laying out the innards of a radio on a glass plate. The glass was fitted to the middle of a racing-car tyre, and thus made the tyre into a table. Kay had got it as a free gift when she subscribed to a car magazine, the issues of which were stacked on a metal shelf behind her. Beside her, on the floor, stood the ravaged wooden housing of the old radio, which she intended to repair with a soldering iron, a bunch of new cables and two new tubes. She was not really attending to what she was doing, picked up a cable, stretched it smooth and stared ahead of her. She thought of Martina and dismissed the thought immediately. No point in nurturing false hopes. Kay bent over the soldering iron, melted half a centimetre of tin and let it drip on a metal bar, stuck the wire emerging from the plastic round the cable into it, and waited for the tin to harden. Evening was slowly drawing in. The rainclouds were making it dark too. She could hardly see the ends of the wires. Kay was about to put the light on, but then forgot it and stared out of the window. Her whole life had been spent in this place. Surprising she didn't have reeds growing out of her head, really. And no wonder Leon was getting so run down. If he had any sense he'd move away from here as soon as possible. If he stuck around he'd rot away like an over-watered cactus. He already looked all squishy. Kay stood up. She didn't feel like welding any more. She wanted to go and see Martina. Right now. She tramped downstairs and put on the yellow gumboots standing by the door. As she was reaching for her waxed jacket Isadora came into the hall in a nightdress, with a jar of fish food in her hand.

'Going over to Leon and Martina's again? I don't think they'll want to see you just now. They've got visitors.'

Kay froze.

'Who?'

'Those two crooks – you remember, the ones with the cucumber dog which bit poor Noah's ear off? I wish I knew why crooks always look like crooks. You'd think it would be in their own interest to hide their profession . . .'

'What?' Kay almost shouted. 'We must go over at once. How long have they been there?'

Isadora shrugged her shoulders, bored.

'A person's allowed to visit friends.'

Kay took her jacket and threw Isadora the cape.

'Come on, get dressed! Quick! Hurry up! We can't leave Martina alone with those two thugs.'

'What do you think's going to happen?' muttered Isadora, but she put the fish food down on the ground, put on the cape and even a pair of shoes, and followed her sister out. It was almost dark, and raining. They walked through the marshes, Isadora panting and snuffling but managing to keep up. Halfway there they heard Noah barking. Barking frantically, without much in the way of pauses. It sounded as if he were trying to send an urgent telegram. Kay and Isadora exchanged a glance and went even faster. Shortly before they reached Leon's garden, Isadora held her sister back.

'Not so fast! We don't know what's going on.'

'I know *something* is. I just know,' hissed Kay. But she continued on her way more cautiously. The only light in the house was in the living room window. They crept up to it sideways. The daylight had not yet entirely disappeared. Kay slowly moved her head forward.

Pfitzner was standing by the hearth, stirring the fire with a poker. Leon was crouched in his chair. His face was swollen, and smeared with blood and tears. He had pleaded. 'Let her go,' he had begged. 'She's never done anything to you.' He had roared. 'Don't touch her,' he had roared. 'No, Harry! Don't! Yes, yes,' he had roared, 'yes, yes, yes, I'll do it. I'll write the bloody book. I will! Stop it! Please, please!' He had wept. He had implored Pfitzner to spare Martina. He was quiet now. He wiped his face with his hand and got blood in his eyes. It stung. He wished he hurt even more. Pain would have been a release from what he was feeling. He was nobody, he knew that now. A shapeless thing without a core. Of no value. Years ago, when he was being questioned on his reasons for conscientious objection to military service, he had been asked what he would do if he had a gun and two enemy soldiers were trying to rape his girlfriend. Would he fire the gun? He had been prepared for this question, had known what to say: *Since I never carry a gun I couldn't get into such a situation in the first place.* Now he would unhesitatingly have given all he possessed for a loaded pistol. He wanted to see these bastards die. And while they slowly bled to death he would trample on their balls and piss in their open wounds. Leon's face was distorted like that of a despairing little boy. First he whimpered and sobbed quietly, then he began to weep uncontrollably. As suddenly as he had begun weeping he stopped again. Pfitzner glanced briefly at him and drew on his cigar.

Harry came into the room, pulling Martina along behind him by her arm. She was naked, and the insides of her legs had dark smears on them.

Kay was on the point of jumping through the window.

'Don't,' whispered Isadora, putting a hand on her arm. 'Stop and think! They may have weapons. And we have nothing.'

'I'll get a spade,' Kay whispered back. 'I'll get a spade from the toolshed and smash that man's head in.'

She shook Isadora's hand off and went away.

Leon did not look at Martina, but stared through her into space.

'Leon,' said Martina, and was startled herself by the hoarse sound of her voice. Her throat was swollen. Leon turned his face away, as if only now was he leaving her alone, as if he hadn't left her alone long ago. Pfitzner cleaned out his ear with his little finger. Harry tucked his shirt back into his trousers. Alone. Martina had thought she knew what that meant. But until now she had not had the faintest idea of how lonely a person could be. Noah's barking was getting louder. He must have freed himself. He was barking as desperately as on the day when he had to watch Harry's bull terrier pissing in his garden. Pfitzner threw his cigar into the fire, went over to Leon and placed a hand on his shoulder. Perhaps it was meant to be a gesture of reconciliation, perhaps it was just the gesture of a lion placing a paw on his prey. Leon did not resist. He did not react at all.

Suddenly there were sounds in the corridor. Harry drew out his pistol and with one long stride got between the door and the wall. The next moment Noah ran round the corner, but then stood there in confusion, growling and not immediately sure whom to attack. Kay came after him. She was dripping wet and had the burner strapped to her back. Her right hand held the thin pipe, with a small flame licking from its mouth. Pfitzner watched out of the corner of his eye as Harry slid out from behind the door. But now Isadora entered the room too, saw Harry and screamed. Kay turned on her heel and sent a howling, metre-long tongue of flame in Harry's direction. He yelled, put his hands to his face and staggered backwards. With a strange, buzzing wail he fell to his knees. Then he twisted and fell to one side. He still had his hands pressed to his face.

Kay regulated the gas outlet and directed the flame at the floor, where it immediately ate a hole in the rug. Kay's glance flicked back and forth between Harry and Pfitzner. Pfitzner and Harry. She must not take her eyes off Pfitzner. He looked as paralysed as all the rest, and did not even react to the fact that by now Noah had decided he was the enemy and was tearing at his 2000-mark jacket and growling, but beneath his lazy lids he seemed to be waiting for something. Was there anyone else in the house? Leon sat there in his armchair. Martina's naked back was pressed to the wall beside the bookshelf, and Isadora, at whose feet the pistol had fallen, positively begging to be picked up, stood there perfectly still and stared at Harry. They all stared at Harry, stared at his blackened hands and waited for him to lower them again. Then Kay saw what had happened, and so did the others: he couldn't. The heat had forced his tie upwards, fusing it with his face and hands. A blistered piece of black and yellow plastic and a bent jetton emerged between his fingers.

'Water,' shouted Pfitzner, kicking the dog in the ribs. 'Why the hell doesn't anyone fetch water?'

With a furious and determined expression he made straight for Isadora, since she was standing in the doorway, and after all he had to get through that door in order to fetch water. Kay hesitated, for a second accepting the idea that he only wanted to help. But she hesitated no longer than that second. Then she raised Kerbel's turbo-burner again and, as Pfitzner flung himself forward, caught him on the right shoulder with the jet of flame. Pfitzner bellowed, his suit was burning, but none the less he made a dive for the ground, trying to pick up the pistol. Isadora kicked it aside. Not particularly skilfully; the pistol slid only half a metre further off, but that was enough to prevent Pfitzner from reaching it. Still howling, he rolled on the floor, tugging at his burning jacket. Kay stood beside him, stony-faced, and let out a jet of fire at a temperature of 1800 degrees. She directed it as slowly and thoroughly over his large, twitching body as if he were a chunk of wet masonry to be dried out.

What Leon chiefly remembered later was how incredibly long it took Pfitzner to die. He must have been suffering the torments of hell, and was screaming all the time as if he were being roasted on the spit. But even when he was already burning in several places he kept trying to grab Kay's legs. The blazing heat she turned on him every time beat him back, forcing him to the floor again, and finally he lost consciousness.

'No,' screeched Martina, 'no!'

Noah ran over to her, sat down beside her and scratched himself behind the ear with the sheer excitement of it all. A gurgling sound came from Leon's chair. When Pfitzner had stopped moving Kay turned the flame down. She was trembling. Her knees shook and she was gasping for air. An oily smell filled the room, a nauseating mixture of burnt hair, burnt plastic and burnt flesh. Martina was sobbing uncontrollably, and her hands seemed as firmly fixed to her face as Harry's to his. Her sobbing grew louder and louder. Kay wanted to go to her and comfort her, but she had underestimated her own need for comfort. After two steps her legs gave way beneath her, and she had to sit down and lean against the wall. The flame-thrower singed the floorboards. Isadora went to Kay, turned off the outlet of the gas bottle and helped her to get it off her back. Then she took hold of the burning rug by an intact corner and dragged it out into the garden. When she came back Leon had risen from his chair. He had picked up the pistol and was aiming it at Harry. That was exactly what Isadora herself had mentally listed as Problem Number Three: Harry. Pfitzner was dead. A child could see that. Dead as a doornail. But Harry looked almost uninjured, even if it was quite some time since he had moved. Only his hands were black, as if he had been digging about in coal dust, and a shiny, red, juicy area had burst open on his left hand. Leon was aiming at Harry's head, his arm outstretched. His lips were pressed together. Martina was weeping more and more hysterically. Isadora frowned like someone trying to concentrate on her work but disturbed by a fly. Then Leon's arm began to tremble, his face slackened again, and suddenly he sobbed and lowered the pistol. A thread of saliva ran from his chin to the collar of his sweatshirt.

Martina pushed herself away from the wall, stepped naked as she was over the bodies of Harry and Pfitzner, crossed the corridor and closed the bathroom door behind her. Isadora knelt down beside Harry and felt his pulse.

'I don't think we'll have to shoot him,' she said, standing up again. 'He probably suffocated.'

Loud and desperate sobbing came from the bathroom. Kay stood up and, with Noah, went to investigate. Martina was sitting on the side of the bathtub, trying to wash as best she could. She showed Kay the hole in the fittings where the shower hose was usually attached.

'I can't shower.'

'You can shower at our house,' said Kay.

Noah licked one of Martina's thighs.

'Is he dead?' asked Martina.

'Yes.'

'I'm glad he's dead.'

'I know,' said Kay. 'How are you? Are you reasonably all right, or do you need to see a doctor?'

'She can't see a doctor,' shouted Isadora from the living room. 'There'd be questions.'

'Oh yes, she can see a doctor,' said Leon. 'All this is your business. You two did it. You killed the pair of them. Martina has nothing to do with it. Nor do I.'

'Oh, you're still around, are you?' said Isadora.

Kay and Martina came back into the living room. Martina was wearing Leon's white dressing gown.

'Yes, I do,' she said. 'I do have something to do with it. And I wish I'd killed that bastard myself.'

Leon looked at her, and then he looked at Kay, who had killed not only Harry but Pfitzner too, just because he was going to fetch water, and then he looked at Isadora, that dreadful fat woman walking around among the disfigured corpses so casually, as if she'd done it thousands of times before. Women really were much harder than men. He'd always known it.

'Do you realise you could go to prison for this?' he asked Martina.

She didn't bother to answer him. She looked calmly at Harry and Pfitzner, lying among the furnishings of her innocuous domestic world like victims of an air disaster.

'We must get them out of here,' she said.

'Yes,' agreed Isadora. 'Help me to wrap them in something. We can't pick them up like that.'

'I'm going to take the Mercedes, drive into the village and call the police,' said Leon. 'If none of you will do it then I will.'

He still had the pistol in his hand.

'Oh no, you won't, you bastard,' said Martina.

'Is that what you're really planning to do?' asked Isadora in astonishment. 'Do you really want everyone to know you sat there in your armchair, watching your best friend rape your wife?'

'I didn't watch,' cried Leon. 'I was . . .'

'That's right,' said Kay venomously, 'it only happened in the next room.' Martina ran out.

'You make me sick! You all make me sick!' she shouted from the corridor. Leon put the pistol on the mantelpiece. No, he would not call the police. But not because he wanted to protect Kay and Isadora, or because he was afraid of Pfitzner's henchmen, simply because he no longer felt like it. Kay could cope. She'd committed murder, now let her see about getting rid of the corpses. He dragged himself back to his armchair and sat down.

After a while Martina came back. She had dressed and was wearing her houndstooth check trousers, another shirt and gumboots. She was carrying two quilts and the sheets that matched them over her arm. Her eyes were still reddened, but otherwise she seemed perfectly calm.

'We can carry them in these,' she said.

'We only need one. One sheet will do,' said Isadora.

'I want to get rid of the lot.' Martina dropped the quilts to the floor. 'And these too.' She added her jeans and the man's shirt to the pile. 'Can I sleep at your place tonight?' she asked.

'You know you can,' said Kay.

She went to fetch the wheelbarrow. Leon watched the three women wrap Pfitzner like a mummy and load him on to it. Kay pushed while Isadora and Martina walked beside the barrow, holding Pfitzner's sides so that he wouldn't slip off, turning his body to get it through the doorway. Much harder than men. Leon had always known it. The dog yapped and jumped around the wheelbarrow as if they were off for a fun outing.

Leon was left alone in the living room, alone with Harry's corpse. He had no friend left, not even a dead one. He rose, made his way to the window like a sleepwalker, and opened it. Cool, fresh air. The rain was pouring down. Ah yes, rain, just as he'd expected. He heard Kay put the wheelbarrow down and say something about a car key. They unwrapped Pfitzner again and searched his charred pockets. A thousand times harder than a man could ever be. With luck the car key would have melted.

'It's in the ignition,' called Martina from the garden gate. So they'd struck lucky yet again.

When Isadora, Kay and Martina came back with the empty wheelbarrow, Leon was still standing by the open window with his back to them. He didn't want to watch the three wet women handling Harry's body, wrapping him up and loading him on the wheelbarrow.

'Not here, though,' said Kay. 'I want people to feel sure that this car has left Priesnitz again. And there must be a driver and a passenger in it. Isadora had better sit beside me. No one will recognise us in the dark.'

'I don't look like that fat man,' said Isadora. 'Martina can sit in front. I'll lie across the back seat.'

'OK,' said Kay. 'There probably won't be anyone out and about. The main thing is for the Mercedes to be heard driving away.'

She turned to Martina.

'Are you all right to come with us? If not we'll come back on foot afterwards to fetch you. We're going to drive right through the village and then out into the marshes beyond. I know a good place. But it will be quite a long walk back to our house.'

'No,' said Martina, 'I'll come with you. I'm all right.'

She went into the kitchen and got her cheque card and the 400 marks of housekeeping money from the coffee container. Then she went into the bedroom, took a bag out of the cupboard and flung a few things into it, went on to the bathroom and collected her tubes and pots of cosmetics.

'People will see where you turned off,' said Leon, without turning round. 'People will see the tracks. The tyre tracks.'

No one answered him. The women took Harry out and loaded him in the boot with Pfitzner. Kay put the wheelbarrow back in the toolshed. When she got back Martina had already started the engine and turned the car. The headlights caught Noah drinking out of the big puddle. His eyes glowed green. Kay climbed into the passenger seat beside Martina.

'Do you want to drive?'

Martina nodded.

'What about Leon? Are we leaving him here?' asked Kay.

'Oh, him . . .' said Isadora from the back seat, opening the side door to let the dog jump in. Noah shook himself, spraying the interior of the car with water.

'I hate him' said Martina.

'But he couldn't have done anything to help you. He's ill. It was a hopeless situation. You can't hold it against him.'

'I hate him,' said Martina, stepping on the gas.

Leon was alone. He closed the window and went into his study. He took the manuscript out of the desk and the disk out of the computer, put a couple of sheets of paper on top, his notes, the rough books, the file – everything he had prepared for his great biography of the great Benno Pfitzner – and took it all over to the fireplace. He threw the whole lot into the embers. Flakes of ash rose. Slowly, very slowly, the edge of a single page caught fire. The page rolled up and flew a short way through the air. Then the first rough book caught as well. The edge of the bound manuscript turned black, began to glow and went up in flames. Leon staggered into the bedroom. Only the mattress was left on the bed. He opened the cupboard, and after some searching found a woollen blanket. Wrapping himself in it, he lay down on the bare mattress. Leon had expected to be too agitated to sleep, but he fell asleep as quickly as if he had been knocked unconscious.

A few kilometres away Kay, Martina, Isadora and Noah were standing on the edge of a large boggy patch in the marshes, watching as a rising air bubble added a full stop to the story of Harry and Pfitzner.

9

Cloudy, but very little rain. Mist may be expected from the afternoon onwards. Visibility less than ten metres. Highest daytime temperatures around 17 degrees.

When the doorbell rang Leon thought it was Kerbel coming to fetch the burner at last. The shopkeeper had not been back, hadn't even come to take Leon for his orthopaedic treatment, although he had definitely said he would. Leon was fervently hoping Kerbel would turn up. He hadn't left the house since the death of Pfitzner and Harry. The fridge was empty. There was nothing left in the larder except rice, noodles, a tin of sweetcorn, two large tins of peas and carrots, four small tins of green beans, two jars of asparagus and half a bottle of rum.

However, it was not Kerbel at the door, but a bearded man in a brown leather jacket, accompanied by a short-haired young woman with glasses in cat-like frames.

'Yes?'

With the word 'Yes' a cloud of bad breath emerged from Leon's lips. He had neither washed nor shaved since Pfitzner's death, he was wearing his dirty white towelling dressing gown, and was as pale as if he had spent the last ten years studying books about mealworms in the windowless underground vaults of a monastery.

'Breunig,' said the man in the leather jacket. His features were hidden beneath his grey beard and bushy eyebrows. 'Detective Superintendent Breunig. And this is Frau Siebert.'

The woman was small and slim, and wore a trouser suit. 'We're from the Criminal Investigation Department,' she said. 'We'd like to ask a few questions, if that's all right with you, Herr . . . ?'

Horrified, Leon stared at them through his smeared glasses. So this was it. Every day for the last three weeks he had expected the police to come and arrest him. He had almost hoped they would. But the police had not turned up. And now that he was slowly becoming accustomed to the idea of getting away with it, here they were on his doorstep.

'What was your name again?' asked Breunig politely.

'Ulbricht,' said Leon like an obedient schoolboy. 'My name is Leon Ulbricht.'

'May we come in?'

Leon reached for his belt and pulled the dressing gown more closely around him. Underneath it he wore a yellowed vest and his black jogging trousers. He was barefoot.

'Yes, come on in.'

The fear receded from his face, giving way to an expression of total resignation. He took them into the living room, where he no longer even noticed the smell. Saucepans encrusted with food stood on the floor among items of clothing, books, old newspapers, and wine bottles both empty and half empty. There was a blackened, squashed banana beside the TV set. Leon dropped into the armchair. Breunig pushed the blankets on the sofa aside and sat down too. Frau Siebert remained standing in the doorway with the corners of her mouth turned down.

'Very well,' began Breunig, opening his notepad, 'your name is Ulbricht, first name Leon, right? Age?'

'Thirty-eight.'

'Profession?'

'Writer.'

'A writer? How interesting. I've always wanted to meet a writer. What kind of thing do you write?'

'Poetry.'

'Poetry. Well, well.'

Breunig handed Leon a photograph.

'I'd like to show you something.'

Leon examined the photograph, and then looked at the superintendent in surprise.

'I'm sure you know that van,' said Breunig.

'Yes, of course. It's Herr Kerbel's. He runs the village shop here. At least, he has a van just like that. I can't say whether this is actually it. I never looked at the number plate.'

'Have you noticed the van from time to time? Have you noticed it standing outside your house on occasion?'

'Kerbel's been here quite often. He regularly delivered food for us and the house over there.' Leon waved a hand vaguely in the direction of the living room window. 'In fact I've noticed that he hasn't called recently. Has something happened to him?'

Breunig turned his pale blue eyes on Leon.

'If you're concerned about your delivery man, why not walk the few metres down to the village and ask after him?'

'You said *us*,' put in Frau Siebert. 'You don't live here alone, then?'

'My wife,' said Leon. 'I live here with my wife.'

'And where's your wife?' asked Breunig.

'With the neighbours. She's just popped over to see the neighbours.'

He didn't want to spell it out to the superintendent and his assistant that Martina had left him. Breunig took six photographs from the inside pocket of his leather jacket and fanned the pictures out on the table in front of Leon.

'Ever seen any of these girls?'

Leon picked up the top photo and looked at it. A shy and insignificant brunette, hopelessly unattractive. He shook his head and picked up the next picture.

'Are they all dead?'

'What makes you think that?' asked Breunig.

'Well, either they're dead or missing or you're running a dating agency on the side.'

Breunig smiled in a genial manner.

The second, third, fourth photographs. Leon thought: none of them worth murdering for. The fifth picture – he was sure he'd seen that girl with the long dark hair somewhere before. If he imagined her face rather more bloated . . . yes, it was probably the drowned body he had found.

Breunig noticed his reaction at once.

'Do you know that woman?'

'No,' said Leon. 'For a moment I thought I did, but I was wrong.'

'Christine Meissner. Does her name mean anything to you? Or have you perhaps seen her with Herr Kerbel, or in his van?'

Gradually, Leon was coming to realise that Breunig was not here because of Harry and Pfitzner but on account of these women, and apparently Kerbel too. Kerbel? A murderer? A pervert? Well, come to think of it, why not? Leon could not suppress a grin.

'What's so funny?' asked Frau Siebert coolly.

'Nothing,' said Leon. 'Do you really suspect our village shopkeeper of murdering these women?'

'I didn't say that.' Breunig shook his head. 'But we're following up every clue. And you say the van was often parked here?'

'Of course – delivering the stuff I'd ordered.' Leon leaned towards Breunig and switched to a confidential tone. 'Do you think a murderer can kill a person and never be caught? Just kill someone, but never be investigated or even questioned, or have to deal with any other awkward situation?'

'Of course,' said Breunig. 'The world's probably full of criminals who have never been brought to justice.'

With some surprise, he observed the way in which Leon was rubbing his hands. The man was obviously a psychopath. Leon began again.

'What do you think goes on in the mind of a murderer like that? Does he eventually forget what he did? Does he get accustomed to the idea of being a criminal? Or does it destroy him?'

'I don't know,' replied Breunig, keeping his eyes on Leon. 'People are all different. I know of one case where someone anonymously sent back money which had been embezzled twenty years later. What would you do? How would you live with it if you'd committed a crime?'

Leon's eyes widened in alarm. His voice rose shrilly. 'Why ask me?'

Frau Siebert cast Breunig a glance indicating how extremely suspicious she thought Ulbricht's conduct. It was this meaningful glance from his assistant which convinced Breunig that the man was innocent, a harmless nutcase, someone who wanted to feel important attracting suspicion to himself on purpose to get attention.

'Just routine. I was only asking a general question,' he said quietly. 'What are you getting so agitated about, Herr Ulbricht?'

'I'm not getting agitated! I'm not getting agitated at all! Not in the least!'

And as if to prove it, Leon instantly fell into a lethargic state, staring apathetically into space.

'Do you know if your neighbours are at home?' asked Frau Siebert.

Leon raised his head, in slow motion.

'My neighbours? Oh, you can't just go over there. All the rain we've had, you know – the path's not safe. You could sink in.'

Frau Siebert cast him a sharp glance.

'Have you any objection to our visiting your neighbours?'

Before Leon could reply, Breunig answered for him. 'Of course not! Herr Ulbricht simply objects to our sinking into the marshes, isn't that right?'

He rose and offered his hand. Leon automatically shook it and then sank back limply in his chair. Breunig left, followed by his furious assistant.

When Leon was alone again he picked up one of the encrusted saucepans from the floor, took it into the kitchen, and found the last tin of sweetcorn in the larder. In his relief that the superintendent had not come about Harry and Pfitzner he had quite forgotten to ask why they were after Kerbel, and whether he was in custody or just hiding away at home. Leon found the tin-opener in the sink, where a stack of used plates had been soaking for days. Sighing, he opened the tin of sweetcorn and tipped its contents into the dirty pan, put it on the stove and stirred it with the handle of a knife. He did not wait for the sweetcorn to be heated through, but took his meal off the stove before it was hot and carried it into the living room. He sat down in the armchair and placed the saucepan on his lap, on the fabric of the towelling dressing gown. No sooner had he sat down than his back hurt again. When I get back to Hamburg I'll try acupuncture, thought Leon. He liked to indulge in such daydreams – what it would be like when he was perfectly well again and Martina had come back to him. Leon found the spoon he had left among the cushions of the armchair and shovelled a few lukewarm yellow grains into his mouth. He picked up the remote control from the coffee table and pressed various buttons with his thumbnail. The batteries were running low. The TV set would come on only if he pressed the buttons at a certain angle. In the days just after the deaths of Harry and Pfitzner he had kept the television on twenty-four hours a day, constantly channel-hopping. He had to know what was going on in the outside world. Had a search for Pfitzner been mounted? Was he at least reported missing? Were his friends on their way to avenge him? There were no news stories on the subject. No one had noticed the disappearance of a brothel owner who in his previous career as a boxer didn't even make it to a World Championship fight. And his friends, if he had any, hadn't turned up either. No criminals or pimps. And no police until today. Leon's publisher had written twice asking about further chapters of the book about Pfitzner. It was probably Kay who had pushed the letters under the door. Leon had written back to his publisher saying that the book was never going to materialise. Insuperable differences of opinion. But of course he had not been able to bring himself to take the letter down to the village. He didn't even want to read these days. Reading was work. And he didn't have to work any more. No one could force him to write, to wash or to tidy up. OK, he was a failure. He was nothing, he was a mess – but he was free. Free and above suspicion. The police were looking for Kerbel, not him.

A dog barked in the garden. Noah! It could only mean that Martina had come back. She couldn't have picked a better moment. Now that Leon finally had the police off his back they'd begin all over again. He would insist on their moving back to Hamburg. Or no, not Hamburg! He didn't fancy meeting any of Pfitzner's acquaintances and having to face awkward questions. But they could move to Berlin, or Cologne. Sometimes a radical life change is necessary. And unless he was mistaken, Martina still had some money. Or she could ask her father for money. And Leon would go on a diet and start jogging or take up squash. Once his back pain was gone he'd exercise every day. And Martina would cook special diet dishes for him.

Leon went to the door of the house and opened it. Noah came in, sniffed Leon's leg in passing and pushed his way into the living room.

'Martina?'

Leon went out on the veranda and looked to the right and left round the corners. She wasn't there.

'Martina!'

No answer. He went out into the garden in his bare feet. The mist had risen from the marshes and was already surrounding the fence. Leon shivered and pulled his towelling dressing gown more closely around him, wiping the sole of his right foot dry on the instep of his left.

'Martina! . . . Martina! . . . Martina!'

His cries became more and more desperate. He put his head back and howled at the sky. He howled like a coyote with a foot caught in a trap.

'Mar-tii-naaaa!!!!'

If she didn't come back to him he couldn't leave this place. He narrowed his eyes and tried to make out the outline of the Schlei villa. But the mist was already too thick. She was over there with Kay and Isadora, having a nice time. The state he was in didn't bother her.

They were all three avoiding him, those bloody women. As if he were a leper. Dressing gown flapping, Leon went back into the house. Noah was still in the living room, sniffing and licking the crockery on the floor. He finally found the saucepan of sweetcorn and began eating it. When Leon, panting, appeared in the doorway he put his tail between his legs and tried to run off. Leon grabbed his collar.

'Good dog,' he said ingratiatingly, pulled the belt of the dressing gown out of its loops and tied it to the dog's collar. Keeping Noah on this towelling leash, he put on his socks and gumboots. The boots were tight. He hadn't known that when you gained weight your shoe size might change too. Leon hobbled out on the veranda, let the dog go over the plank first and flicked the belt encouragingly at his back. Noah snapped at it and began to skip about, growling with pleasure and trying to wrench the belt out of Leon's hand.

'Off you go! Go on! Seek!'

If the dog had guided Martina through the marshes safe and sound, then he could lead Leon to the Schlei house too.

Noah trotted a few steps straight ahead, in entirely the wrong direction. Leon pulled the leash taut. With difficulty, he got down on his knees beside the dog, raised Noah's front legs and turned him through an angle of 180 degrees. His back had improved. He could already lift a fat dog. Not much longer and he'd be completely better.

'Go on, seek!'

The mist billowed towards them like spilt porridge, and Noah plunged right into it. He undoubtedly knew his way; the question was, which way was it? He didn't always go straight ahead. He splashed through most of the puddles, but would suddenly take the long way round some of them. Leon tugged the improvised leash twice more and corrected Noah's course, but then he no longer knew where he was. Whatever way they turned, the thick mist was waiting for them, making everything look blurred and milky. Leon wished he had put on something warmer than the flapping dressing gown, his vest and his jogging trousers, but they were the only garments which still fitted him. A small animal shot in front of his gumboots and swiftly disappeared in the tall and already yellowing grass. There were sounds of crawling and rustling in the branches too. Branches! They must have reached the drowned wood. Leon held Noah back again and went closer to a thin tree trunk. It was black and felt soapy. So they were on the right track. But Noah tried to bypass the wood. There was a short struggle between them, from which the white dressing gown suffered most. Then Leon managed to steer Noah into the little wood. Duckweed was floating on the swampy water, strands of it coming to the surface and running into Leon's gumboots, drenching his socks and making his chafed heels even more uncomfortable. But finally, veiled in the omnipresent mist, Isadora's villa stood before them. Leon untied the dog. Not without difficulty: the belt was now wet and dirty, and Noah had tugged hard. Leon pulled his dressing gown together, threaded the belt through its loops and tied it in front. He looked round for the dog. Noah had made off, dissolving in the swathes of mist. Obstinate animal. Leon wiped his hands on the dressing gown and pushed the hair back from his forehead. His hair was too long as well. The first thing Martina must do was cut it for him. He felt for a bell and found none. Then he saw a lion's head with a ring in its mouth, and knocked twice. It was Kay who opened the door.

'I want to see Martina,' said Leon, pushing Kay aside and marching into the house. 'Martina? . . . Martina?'

He pushed a door open. The kitchen. Old-fashioned cupboards with flowered curtains behind the glass-fronted doors, an old gas stove, high-backed wooden chairs, squat pots, huge pans hanging on the wall. Isadora was standing in the middle of the kitchen at a large table. She wore a white apron and was using a ladle to scoop batter out of a pale blue plastic mixing bowl and into a waffle iron. She closed the iron, and batter overflowed the sides and dripped on to the already filthy table.

'Where's Martina?' Leon bellowed at her.

'Hi, Leon,' said Isadora. 'You're looking good. Nice and fat. Want to try one?'

She pointed to a plate of cooked waffles.

'Where's Martina?' asked Leon, more calmly this time. The fragrance of the waffles rose to his nostrils. For days he had eaten nothing but noodles, rice and canned vegetables.

'Oh, what a pity,' said Isadora. 'She left the day before yesterday on the afternoon train from Freyenow. When we passed your house I did ask whether she wanted to say goodbye to you. But she said no, not in any circumstances. She said to tell you that you can keep the furniture and everything.'

Leon felt dizzy. He had to sit down on one of the kitchen chairs. Martina gone! His last chance.

'When will she be back?'

'She didn't say that she was coming back at all.'

'Why did she go? Where is she?'

'Well, first she was going to someone she knows. I don't know who. Someone from the television. As for why – you'll have to ask Kay that.'

Isadora pointed to her sister, who had just come into the kitchen.

'Leave me alone,' said Kay, putting her hands in her trouser pockets. Isadora opened the waffle iron, took the waffle out and put it on a spare plate, sprinkled it with icing sugar and pushed it over to Leon. Leon rolled the waffle up like a cone and put it into his mouth. It tasted delicious. Isadora moved the plate with the rest of the waffles in his direction.

'Why did she go?' he asked with his cheeks full. He rolled two more waffles up at the same time and stuffed them in his mouth too.

'What a revolting sight you are, pigging out like that,' said Kay. She turned and left the kitchen, and started noisily tidying up the hall.

'They quarrelled,' said Isadora. 'Over Noah.' She sat down beside Leon and placed her hand on his leg. He let her.

'Over Noah?'

'Yes. Noah was missing all week. He's started wandering about on his own again. Martina took it personally. And I suppose Kay had false hopes.'

Leon rolled up a fourth and fifth waffle, dipped the ends in the icing sugar and bit into them. It was warm in the kitchen. Cosy. Even the water in his gumboots was warming up. Isadora's hand slowly kneaded his thigh.

'What happened?'

'Martina began crying and said nobody loved her, not

even the dog. And Kay said, "I do. I love you." And Martina sobbed, "I couldn't care less." And then Kay shouted, "Great! Now at least I know where I stand!" Very sad, the whole thing. Everyone's so irritable at the moment.'

Isadora let go of Leon's leg and filled the waffle iron with batter again.

'Aha!' said Leon with malicious satisfaction, and stuffed his sixth waffle into his mouth. He already felt sick. None the less, he couldn't stop eating. For a moment they were silent. Isadora ran water into the empty plastic bowl, and Leon went on munching quietly.

'Who took her to the station? Kerbel?' he asked, when he had swallowed.

'Oh,' said Isadora, 'didn't you know? Guido's in police custody. On remand.'

'Yes, of course I know. What's he done?'

Kay came in again. It was clear that she had been listening the whole time.

'Kerbel had a dress in his car,' she said. 'It belonged to a missing girl. They found it in his van at a traffic checkpoint. He tried to stuff it under the seat, and acted so stupidly he attracted the police's attention.'

'Kerbel doesn't have the guts to kill anyone,' said Leon.

'Of course it wasn't him,' said Isadora.

'I'm not so sure,' said Kay. 'Even the biggest coward has to feel superior to someone.'

Leon jumped up. The plate fell to the floor, but did not break.

'Do you mean me? If you mean me you'd better say so straight out!'

'Why are you all so edgy?' said Isadora. 'None of us seriously thinks Guido would do it. And so far there isn't even a body – or at least, not of the girl the dress belongs to. Let's hope the police don't get the idea of poking about in the marshes here.'

She grinned cheerfully, but then suddenly cried, 'Oh no, oh no, oh no!,' and now Kay and Leon smelled the burnt batter too. Isadora pulled the plug of the smoking waffle iron out of the wall, opened a window and threw it out into the garden.

'You slut!' cried Kay. 'You know I hate clearing up after you. Leave the garden alone!'

'But it stinks!' shouted Isadora back. 'We sleep in the house, not in the garden. Would you rather sleep in this stink? If so, go and fetch it in again!'

'Fetch it yourself!' snapped Kay.

Leon went slowly out of the kitchen, opened the front door and stepped outside. The waffle iron lay a few metres from the door. The sisters were still shouting at each other with unabated vehemence on the other side of the open kitchen window. Leon belched quietly. The mist was thicker than ever. Only the pollarded treetops and a few long branches emerged from the vapour which had spread over the dead and swampy wood. Leon closed the door behind him and went out into the garden. Scraps of vapour crept towards him, winding round his feet. He wanted to go home. At once. If he went very slowly and carefully he could manage on his own. After all, he had found his way here alone. Leon stopped at the end of the garden and tipped the water out of his gumboots. He listened in case Kay might be coming after him to guide him home, but he heard only the distant tapping of a woodpecker. Then he set off.

The mist enveloped him. It caught in his dressing gown and formed droplets in the towelling. Leon was shivering. Air even colder than before seemed to be descending on him from the branches. He smelled something rotting which he hadn't noticed on the way. It must come from the duckweed already slipping into his boots again. It was quiet, extremely quiet. Even the woodpecker had knocked off work. No sound but the cracking of the twigs which Leon snapped as he clambered over the tree trunks, and now and then the splashing of some small, invisible creature. Leon couldn't see more than four or five metres ahead of him. His dressing gown became heavier and heavier. The moisture penetrated his vest and jogging trousers. It took over every particle of his skin, until he felt utterly cold, wet, stiff and helpless. It seemed as if he hadn't been properly dry for months. He tensed his muscles because he felt so cold, and his back was giving him warning again. Not just his back: his ankles hurt too, and so did his right knee. Not to mention the chafed heels. Grimly, however, he put one foot in front of the other. The tree trunks seemed to become darker and stouter, and the wood struck him as much larger than he remembered it. He didn't know where all these trees had suddenly come from. Even if he'd been crawling on all fours he ought to be on the other side of the wood by now. Leon undid the heavy, wet dressing gown which was now only sucking the warmth from his body, and placed it on a reasonably dry hummock of moss. Without its weight he walked faster. The waffles were churning about in his stomach. The duckweed pond became shallower, and Leon reached soft but reasonably firm ground with countless little streams running through it. He didn't remember those little streams, but after all he had been struggling with a refractory dog on the way. Finally the trees came to an end. Leon emerged from the wood and almost fell into a large ditch. Now he knew he had never been here before. He had lost his way. The best thing would probably be to turn round and retrace his steps. But the idea of going through the eerie wood again did not particularly appeal to him, so he decided to go round the edge, skirting it until he had at least found Isadora's garden. With a little effort you could also make out a kind of damp marshy path going round the wood on the left. He was running now, he began to sweat, forgot about the dangerous places where the ground might swallow you up, thought only of making progress as fast as possible. It would soon be dark, and then he'd be done for. His back hurt. Dear God, did his back hurt! And his knees and his ankles. They were sure to be swollen. He had to sit down for a moment on a stone. But no sooner was he sitting than he began to freeze. Leon picked some of the blue-bloomed, red-fleshed berries growing at his feet, crushed them in his fingers, sniffed them, and threw them away for safety's sake. He was shaking with cold and exhaustion, his teeth were chattering, and his breathing was wheezy and spasmodic. For several seconds he gave himself up to the vision of a comforting bath: a big tiled bathroom with a powerful shower head from which hectolitres of hot, crystal-clear water sprayed at high pressure. He forced himself to get up again, ignored the fact that his body was crying out for peace and a rest, and hobbled on. After only a few steps he stumbled over a root and fell on damp moss. He lay there in resigned despair. His pulse throbbed in his throat and rushed in his ears. He felt as if he himself were now becoming one of these squashy, worm-eaten tree stumps everywhere around the place, so soft that they didn't even make a sound as they broke up. In front of his face he saw a branching blade of grass on which dewdrops had gathered, gleaming like a chandelier even in this diffuse light. A large spider's web full of water drops hung, quivering slightly, between a bush and the tree root which had brought him down. And Leon's fall had alarmed something else too. First he heard a soft rustling by his right ear, then something touched his cheekbones, climbed higher and higher, and glided, cool and scaly, over his face. Leon froze in icy horror. A snake, a poisonous snake! Whatever he did he mustn't move, or it would sink its long poison fangs into his face. The snake crawled over his mouth and chin, down his throat, and back to the ground again. The sensation was like having the blunt back of a knife drawn across his throat. Leon jumped up, screaming with disgust, and spat several times. He could just see the grey and black reptile disappearing among the grasses. He staggered on. There – there was another snake. It was dead, hanging draped over a branch right in front of his nose. He must have disturbed a bird eating its dinner. This snake too had a grey back and a lighter belly, and a lemon-yellow, crescent-shaped patch each side of the back of its head. The place seemed to be swarming with poisonous adders and vipers, amphibians lying in wait, slumbering newts. Twilight had already set in. He now walked further away from the edge of the wood, fearing a snake might fall from a tree and land on the back of his neck. Whenever something moved in the grass it made him jump. There were creeping, rustling, sliding, gliding sounds every-where. The path became wetter again. For some time there had been a monotonous belt of reeds of melancholy appear-ance on Leon's right, higher than a man, which sighed and rustled mysteriously. Suddenly Leon's childhood fear of the dark, overcome long ago, returned. Once, he startled a very large bird, which flew up with wings flapping. There was another of those strange sounds from the reeds. It was like something clearing its throat – in fact rather like a gigantic duck clearing its throat.

'Hello?' called Leon, trembling. 'Is there anyone there?'

He was a modern man who had passed his school-leaving exams, and even if he had not acquitted himself very gloriously in the natural sciences, he was familiar with their basic principles. But when the giant duck cleared its throat again he ran in panic, without even looking round. His feet splashed into cold puddles, mud spurted up to his left and right, branches whipped into his face and broke one lens of his glasses. Leon ignored it, he ran on, on and on, ran out of the wood and crossed a broad expanse of brown and hostile-looking grass. Amphibian creatures proclaimed their unchristian gospels to him from all sides. He reached another marshy wood full of dead trees. Here the mist was only a thin veil hanging in the branches. Breathing heavily, Leon clung to a slippery tree trunk. Twigs cracked. He whipped round and stared in the direction from which the cracking sound came. There was something approaching. Something large. A human being or a heavy animal. Leon felt the hairs rise on the nape of his neck. Then he saw the animal. It was Noah. He was trotting past a line of trees only ten metres away. He must have changed his mind and had come back to look for his master. Leon sobbed with delight.

'Noah!' he shouted. 'Noah, here.'

The dog turned his head, but trotted on as fast as ever.

'Good Noah! Come here. Come here, good boy, Noah,' begged Leon, crouching down and putting out his hand. The dog disappeared behind a bush. Leon jumped up and ran after him, but had to abandon the pursuit at once. He was worn out, with no reserves of strength left.

'Noah! Noah, come back!'

Far away, he heard a cracking sound again.

'Noaaaah!'

His voice echoed through the wood, and then everything was still once more. Half unconscious, Leon staggered on. How dark it was already! He felt like simply dropping to the ground and closing his eyes. But then, a little way off, he spotted a pile of something with a curiously white gleam, and forced himself to approach it. It was his dirty old dressing gown, lying in the moss beside a toadstool. Just beyond it he saw a shallow pond, its surface covered with streaks of green. Leon summoned up hope for the last time. Isadora's house was not too far from this spot. He put on the wet, heavy towelling dressing gown again, tied the belt in front, and turned in what he thought the most likely direction. Once again he waded through the duckweed pond, slipped on slimy roots and clambered over mossy tree trunks. He was shivering and freezing. His feet were frozen lumps. His heels felt as if he had worn right through them to the bone. But at last, when he was abandoning hope of ever getting anywhere again in this life, he made it out of the wood, and when the mists parted for a moment he saw his house, his own house, not too far away.

An hour later Leon was sitting in his armchair, sipping hot rum from a mug. He had stripped naked and wrapped himself in a blanket. The jogging trousers, vest and dressing gown were hanging in front of the fire to dry. Leon felt the warm drink spreading through his body, relieving his poor knees, relaxing the veins in his feet. He sneezed.

Glancing out of the window, he looked into the dark and listened to the rain beginning to fall. He started to weep.

10

A depression with violent storms is building over the Atlantic, and will move over northern Germany during the night. Showers and in some places thundery rain. Winds will reach speeds of up to 120 kph. The rain will slacken during the day. Skies clear to cloudy. Temperatures of around 9 degrees.

The autumn turned out no better than the summer. A rainy September gave way to a cold, wet, windy October and then a stormy November. Any leaves that had not already rotted fell from the trees in Leon's garden. No one swept them up. They lay like a blanket over the grass and the flower beds. Gusty rain tore at the remaining foliage which hung limp and black from the branches, too heavy to blow away. It was a cold, useless rain, quenching no one's thirst, filling the roof gutters, running down the windows and flooding all the holes Leon had dug in his garden. The house creaked and groaned more often and louder now. Leon had given up any hope that his situation might change; he no longer even wanted to leave the place. A stubbly beard had grown on his chin and cheeks. There was nothing he wanted to do. The easiest of all the things he didn't want to do was watching television, so he sat in his armchair with the set on all day. Only occasionally did he get up from the chair, shuffle off to the kitchen in his slippers, ignoring the dripping tap, and look to see if he could find anything to eat that wasn't rice. He had eaten nothing but rice for weeks. Rice, rice and yet more rice. Kerbel had given it to him as a present when he drove up to say goodbye. Kerbel was innocent. Of course he was innocent. The girl whose dress had been found in Kerbel's van had turned up when some divers were doing work on a weir. Although the body was badly decomposed, marks of some kind or other on it showed that Kerbel could not be responsible.

All the same, he wanted to leave Priesnitz.

'There's nothing to be got out of this place,' he had said. 'Deciding to run the shop in a dump like this was a bad idea. I'm leaving.'

He had not said how the dress got into his van, nor did he say where he was going. His farewell gift to Leon was a box of provisions plus six kilos of rice. The box was soon empty. Leon boiled the rice and then fried it in oil. He tipped a little flour and sugar into it and made the mixture into a kind of cake, which he ate alternately with or without seasoning. And although he did not enjoy it, he watched his stock of rice dwindling with concern. His life in front of the TV was no fun, but it was peaceful. He kept the fire burning, he did not write, he did not read, he did not think. He simply existed, and was glad not to have to talk to anyone.

So it was a shock when he heard the car coming. Voices outside his house. Were they never going to leave him in peace? Hadn't he suffered enough? Surely at some point the time must come when misfortune tired of striking the same victim down over and over again. Leon crept to the door of the house and opened it a crack. The police! Two green and white cross-country vehicles with barred windows had drawn up outside the gate. Breunig, his female assistant and a young policeman with a moustache got out of the first vehicle. Two more uniformed officers and a man in a jogging suit emerged from the second. The man in the jogging suit opened the back of the second vehicle, and out jumped Noah, shaking himself. The man put him on a leash and led him into Leon's garden, where a film crew was already crowded together under an umbrella, passing a thermos flask from hand to hand. The TV station's logo, a large orange 'V', was prominently displayed on the umbrella and the thermos flask. Suddenly Kay and Isadora were standing at the gate too. Leon was enormously relieved to see them. He went over to them.

'What's going on?' he whispered.

'They're going to dig him up,' Kay whispered conspiratorially back.

Breunig's assistant pointed to the far end of the garden, and the entire company – the police officers, the film team, the photographers and a group of curious onlookers who had now turned up too – marched past Leon to the point she had indicated, led there by the dog. No one spoke to Leon or took any notice of him. Even Breunig acted as if he had never seen him before. At the end of the garden the cameraman focused his lens on the dog handler, and the woman in the blue anorak held a microphone out to him.

'Can you tell us to what depth Noah can scent something?'

The camera zoomed in on Noah's head with its single ear.

'About two metres deep, depending how strong the smell of the ground-water itself is. His sense of smell is ten thousand times better than a human being's.'

'And what has he found so far?'

'Sorry, but we have to start now. The rain's just stopping, and the dog will be able to pick up scents better then.'

The cameraman followed Noah, filming as he wandered through the garden. The dog looked aimless; apparently he hadn't even found a trail. Leon watched him anxiously. Superintendent Breunig came up behind him and put a hand on his shoulder.

'Don't worry,' he said. 'That's an old dog. He's lost his sense of smell.'

'But Kerbel is innocent,' cried Leon. 'What are all these people doing in my garden? What do they want?'

'The truth,' said Breunig. 'The truth will always come to light.'

Leon felt like running away. He wanted to go into the house and hide, but when he turned round there were so many people behind him that it looked impossible to get past them.

'It wasn't me,' he cried. 'It was those bloody women! There's no one buried in my garden.'

Nobody took any notice of him except Kay, who put her mouth to his ear and whispered, 'Yes, there is. We buried Harry outside the house, and you didn't even notice. He's been there in your garden all this time.'

At that moment a general murmur arose. Noah had picked up a scent. Leon caught it too: a penetrating, sharp smell, like Maggi seasoning. The dog barked. He seemed more surprised and touched than anyone to find that he still had his faculties as a tracker dog. Two policemen fetched spades and drove them into the ground. The TV team directed its light and camera on to the spot where they were digging. Before long something white came into view. Everyone moved forward, and Leon was pushed to the edge of the pit. More and more people had gathered in the garden. Leon saw the youth from the filling station in his Heavy Metal T-shirt; behind Isadora's ample hips he saw Dr Pollack; and over there beside the toolshed stood Kerbel. Kerbel did not want to be seen, and signalled to Leon not to give him away.

'The body,' cried the youth from the filling station. 'There's the body.'

'That's not a body,' shouted Dr Pollack indignantly. 'A body doesn't look like that. It moves more! A body would move much more.'

The white thing was not an item of clothing or a pale arm. It was paper.

'Stasi files!' whispered the cameraman enthusiastically. The police officers hauled the stack of papers out. Leon wanted to make a break for it again, but the inquisitive and ever-growing crowd kept him back.

'Stasi files, you fucking bastard!' bellowed a voice behind him. It was the voice of Martina's father, and when Leon turned round there he was. 'I always knew it,' shouted Martina's father. Two little boys in bright red raincoats began throwing mud at Leon.

'Those aren't Stasi files,' called Breunig's woman assistant, 'they're newspapers. It's the *Echo*.'

And now Leon remembered: the *Echo* was a free local paper consisting largely of ads and distributed to all households. He was supposed to be delivering it – for three pfennigs a paper – but being no fool he had pocketed the money and simply buried the two bundles of newspapers.

'Leon,' cried his mother, 'Leon, why did you do it?'

She was standing opposite him on the other side of the hole in the ground. Leon was not at all surprised to see her there. She looked good, his mother did. So young. But she was crying.

'I'm going to thrash you to within an inch of your life,' shouted Leon's father. He was dead, and he was as large and terrible as Leon remembered him. Then he turned into Pfitzner.

'A week,' roared Pfitzner. 'You have a week to deliver those newspapers or I'll thrash you to within an inch of your life.'

And then it was his father again. Leon found a gap between all the onlookers. He could see Martina through the gap. She was standing on the veranda, waving to him. He wanted to go to her, began to run, but then his mother grabbed his leg and called, 'I've got him, Paul, I'm holding on to him. Go on, hit him!'

Leon couldn't breathe; her weight was constricting his lungs. With a loud snort, he woke up.

He found himself back in his bathroom. The ceiling light was on. He was lying in cold, dirty, brown water in the tub and freezing. A storm was raging outside. The wind howled, shaking the house, and rain pattered down on the roof as if someone were flinging small pebbles at it. The branches of the pear tree drummed against the bathroom window with a bony sound. Leon remembered running a hot bath the previous evening to relieve the persistent pain, which had moved from his backbone to his legs. Yet again the water had run brown, but his ambition had not been to get clean. He must have fallen asleep. The bath foam had dispersed long ago, leaving a second tidemark on the enamel above the existing ring of dirt. There was not much water in the tub. Leon himself took up most of the room, his body swollen and wrinkled from lying in the water for hours, and fitting the shape of the tub like dough. That was one of the few advantages of being fat – you didn't need much bathwater. Groaning, Leon leaned forward, fishing for the chain with the plug on the end of it. His fingers felt something spongy and disgustingly wobbly. He let go of it in alarm, but then realised that what he had felt was part of his own body, and he went on groping until he found the row of small silvery beads which made up the chain, and could pull it out. Most of the water ran away. All that kept back the rest of it was the fat around Leon's hips. He put the plug back and turned the tap on, letting more hot water run in, until it was pleasantly snug around him.

What's happened to me? he wondered, leaning back and bracing the wrinkled soles of his feet against the side of the tub. I'm a mess, an ugly fat mess.

He looked at the two islands of his drooping breasts, with a brown nipple instead of a palm tree in the middle of each.

Disgusting, he thought, and then: at least there isn't any milk coming out of them.

His prick rose. His prick was still big, even when he compared it to the size of his fat body. He groped for it with his swollen hands and tried to think about sex. The average German male thought about sex eighteen times a day. When did he last think about it? Two weeks ago? He couldn't remember.

A flash of lightning lit up the window, and at the same moment there was a roll of thunder and the bathroom light went out. Leon lay in the tub, listening in the darkness. The eternal rain had stopped; at last the wind was holding its breath. In the midst of this silence, the house made a strange, grating sound, like a blocked machine, a crushing mill into which someone had got his arm or foot. Next moment there was a dull wailing sound, and Leon heard something crackling beneath the wallpaper beside him, although he could see nothing in the dark. When he touched the place he felt a jagged crack as thick as a finger, which stretched higher up than his arm could follow. There was loud crashing outside. A couple of tiles slid off the roof and broke into pieces. Another grating sound, louder this time. Then the house seemed to sway, a wall fell somewhere, the ground trembled, and suddenly the water in the bathtub was on a slant and running over the rim. Leon felt for the tap and turned it on. Surprisingly, it still worked perfectly well. Leon let a little more swampy hot water flow in, and then leaned back and went to sleep again.

Outside, the storm began again, sweeping over Priesnitz. Branches broke, trees fell over. The bicycle stand outside Kerbel's abandoned shop sailed along the street, clattering. The foaming stream burst its banks, flooded the gardens and washed paving stones out of the ground. The satellite dish was blown off Leon's house, driven through the grass by the wind, and caught on the fence. But all the clattering, howling and moaning around him, all the pattering and crashing could not rouse Leon again from his sleep, this time a deep and dreamless one.

On the morning after the storm Kay set out for the village to see how much damage had been done. She and Isadora had got off comparatively lightly. They would merely have to replace a few pantiles. The wind had dropped. Now and then the sun even shone through a break in the clouds. Fallen branches lay everywhere. As Kay approached Leon's house she automatically walked faster. She did not want to meet Leon. Not that there was much danger of that. Over the last five weeks he hadn't shown himself once when she passed his house. Kay always looked up at the chimney. As long as there was smoke from the fireplace he must still be alive. What was he doing there all by himself day and night? Probably wallowing in his sorrows. Or writing the Great German Novel.

But this time, when she glanced up at the chimney out of habit, there was no chimney left, and the dark patch on the roof was not just a patch but a hole. So the house had indeed subsided. As she had predicted it would. And Leon might have been hit by the ruins. Kay began to run. Even as she was climbing the back fence of the garden, she called his name. Leon did not answer. Kay ran past the kitchen window and the fallen pear tree to the door. But the planks of the wooden porch were at such an angle that she dared not go any further.

'Leon! Leon, are you in there?'

When she turned the corner and reached the other side of the house, she saw the full extent of the damage. The house had actually broken in two, and the window on this side was buried. But Kay had only to stand on tiptoe to look into the living room through the half-metre-wide crack in the upper part of the outside wall. The formless mass that was Leon sat in the armchair in a dark grey towelling dressing gown, holding his fat bare feet out to the smoke which was issuing from the half-submerged fireplace, spreading over the floor, and then rising up to the crack in the wall through which Kay was looking. The bookshelves had fallen over. Leon had left everything lying where it was.

'Leon,' called Kay, hooking her large hands round two projecting bricks, 'are you all right? Everything OK?'

Leon did not move so much as his little finger.

'Leon,' called Kay again, 'you have to climb out this way, where I am. You can't get through at the front. It's much too dangerous. Come on!'

He did not react.

'Oh, very well,' said Kay, 'stay where you are! Don't move from the spot, right? The house could fall in any moment. I'm coming in to get you.'

He followed her instructions to the letter, and did not budge. Kay hauled herself up to the crack and tumbled into the room in an avalanche of stones and mortar. For a moment she sat there, listening, in case any more masonry was about to follow. When nothing happened she got up and went over to Leon. He turned his head towards her and smiled. One of the lenses had fallen out of his glasses, and his eyes were as dull as hardboiled eggs.

'Kay, how nice. Sit down with me and get warm by the fire.'

There were dirty plates and dishes all over the floor. Leon picked up the saucepan at his feet, which was half full of a grainy mass of something covered with green mould. Woodlice scurried out from under the pan.

'Help yourself, there's plenty. Rice. Delicious. Nice nutty flavour.'

Kay looked more closely at Leon, wondering if something had hit him on the head, but she could see no injuries.

'Great outfit,' she said, glancing at his dirty dressing gown. Leon dreamily stroked its sleeves. Smoke billowed more thickly from the fireplace. Kay saw that Leon must have started burning the furniture as fuel some time ago. A table leg and the back of a kitchen chair stuck out of the ashes. Apart from the ruined masonry and overturned bookshelves, the living room was strikingly empty. Mould and a white coat of fungus were spreading over the walls. Kay grasped Leon's shoulder.

'Get up! What the hell do you think you're doing sitting about here?'

'Thinking about death,' said Leon, staring through the broken ceiling and the hole in the roof of the house, and up to the sky. A sunbeam fell on his bald forehead. 'Do you think there's life after death? Or does it all end in emptiness and nothing?'

'A very original question,' said Kay. 'Anyone can see straight off you're a writer. OK, let's get moving!'

'But if death isn't the end of everything, and we do go somewhere or other, that means that Martina's father and Guido Kerbel and that lad from the filling station, you know who I mean, the one with the Heavy Metal T-shirt and that awful haircut – well, it means they'll all be there too. And what sense is there in someone like that Heavy Metal character still surviving after death? I mean, I ask you!'

Kay took his hand and pulled gently at it.

'No,' said Leon, 'I don't want to be mixing with Martina's father for all eternity. I want my peace. I want to get off the eternal cycle of reincarnation.'

'Are you drunk?' asked Kay, sniffing his breath and pulling harder. Leon's hand was warm and soft and limp. 'Come on! You're going to stand up now, and then we'll get out of here!'

Leon bit his lower lip and obstinately shook his head. His dressing gown fell open beneath its carelessly tied belt. He was wearing nothing underneath it, and his hugely fat belly and other unedifying details of his anatomy were visible. Kay took hold of the two flaps of the dressing gown and over-lapped them.

'For God's sweet sake, pull yourself together! Are you a man or aren't you?'

Leon looked up at her as if he had to consider this question seriously.

'No, I don't think I am,' he said.

'So what's that?' Kay opened his dressing gown again and pointed to Leon's penis lying limply on the armchair.

'A slug,' said Leon, 'I think it's a slug. Must have crawled under my dressing gown. Take it away, please.'

Plaster trickled from the ceiling. Kay tried to haul Leon to his feet, but he evaded her grasp and threw himself on the floor, where he rolled into a ball and pulled his knees up under his chin.

'Leave me here. I can't.'

Even more plaster trickled from the ceiling. Kay looked around her, and thought. She'd never get Leon through the hole in the wall. He might not even get through the kitchen window. So they'd have to use the front door, and move fast. She knelt down beside him, pulled the belt of the dressing gown out of its loops and tied it round his neck. She held on to the other end. Taking the wooden leg, which had once probably belonged to the coffee table, out of the hearth, she blew on its faintly glimmering end until it glowed red.

'Come on,' she said. 'You think I want to get buried here on your account?'

Leon only clasped his knees more tightly. Kay flicked up the dressing gown over his buttocks and held the glowing wood to the hairy, white flesh. Yelling, Leon jumped to his feet. The belt stretched taut. Leon gasped and tried to get a hand under the belt round his neck. Kay tugged at the leash and pulled him out into the corridor behind her, like an animal.

'Why did you do that?' whimpered Leon. When Kay opened the door of the house he stopped again.

'No, no, no,' he whined, clutching the door handle. Kay pulled on the belt. Leon stumbled forward and out on to the veranda, which was making alarming creaking noises. Two shingles fell.

'Come on, run!' shouted Kay.

'No,' cried Leon, clutching a plank. The plank gave way and the porch fell in. Kay and Leon staggered into the garden through a cloud of dust and rubble. Kay sat down on the lawn and held her head. Leon had lost his dressing gown and his glasses. Stark naked apart from the towelling belt hanging round his neck like an over-long tie, smeared with grey dirt and scratched all over, he simply ran straight to the end of his garden, scrambled nimbly over the fence, for all his obesity, and ran on, on and on, straight into the marshes. Kay was going to stop him, but when she rose to her feet she felt dizzy and had to sit down again.

Martina was on the way to her parents' house. The make-up artist whose place she had been using had come back from filming in Spain at the beginning of November, and suddenly found it inconvenient to sublet her flat. In short, the summer was over, colder weather was beginning to set in, and she wanted Martina out. At once. After all, Martina could live with her parents. The make-up artist had to think of herself too.

'Want to come back, do you?' Martina's father had said on the phone. 'You're lucky it's all so easy, aren't you? First you chuck in the job I got you, now you come back with nothing, and I can pay again, is that so? But of course your stupid old Dad has no idea of literature. Can't see what great talent the bloke has. I hope you had fun at least.'

In the suburban train a man in a business suit sat down opposite her and kept looking at her over the top of his newspaper. Obviously wearing wide cord trousers, stout boots and two baggy pullovers wasn't enough to deter such glances. The man opposite rustled his newspaper, and when she looked up smiled at her and said, 'What a bad year it's been. A bad summer. Nothing but rain.'

'Yes, a bad summer,' replied Martina. There was no one at the station to meet her. Her mother didn't come because she had to bake an apple cake for the bring-and-buy sale organised by Pastor Spangenberg in aid of a family of Kurds. Her father had not considered it necessary to think up any excuse.

Martina took a taxi. During the journey the taxi driver embarked on a conversation conducted almost entirely with himself, bewailing the poor state of business.

'You don't have much luggage, do you?' he concluded. 'Got everything you need? If not you can buy the essentials from me.'

He opened his glove compartment. It was unusually large, and crammed full of toothbrushes, toothpaste, boxes of tampons, mini-soaps, packets of condoms, chocolate bars, batteries, biros, sticking plasters, aspirins, cigarettes and matches, and a bottle of shampoo.

'I can sell you tickets for musicals too,' he said. 'How about the Buddy Holly show?'

Since the man's eager and senseless business acumen reminded her of Kerbel, Martina bought one of the miniature soaps and a box of matches for one mark fifty. The soap came from a hotel.

When the taxi turned into Rebhuhnstrasse and reached the scrapyard, Martina asked the driver to let her out. She was going to walk the last few metres.

'Eighteen marks forty,' said the taxi driver. She gave him a twenty-mark note. The taxi driver kept on jingling his coins until Martina finally got the message and said, 'Keep the change.' She climbed out with her bag. As usual, young men were bending over the empty bonnets of cars behind the wire-netting fence, and their girlfriends were walking up and down beside them, arms folded. Martina was shivering. It was no longer raining, but the air was full of moisture which even penetrated her two pullovers.

And then she was home. The yellow car was still there – a

little rustier, with a little more grass growing under it. Two used VW Golfs with prices in their windscreens stood beside it, and rather further away a nearly new Jaguar, which her father must have acquired for himself. She went to the house and stood in front of it for a while in silence. Her return would mean nothing but satisfaction to her father, as well as being a nuisance to him, and to her mother it would be a disappointment because it was she and not her sister Eva coming home. Martina turned and walked away again. The taxi was still standing outside the yard. The driver had opened all the doors and was taking the mats out one by one, beating them against one of the doors. Martina went over to him.

'Can you take me back into town, please?'

'Weren't they pleased to see you?' he asked, grinning.

Not realising that he was joking, she felt she had to justify herself.

'I wasn't going to visit anyone,' she lied. 'I only wanted to fetch my car. I'd left it here. But it won't start.'

'Oh, we'll soon have that sorted,' said the taxi driver, opening his boot and taking out some jump leads. 'Where's your car?'

'No, no, that's no use,' said Martina quickly. 'It's not the battery.'

'How do you know? Let me try.'

Martina began to perspire. An idea occurred to her: 'The tank's empty,' she said. 'I'm out of petrol.'

The taxi driver put the jump leads back in the boot and took out a spare can of petrol.

'Here you are,' he said. 'Thirty marks with the can thrown in.'

'But I . . . I don't need petrol. I mean, it's diesel. And I need super diesel,' said Martina.

'There's the super,' said the taxi driver, pointing to his boot, which contained two other cans. 'I always carry everything with me.'

'Oh. Well, thanks.'

Resigned, she took the can and gave the taxi driver thirty marks. He got into his pale yellow Mercedes and drove off, disappearing irrevocably round the next corner. Tears of anger and despair came to her eyes. Why, she wondered, why do I tell such silly lies? With the petrol can in her hand, she went back to the sandy area which her father described as his garden. Once again she stood in front of the yellow Audi. And then she realised what it all meant – her hesitation outside the house, the taxi driver's extensive range of wares, the idiotic lies she had told him, the petrol can in her hand. Her pulse beat faster. This was no coincidence! This was something elaborately arranged by Fate: a woman's encounter with her opportunity – the opportunity to do something she ought to have done long ago.

Martina unscrewed the cap of the petrol can. She tipped the fuel into the Audi through one of the broken side windows, drenching the rotting upholstery. She sprinkled it over the roof and the flat tyres, and poured what remained over the bonnet. Then she struck a match and let it drop.

Leon had gone straight ahead for hours. He had left his house and garden far behind. By now the marshes surrounded him on all sides. Without his glasses, the landscape appeared to have no contours, was nothing but brown, yellow, black and grey flecks of colour merging into each other. Leon was frozen and exhausted, and too confused to think clearly. He kept treading accidentally on the end of the towelling belt which still hung from his neck. Then there would be a jerk, and he'd stumble and briefly retch. He staggered on until twilight began to fall, and he came close to a pond with bare trees and bushes bending over the weedy, black water of its dead-end arm. The pond was a stretch of boggy water, one of those pools which carry their own death within them, layer upon layer of it. Withered wild hops and creepers wove the bushes and trees together into a jungle-like leafless wilderness, at once luxuriant and lifeless, attractive and alarming. A heron, which Leon saw only as a vibrating pattern, perched swaying on a silvery branch. A single raindrop from the eternal cycle of water fell on Leon's head, as cold and wet as when it had fallen on the head of an iguanodon a hundred million years before. The bank gave with every step he took. Mud welled up between Leon's toes, and his footprints filled with water. He dropped to all fours, dipped his hands into a muddy hole and smeared his face. He grunted with satisfaction. When he raised his head again he saw Isadora standing on the opposite bank. She was naked too. And she was wonderfully fat. The reflection of her white body floated on the surface of the water.

'Come along, my lonely Leon,' she called to him, reaching out her arms. Her voice was a rushing and murmuring sound. 'Come along, come here! I've missed you so much. Autumn is so chilly. I'll hug you and warm you up.'

Leon rose and went towards her, right into the middle of the boggy depths. He immediately sank into them up to his knees. Far from being alarmed, he pulled his legs out of the squelching mud and walked boldly on.

'Come here, my poor Leon,' cried Isadora. 'Come here! You will never be alone again, you'll never have to be afraid of anything again.'

She smiled and played with her breasts with one hand. Her long, black hair was closely interwoven with the branches of the trees. Full of longing, Leon reached his arms out to her. He took another step, and then another. He lost his footing. His hands grasped damp, warm mud, and the bog closed, gurgling, over his head. Leon sank into a world of total darkness and swelling softness. He buried his face in the rotting plant fibres. They felt warm. He rammed his head and hands into them. Mud made its way into his mouth and nose, mud filled his ears and every fold of his body. Leon smacked his lips and swallowed, filling his stomach with mud and darkness. How good it was to be mould beneath the mould. Leon sank back into the womb of his true mother. At some point he had been born, and now he was dying, and what had happened in between, if you looked at it critically, did not make much sense. Sighing, he gave himself up to that damp embrace. Immediately the mud burst into his lungs with fierce pain. Leon struggled for breath, and swallowed nothing but quagmire. The marshes were not warm and gentle now; they were brutal, taking possession of the cavity of his chest, trickling into his bronchial tubes, mingling with the water of which he himself was made and filling him entirely, like a ship wrecked in the silt. He twisted and turned in his death agony. At last he lost consciousness, and Leon left the body in which he had never really felt at home for thirty-eight years. All that was left was darkness, and a fat corpse with the belt of a dressing gown round its neck.

Last night's storm had washed a great deal of flotsam and jetsam up on the beach on Sylt. The two little boys aged four and seven, on their way to the southern tip of the island with their parents, had already found, picked up and sometimes thrown back into the North Sea a container full of holes, a damaged buoy, a Spanish plastic bag, a piece of fishing net, any number of starfish, and various stones which might be amber. There was still a strong wind, and the waves were high. Something was drifting in the surf. Something large. The elder boy had been told to keep an eye on his brother, but did not let the burden of this responsibility trouble him too much. He waded out into the sea and angled for the thing with a stick. It was an animal, a dead animal. His brother picked up a stick too and went to help him. The boys' parents, who had dropped a little way behind to look at the sunset, shouted something. The boys looked up. Their parents were waving and running towards them. The children hurried to get the animal ashore before they could be told to leave it alone. They pushed their sticks into it and got it up on the belt of pebbles. Surf washed round their yellow gumboots.

'Didn't I tell you not to go into the water?' gasped their father, but he was already looking at the corpse with interest.

'Come away from that,' said their mother. 'It's disgusting.'

She tried to take her younger son's hand and pull him away. He struggled and kicked until she let go of him again.

'What is it, Dad?' asked the older boy. His father looked at the animal's curiously cucumber-shaped head with the wire wrapped round it, and at its bloated and partly decomposed torso. The ears and all the extremities were missing. The boys' father cast a knowledgeable eye over the creature's short white coat.

'A seal,' he said. 'A baby seal. See that? Its coat is still white.'

He borrowed his older son's stick and poked the body with it.

'Oliver, please . . .' said his wife.

'OK, wait a minute,' replied the man. He just had to know if the skin would tear. It did.

A Note on the Author

Karen Duve was born in 1961 and lives in Hamburg.
She has been awarded numerous awards for her short stories.
Rain is her first novel.

A Note on the Translator

Anthea Bell, who lives in Cambridge, has translated many
works of fiction and non-fiction from German and French
and has won various translation awards, most recently the
2002 Independent Foreign Fiction Prize and (in the USA)
the Helen and Kur Wolff Translator's Prize for W.G. Sebald's
Austerlitz.

A Note on the Type

The text of this book is set in Linotype Sabon, named after the type founder, Jacques Sabon. It was designed by Jan Tschichold and jointly developed by Linotype, Monotype and Stempel, in response to a need for a typeface to be available in identical form for mechanical hot metal composition and hand composition using foundry type.

Tschichold based his design for Sabon roman on a fount engraved by Garamond, and Sabon italic on a fount by Granjon. It was first used in 1966 and has proved an enduring modern classic.